· T A L E S   F R O M ·

· **TALES FROM** ·

Short Stories for Young Adults

Selected by Eleanor Sullivan and Cynthia Manson

With an introduction by Joan Lowery Nixon

Harcourt Brace Jovanovich, Publishers
San Diego   New York   London

Library of Congress Cataloging-in-Publication Data
Tales from Ellery Queen's mystery magazine.
Summary: A collection of seventeen short stories of mystery, detection, and suspense, emphasizing young protagonists such as a computer genius who breaks a failsafe security system on his trusty Apple computer and a selfish teenager who meets her mother's teenage ghost.
1. Detective and mystery stories, American.
2. Detective and mystery stories, English. [1. Mystery and detective stories. 2. Short stories] I. Sullivan, Eleanor. II. Manson, Cynthia. III. Ellery Queen's mystery magazine.
PZ5.T23   1986   [Fic]   86-7634
ISBN 0-15-284205-5

DESIGNED BY FRANCESCA M. SMITH
PRINTED IN THE UNITED STATES OF AMERICA
FIRST EDITION
A B C D E

TABLE

OF

CONTENTS

INTRODUCTION

A cross the street from our house is a large patch of un-developed woods, with crowded clusters of stiff-branched pines and scraggly tallow trees rising above a tangled scrub of wild grasses and vines. Since we rise early, it's usually dark as I walk to the curb—and toward the woods—to pick up our morning paper. With only our flickering gas lamp and an occasional low, thin moon to provide light, the woods are darkly menacing. Nervously, I sometimes wonder if I've seen the subtle movement of a shadow or heard a rustle that barely stirs the bushes.

Someday, in my imagination, someone—or something—might creep from the woods and silently follow me to our front door. From such are mystery stories born.

Since 1841, when *Murder in the Rue Morgue* was written by Edgar Allan Poe, father of the detective story, the mystery has grown in popularity and expanded its dimensions.

The traditional mystery—the Detective Story—in which a hired private investigator sets out to solve a crime, is exemplified in this collection by "How I Became a Jeweler."

But, obviously, not all fictional detectives are professionals in law enforcement. Many mysteries come under the category of the Innocent Bystander Story, in which the protagonist has a solid reason for working to discover the identity of a criminal. Mystery readers who write down license numbers of cars parked in lonely places at strange times or who memorize physical descriptions of people who they see loitering outside bank buildings will strongly identify with five of the stories in this collection. Jacques, in "The Boy Who Read Agatha Christie," models his sleuthing on his hero, Hercule Poirot, while Mr. Strang, in "Mr. Strang and the Purloined Memo," bases his method of detection on a story by Poe. Brian, in "A Crime Child," is aware of an ideal situation for a bank robbery and takes precautions to keep it from happening. Dr. Sam Hawthorne steps into the job of sleuthing in order to help his friend in "The Problem of the Fatal Fireworks," and an intrepid journalist, Sweeney, becomes involved in solving the murder of a marathon runner in "The Death Triple."

The situation itself can be a strong factor in the evolvement of a mystery plot. It can lend itself to the detective story, as in "The State of the Art," in which a code-breaker who indulged in theft by computer must be tracked down. Or the situation can create a story of Suspense, as it does in "Night Run," a fast-paced tale about college track stars, one of whom is a would-be murderer.

Location plays an important part in many stories of suspense. Would Lindsey, in "A Name for Herself," have been stalked as she was in any city other than New York? Or would the thirteen-year-old boy in "The Punchboards" have been able to solve the murder if the characters didn't live in a small town in which everyone knew the personalities and habits of everyone else in town? The history of the city of Tombstone, Arizona, is essential to "Return to the OK Corral," and Clark Howard's depiction of the New Orleans–Baton Rouge area in "New Orleans Getaway" is as vivid as the locals who people his story.

Stories of Psychological Suspense depend heavily upon strong characterization. In "They Never Even See Me," readers dwell inside Raymond's mind as he wonders why no one in his family has noticed that he's dead. Readers question, as does David in "Dead-Letter Drop," the possible menace of dreadful Cousin Edna; and, with Lorna, they feel the touch of the occult in "Don't Be Frightened."

Occult? Ghosts? Yes, ghosts and demons, whether real or imaginary, have a well-established place in stories of mystery–suspense, as evidenced in "Spirit Weather" and in "The Calendar Chest."

Edgar Allan Poe and his fictional detective, C. Auguste Dupin, created a genre that has captured readers ever since, reaching a current peak of popularity. Is it because of the strong plot essential to the mystery story? The mental challenge offered to readers? The reassurance that "justice will prevail"? Or do readers share the same adventurous spirit that propels authors into writing mystery stories in the first place, so that together they delight in watching something slither from the woods, clutch their imaginations, and rush with them into a make-believe world of potential danger?

Here, in some of the best of the tales from *Ellery Queen's Mystery Magazine,* may lie the answer.

Joan Lowery Nixon
May 1986

· TALES FROM ·

ELLERY QUEEN'S

MYSTERY MAGAZINE

THE BOY
WHO READ
AGATHA
CHRISTIE

William Brittain

Young Jacques has a literary hero who inspires him to solve the strange happenings in Larkin's Corners.

I n the weeks following that insane Monday in Larkin's Corners, there were many versions of What Really Happened. However, the village gossips were generally agreed that the first person to be approached by the young madmen when they entered the town was the proprietor of the drugstore, Rad Simpson.

It was shortly after eight o'clock, and Rad had just unlocked the cash register. He heard the bell jingle on the front door, and two youths entered. Rad put on his best smile; they were strangers, and from the looks of their clothing, they were used to spending money freely. *College boys,* thought Rad to himself.

"Got any razor blades?" asked one. "I want the injector kind."

"Yep," replied Rad, tossing a container on the counter. "Ten blades for a dollar. Special this week."

Without a word the boy drew a razor from his pocket, fitted the container to it, and clicked in a new blade. Then he tossed the container and a dime on the counter. "I only need one," he said.

"Hey, wait a minute!" Rad yelled. "You got to buy the whole thing. I can't sell nine blades to somebody when it says ten on the box."

"But I only need one," the youth repeated.

"That don't make no difference, son," said Rad. He came out from behind the counter. "Take the blades or leave 'em. But you owe me ninety cents, irregardless. And you either pay up, or I'm callin' the police."

The boy's companion walked up to Rad and smiled blandly. "Excuse me, sir," he said, "but is there any way I can purchase nine injector razor blades? You see I have only ninety cents and—"

Immediately, Rad was all smiles. They were playing a joke on him. He gave the second boy the blades, and like the first, he took a razor from his pocket and put in a fresh blade. He walked to the soda fountain at the front of the store, took a tube of brushless shaving cream from his pocket, and began to apply it to his cheeks. Then, facing the huge window, he started to shave.

Rad picked up the phone and called the police.

At about the same time another young man entered the Acme Hardware Store, two doors down the street. He purchased a mop and a bucket, requesting that Larry Nash, the owner of the store, fill the bucket with water. When the request was granted, he began, with great diligence but without Larry's permission, to mop the floor of the store.

Larry picked up the phone and spoke to the operator in a low tone.

Within twenty minutes the main street of Larkin's Corners was in a state of shock.

Item: In the firehouse two of the college-age boys were hard at work polishing the already-gleaming brass fittings on the trucks.

Item: Fedder's Grocery was in a turmoil because one lad was busily carrying boxes of jelly doughnuts to the diet foods section while his companion was just as busily replacing them where they belonged.

Item: In the bank a boy was repeatedly going from teller to teller, getting a nickel changed into five pennies from one and exchanging the pennies for a nickel at the next; he kept this up for fifteen minutes before the bank president decided to call the police.

In his office in the rear of the village building Max Cory, the town cop of Larkin's Corners, was still unaware of the deluge of calls about to descend on him. He smiled across his desk at the boy who had come to visit him.

Jacques duMonde had arrived in Larkin's Corners from his home in Belgium six weeks before as part of a student exchange program. Although his command of English was excellent and his tests had shown that he was perfectly capable of handling the work of a high school senior, the school authorities had been somewhat shaken when they first set eyes on the boy; they promptly made a note that hereafter they would insist on knowing the age of any exchange student coming to their school.

Jacques duMonde was just ten years old.

When spoken to by the school authorities, Max and his

wife, Jean, had quickly agreed to let the boy live with them. And certainly he was no trouble. In fact, the neat and orderly condition in which Jacques always kept his room sometimes embarrassed Jean Cory, who was inclined to let her housework slide at times. His stamp collection was painstakingly mounted, catalogued, and annotated in a manner to put an expert philatelist to shame. He was never late for meals or for an appointment. Order and precision seemed to govern the boy's life.

The village librarian was fascinated by Jacques. On his first visit he took out Darwin's *On the Origin of Species by Means of Natural Selection* and returned it in less than a week. When the librarian asked him how he enjoyed the book, she was treated to a short lecture on Darwin's system of classification, including improvements he might have made. Jacques was impeccably polite, but it was obvious to the librarian that he had gained more from the book than she could ever have hoped to.

And then Jacques discovered Agatha Christie's stories about Hercule Poirot. In his fictional countryman Jacques found a kindred spirit. He read and reread the stories, discussing the techniques of detection with Max. That was the reason for his early-morning visit to Max's office.

"I have yesterday completed *The Murder of Roger Ackroyd,*" said Jacques. "And surely, *mon ami,* you will agree that to a person with the tidy mind of Hercule Poirot, it must be clearly evident—"

"Wait a minute, Jacques," said Max, holding up his hand. "My main job here is to give out speeding tickets. We've never had any wild crimes in Larkin's Corners. Besides, I haven't read the book."

Max looked at the small figure sitting across from him. The boy's short blue pants had a sharp crease and were, as always, spotless. His shirt was so white that it almost glittered, and below the kneesocks his patent leather shoes with the pointed toes were dazzling in their brilliance.

And what was that odd movement that Jacques made with his thumb and forefinger beside his nose? It looked to Max almost as if he were curling the end of a nonexistent mustache.

Then the telephone began to ring.

During the next few minutes Max Cory almost went out of his mind. From drugstore, hardware store, fire department, grocery, and bank came the same message. The main street of Larkin's Corners had suddenly gone berserk.

Max jotted down each complaint in his notebook. He started to rise, looked once more at the notebook, then sat down again. He reached for the telephone.

"Rad," he said when the connection had been made, "I want you to do something for me. . . . Yeah, I don't know what's going on either. . . . Look, I'll investigate, but let me do it my way. Now here's what I want you to do. Close the store—that'll keep 'em out for a while. Then go find Larry Nash—he's at the fire department, so that's covered as well as his hardware store. Then get Al Fedder at the grocery and Sam Donohue from the bank. Bring 'em all down here to my office . . . and stop worrying about losing business. You don't sell that much on Mondays anyway."

Max hung up the phone and turned to Jacques. "Bunch of college boys are pulling some stunts down on Main Street," he said. "It's crazy. There's no rhyme nor reason for—"

"Pardon, monsieur," replied Jacques. "There is always a reason. Are we to believe that these individuals, after being exposed to the glories of a higher education, have taken leave of their senses? I would like very much to hear what the merchants have to say. Of course, if you—"

"Sure, kid, stick around. The whole world seems to be nuts today. I guess a little informality around here wouldn't hurt any."

Ten minutes later the four businessmen crowded into Max's office, muttering complaints about a policeman who wanted to do his job without getting off his big fat overstuffed—

"Hold it!" shouted Max. "Now I'm just as concerned about all this as any of you. But tell me something. Just what horrible crimes did these guys commit?"

The others looked at one another in silence. Max continued in a lower voice.

"Look, Rad, a young man took a shave in your window. We've got no law on the books against that."

He turned to Larry Nash.

"Larry, that store of yours has needed a good cleaning out since you bought it. That boy was performing a public service. And as far as the grocery is concerned, you said yourself, Al, that they put everything back just the way they found it."

Max spread his hands. "Look, I don't say you haven't good reason to be annoyed. It's just that they haven't done anything we can arrest them for."

"Yeah," Al Fedder growled. "Well, why can't they do their fraternity initiations somewhere else?"

"No, I checked on that," Max replied. "They're from Cutler College, according to the stickers on their cars. And Cutler has its initiations in the spring, not in the fall."

"But why are they doing it?" asked Larry Nash.

"I dunno. But all I can do is keep an eye on 'em. Now take it easy; at least nobody's been hurt."

The phone rang again. Max answered, and as he listened, his eyes became grim. He hung up the phone and turned to the others.

"Come on," he said. "That was Les Kincaid at the post office. A couple of those guys just roughed up old Mrs. Nearing."

At the post office, Max found eight youths backed up against a wall and guarded by Postmaster Kincaid, who was armed with an ancient shotgun. The eyes of all the boys were wide with fear.

Victoria Nearing had settled her trembling body into a chair. "They really didn't do much, Max," she said. "They just frightened me a little, that's all. I wouldn't want to see them get into trouble."

"Well, I would," snarled Kincaid. "They all came in here at once, Max, all eight of 'em. Stood looking at the bulletin board, they did. I figured they was up to no good, so I got my gun ready.

"Anyway, one of 'em steps up to the window and orders one hundred and two five-cent stamps. One hundred and *two*. So I gives him the sheet and tears off two more singles. He'd no sooner got out of the way than the next one wants the same thing. Why one hundred and two? Just to make more work for me, the way I see it."

"They've made more work for most of us, Les," said Al Fedder. He quickly filled the postmaster in on the events of the morning.

Kincaid nodded. "Just troublemakers. Anyway, after the second one had ordered, Mrs. Nearing walked in and got in line right behind him. She asked for some stamps, but just as she was leaving one of these galoots grabbed her by the arm and whipped the stamps out of her hand. That's when I called you and grabbed my gun."

"But they didn't hurt me," said Mrs. Nearing. "In fact, they gave me all the stamps they bought. I don't think they meant any harm."

"How about it, Max?" asked Larry Nash. "Have you got enough to arrest them now?"

"I guess I can at least question them. As far as arrest goes, that'll depend on Mrs. Nearing. But I wish I knew just why—"

"Monsieur Kincaid!" Jacques's small voice could be heard

over the general din. "I wonder if I might ask you something."

Kincaid looked at Jacques and smiled. "Say, you're the boy living with Max, ain't you? Sure, boy, ask me anything you like."

"Have you seen any of these gentlemen before this morning?" Jacques waved his hand at the frightened young men along the wall.

"No," Kincaid replied. "I don't think—say, wait a minute! That one in the green cap. Yessir, by golly, he was in here Saturday just before closing time."

"Did he come behind your little window at any time?"

"Nope, that's against regulations."

"Then allow me to ask whether or not he assisted you in picking up the stamps which you dropped?"

"Yeah, he did. When I was unpacking the sheets, a couple of 'em fell through the window, and he—hey, wait a minute! How did you know I dropped any stamps?"

"Because, Monsieur Kincaid, that would go far in explaining why these gentlemen are acting in this ridiculous fashion. *Sont ils fou?* Are they crazy? I very much doubt it."

Jacques turned to Max. "While you are attending to these men, *mon ami,* I wish a few more words with Mr. Kincaid. Then perhaps I can assist you in explaining this little mystery."

Max threw up his hands in amazement. But he left, taking his eight prisoners with him, and Jacques turned back to Kincaid.

Half an hour later Jacques walked into Max's office. Seated on the floor on both sides of the small room were the eight college boys. Jacques turned to the one whom Kincaid had identified as the boy who had been in the post office the previous Saturday.

"I know why you did these crazy things," said Jacques, "and I am a friend of Officer Cory. Now if I can convince you that your work here is at an end, and if Mr. Cory gives his permission, will you agree, with haste, to leave Larkin's Corners in peace and go back to your studies?"

The youth in the green cap shrugged. "I don't even know what you're talking about," he mumbled.

"Perhaps I can convince you that I know all about your scheme. But what have you to say, Monsieur Cory? Will you allow them to leave?"

"Leave? I'd be tickled to death if they were gone now. But first I've got to know what they were doing. And what did you mean about convincing them that their work was at an end?"

"*Un moment,*" replied Jacques. He took a thick pencil from Max's desk and entered the small lavatory off the office. Returning a few seconds later, he faced the boys, who looked at him in astonishment and then at one another.

Jacques had drawn in pencil on his upper lip a huge, sweeping mustache.

Without a word the eight collegians rose and left the office. Staring wide-eyed at the door, Max could hear the roar of their cars as they headed for the village limits.

"But it was simplicity itself, *mon ami,*" said Jacques as he and Max sat alone in the office. "As Hercule Poirot himself has taught me, there is a pattern in what is seemingly the most foolish of human actions. To determine that pattern requires only the proper use of the little gray cells.

"What have we in this case? These strangers entered the town and committed several pointless acts. Obviously, however, if they are not all insane, one of these acts is not so pointless. The rest are designed to conceal the one deed that they wish to accomplish in secrecy. They are—how do you say it?—'red halibuts.' "

"I think you mean 'red herrings,' " said Max with a smile.

Jacques ignored the comment. "But where does one find the significant deed?" he continued. "Consider, Mr. Cory, that the boys began by spreading themselves all over the village. And yet all of them came finally to one building—the post office. Is it too much to assume, then, that the post office is the real place of interest to them?

"But what is of so great interest in a post office? Obviously the stamps. After all, Mrs. Nearing was set upon so that those gentlemen could look at the stamps she purchased. This event also told me that they were looking for a particular copy of the current George Washington five-cent stamp which, incidentally, the youths were purchasing in such an odd manner."

"But how did you know that one of those guys had been in the post office before?"

"I assumed that the postmaster did not know of the existence of the particular stamp which interested our eight friends. I asked myself how this could be, and there seemed but one answer. In some way a sheet of stamps had made its way in front of the window and back again. Since I could think of only one manner in which this might have happened, I put the question which so amazed Mr. Kincaid."

"Sounds good so far," said Max. "But why didn't those boys just come in and buy sheets of stamps until they found the particular one they wanted? Why panic the whole town?"

"Ah, Monsieur Cory, to understand this, one must have some knowledge of rare stamps. Perhaps the most famous example in United States stamps is the 1918 airmail which has an error showing the airplane flying upside down. Each such stamp is worth several thousands of dollars.

"But in the fall of 1963, in New Jersey, a similar mistake was found. In that case there was an error in printing the colors. The person who purchased the stamps realized they were a rarity but made the mistake of boasting about his discovery. At this point the government printed many copies of the error, making the man's discovery almost valueless.

"This is what the eight gentlemen were guarding against. They wanted the stamp, but they had to get it in such a way that attention would not be drawn to it. And who would suspect a purchase of stamps after the other fantastic events of the day?"

"And that would explain why they grabbed Mrs. Nearing. They wanted to make sure Kincaid didn't sell her the sheet they wanted."

"To be sure. All the events of the day were for the single purpose of buying an improperly printed stamp without giving anyone reason to believe it existed. One of the eight—probably without any knowledge of the stamp's worth—saw it on Saturday. He mentioned it at college to a friend who realized its value. So they came back today to purchase it."

"Jacques, I've got to know," said Max. "What in blazes was the matter with that stamp to make it so valuable?"

"At times the plate from which stamps are printed becomes marred or damaged. When this occurs, normally the plate is replaced and the imperfect stamps are discarded and destroyed. But once in a million times, perhaps, an error escapes the examiners. Such an error I found in the stamp rack at the post office which Mr. Kincaid so kindly allowed me to inspect. Observe, Monsieur!"

Jacques held up a sheet of five-cent stamps, each bearing the head of George Washington. At first Max could find nothing out of the ordinary.

"The third stamp from the bottom in the second column, *mon ami,*" said Jacques.

There it was. On that single stamp in the entire sheet of one hundred a flaw in the plate had caused the ink to print in such a way that the Father of His Country seemed to be sporting a magnificent mustache.

"So that's why they left after—"

"Precisely. They realized that I had detected their secret. Unfortunately, I must return this sheet to Mr. Kincaid. He will send it back to Washington where it will be destroyed. Sad, *n'est ce pas?*"

"Yeah, Jacques. That would certainly be a great find for your own collection."

"That is so, but that is not what makes me sad." Jacques held up a book—Agatha Christie's *The Labors of Hercules*—which had on its jacket a picture of Hercule Poirot, his superb mustaches stretching from one side of the cover to the other. He placed the book next to the sheet of stamps. Max chuckled at the similarity between Hercule Poirot's and George Washington's mustaches.

Jacques passed his hand across his own hairless upper lip. "It is indeed a pity," he sighed, "that even one example of such magnificent facial adornment must pass into oblivion."

WILLIAM BRITTAIN teaches junior high school in Long Island, New York. He has published more than sixty-five stories in Ellery Queen's Mystery Magazine.

THE
CALENDAR
CHEST

Marilyn Pribus

Pauline receives a gift from a long-dead relative, a chest of 366 tiny compartments that hold her future—and her past.

On the day before her seventy-fourth birthday Pauline received the chest. The moving men uncrated it in the foyer below and struggled up the wide, curving stairway. As they brought it through the bedroom door, scratching the jamb, Pauline noted sourly, she felt a sudden shiver of recognition. "Against that wall, I think," she directed, then dismissed them with a preoccupied wave of her hand as she surveyed the chest, at once familiar and mysterious.

As a child Pauline had often visited her great-aunt Belinda.

Even as a young woman Belinda had been ephemeral and fey. At family reunions the children whispered stories about Belinda having been kidnapped by gypsies at the age of three, about a lover who took his own life, about wild birds from the woods landing at her feet for crumbs of her breakfast toast.

Pauline remembered the last morning they'd been together. "Pauline," Belinda had said in her strange way of speaking, "some day you will have my chest of many drawers. The other children sometimes ventured to open the drawers, but you had respect for the things of others and respect for things we cannot understand. The chest shall be yours."

It must be thirty years since I've seen the chest, Pauline mused as she studied it. It was about one foot deep, four feet wide, and five feet high. The top was shaped like an old European city house in three decorative fan shapes, the middle one being the tallest. The entire chest was stained a dark color, and a gold stencil design was faintly visible through the cracked varnish.

There were twenty-four horizontal rows of tiny drawers, fifteen drawers across in each row, and down the left side were five evenly spaced drawers, each the same miniature size. On the right side was a tiny door bearing the words ONE YEAR IN FOUR. The actual workmanship of the chest was crude, and the drawer pulls varied from elegant crystal knobs to the head of an old wooden clothespin. It was just as she had remembered —a drawer for each day of the year and the door for the twenty-ninth of February.

She remembered Belinda consulting the chest. "Seeing my fortune for the day," she would announce solemnly as she opened a drawer and read from a slip of paper inside it. Pauline frowned slightly. She knew that there had been a sequence for the drawers, but did one start the first drawer on New Year's Day or one's own birthday? She recalled seeing the pale-blue slips of paper with angular copperplate handwriting as delicate as a spider's silk, but she had never actually "read a fortune," as Belinda had referred to it.

"Here you go, Miss Pauline," said Cindy as she brought the dinner tray. Cindy was one of a long line of college students who stayed with Pauline to help her into her wheelchair in the morning and into her bed at night. For nearly twenty-five years, ever since the accident, she'd hired the girls. Some were businesslike, some were kind, and several still wrote to her years after they had graduated and moved away.

"Sure is a funny-looking chest," Cindy commented.

"It's quite old and all handmade," replied Pauline, a trifle nettled.

"Oh, I didn't mean it wasn't nice," said Cindy hastily. "But, I mean, what could you keep in all those teeny drawers? I don't think you could even get a deck of cards in one. Is it some sort of jewelry cabinet or file or something?" She started to open one of the drawers.

"You shouldn't poke into other people's things," said Pauline sharply, hearing an echo of Belinda in her own words. "You should have respect for the things of others."

"I'm sorry, I'm sure," said Cindy in an injured tone. "I didn't know there was anything in the drawers."

"That's all right, there probably isn't," said Pauline more mildly. But she wasn't sure. That night she lay shivering in her bed. The darkened room seemed to be filling with a pervasive dread, like fog filtering through a window screen. The chest loomed dark in the faint light from the hall.

"Fiddlesticks, Pauline," she scolded herself. "You are a practical woman."

She'd been a teacher of mathematics in a fine private school before her marriage to an older man with an excellent position. She prided herself on her orderly mind and logical thinking, and she wasn't going to be intimidated by a piece of furniture.

She dismissed the "fortunes" of the chest as superstitious foolishness and her great-aunt's reliance on them as a mild de-
mentia.

"Really, Pauline," she chided herself in the morning, speaking aloud as she often did. "There is probably nothing at all
in the chest after all this time." Nevertheless, as soon as Cindy
had settled her in her chair and left, Pauline slowly and painfully wheeled herself to the chest and stared at it. It was small
enough to reach across easily, and she rubbed her fingers up
and down on the sides. She walked her fingers from knob to
knob across several rows of drawers, then taking a deep breath
she said, "Well, let's see what you have to say."

She reached up and pulled out the first drawer. She lowered
it to her lap and was only slightly surprised to see that it *did*
contain a small piece of paper. She extracted it and gently
unfolded it. It was blue paper, brittle and faded, and the ink
was faded to a rusty color rather like dried blood. In fine
penmanship a brief statement read *a message from the past.*
There was no punctuation, no capital letters.

After looking at it for a few moments she refolded the paper
and put it back in the drawer. As she replaced the drawer in
the chest she said to herself, "Now you see, Pauline, a message
from the past. That's what the chest is."

That afternoon when Cindy brought her the mail, Pauline
received a large, heavy, white envelope with the return address
of Nicholson, McDaniels, Glenn & Glenn. A bunch of lawyers
for sure, she sniffed. Enclosed was a sealed envelope dated
twenty-five years ago and addressed in faded ink: "To My
Great Niece Pauline on Her Seventy-Fourth Birthday." The
letter inside read

Dear Pauline,
   I am writing this in what will be the fairly distant past when
you read it, and I will no longer be living. I know that people

laugh at me and what they call my strange ways, but I know what is going on and I see the disaster that awaits.

I have recently written my last testament and directed that the Chest of Many Drawers be yours on your seventy-fourth birthday.

Belinda Hartford

Pauline felt a prickle pass over her body like a wave of chilly fall air. This was it then, not the chest itself. This was the message from the past, a message from Belinda.

For three days she regarded the chest with an obscure foreboding, refusing to approach it. On the fourth day she could resist no longer. She had decided to treat the chest like a calendar, so she skipped three drawers, opened the fourth, and read the slip of paper written in the same elegant hand: *a beautiful child with flaxen hair.*

She considered the phrase at length, but she could think of no blond children from the past and she rarely saw children these days. After lunch she dozed until Cindy awakened her with a gentle touch on the arm. "Miss Pauline?" she said softly. "You told me before to always bring the Girl Scouts up to see you when they came with cookies." Pauline opened her eyes and saw a lovely child, her long yellow hair topped by a Girl Scout cap. *The flaxen-haired child,* she thought with amazement. *Simple coincidence,* she told herself briskly after the girl had left, yet she felt uneasy.

Each day Pauline tried to ignore the chest that dwelt darkly against the wall, but each day she was compelled to open the next drawer. On the day the message read *an old friend's greetings,* she received a letter from a woman she'd taught school with many years before. Another day the slip said *a visitor of tender years,* and in the afternoon Sally, one of her college girls from several years before, stopped by with her six-month-old daughter.

Against her will Pauline began to believe in the chest. Summer turned to fall, and each fragmentary message seemed to be like a piece in a jigsaw puzzle, defining and labeling her day. The chest seemed to grow larger and darker with each passing week, although she told herself repeatedly that the chest could in no way retell her past or predict her future.

One day she opened a stubborn drawer with a knob of white porcelain. The slip said *a recollection of deceit and guilt.* She read it with a frown, and as she replaced it she heard a slight rattle. She pulled the drawer more fully open and looked into it, for she was now opening drawers in the middle of the chest and could reach them easily from her wheelchair. In the drawer was a ring with a single small blue stone.

She lifted it out and tried it on, but it was too small. She stared at it for several minutes, then with a shock she recognized it. She flushed hotly and thrust it back into the drawer, remembering her own impassioned denials to Belinda, swearing to her great aunt that she would *never* have taken her ring, but knowing all the time that it was in her own shoe in the closet.

She shut the drawer quickly, wheeled around with her back to the chest, and sat trembling. "I don't understand," she said. She turned around to face the chest. "I don't understand how you knew that."

A few days later the message read *a lie causes lifelong sorrow.* Pauline searched her mind for a terrible lie but couldn't recall what it might be. She was still thinking about it when Cindy came with her lunch. "Hey," said Cindy, looking out the window, "the people across the street got their flag out on the porch. Is today something special?"

Then Pauline remembered. Today was November 11; today was Armistice Day. Years ago Belinda's beau had come to take her to the Armistice Day parade in town. Pauline had been visiting, and she met him at the door. "But Belinda's not here," she'd declared. "She's gone to the parade with someone much more handsome."

The next day the young man had been found dead where he'd fallen from his horse on a wild gallop through thick woods. Pauline had not meant it to be a wicked lie, merely a prank. She had panicked when the body was found, though nothing had ever been said, and she finally pushed it from her mind. But Belinda had known, she thought to herself now. Somehow Belinda knew.

On January 14 the slip of paper said *a marriage of convenience only,* and she realized that it was her wedding anniversary, although she'd been a widow since the accident twenty-five years ago. Well, she ruminated, it certainly had not been a love match, but it had been a comfortable relationship until she'd learned about the other woman.

On Valentine's Day she pulled open a drawer with a knob in the shape of a heart. *A gift of pure malice,* the fortune read. Oh, she remembered that, all right, but the woman had deserved it. She recalled finding the monogrammed, scented handkerchief in her husband's pocket along with an address on a piece of paper. She'd laundered and ironed the handkerchief carefully and packed it in a fancy, heart-shaped box along with a miniature lady's pistol, loaded. She sent it to the address in her husband's pocket, and on an enclosed card she wrote, in an excellent imitation of her husband's hand, "All is lost. We are discovered."

For weeks thereafter Pauline watched her husband appraisingly as they sat silently in the living room after dinner. His late nights at the office had ended abruptly, and he read night after night, staring at a single page for many minutes, an impassive mask on his face. Pauline kept stitching row after row of tidy needlepoint.

On a bitter, sunny day in March the slip read *a cup of coffee.* Pauline gasped. It had been on the day she had told her husband about the Valentine "gift." He was seeing another woman, and she had meant the telling only as a warning. Instead, he coldly announced that he would terminate the marriage.

"You can't mean it," Pauline had protested.

"I do indeed. I will pack a few things and move into a suite at the hotel," he said. "Tomorrow."

The next day she had stolen into the kitchen and put sleeping pills into the thermos of coffee that the cook always prepared for him in the morning. The car crashed six miles from the house, and any question of foul play was minimized by Pauline's convincing swoon at the top of the stairs when she received the news. She had relied on the policeman to catch her, but instead she had fallen down the stairs.

After several months in the hospital she had returned, still paralyzed, to the spacious house which was now hers alone. She was financially comfortable, with sufficient means to retain the cook and to hire her college girls. She read many books, played solitaire in many varieties, and continued her needlepoint.

But that was long before the chest that now occupied her every waking moment. Rationally she knew there was no possibility of fortunes being told. "Merest coincidence," she told the chest accusingly. She would waken in the morning determined anew not to open another drawer, yet she always succumbed to the irresistible power of the chest.

One cold morning in late spring she opened her message and read *a day of reckoning*. She sat staring at the rows and rows of drawers, weary and bemused. Only a few remained unopened. "Miss Pauline?" Cindy interrupted her thoughts. "Here's the mail."

There was another imposing white envelope from Nicholson, McDaniels, Glenn & Glenn. She opened it apprehensively and found another sealed envelope. The letter enclosed read

Dear Pauline,

By now you know that I knew many things. I should have said something sooner, but I remembered you as a child and somehow could not.

Nevertheless I now feel justice should be served, and I must inform the authorities. Therefore I have written a letter which now rests with my attorney and which will be mailed to the police on your seventy-fifth birthday. I hope that the past year has served as one of reflection for you, and may God have mercy on your soul.

Belinda Hartford

P.S. The letter will be destroyed unopened in the event of your death.

Pauline was stunned. The past overwhelmed her, and the terrible memories she had forced out of her mind swept over her. All day she watched a sullen drizzle saturate the soggy ground. She could not eat. She shifted uncomfortably a hundred times in her chair, and when Cindy finally settled her into bed she couldn't sleep.

Her thoughts were chaotic. What did Belinda's letter say? Would it be believed? Would the police put a woman of her years into prison? She considered burning the chest. She could sell it or *give* it away. Perhaps the Salvation Army would take it. If only she could open her eyes in the morning and it wouldn't be there. "I wish you would disappear," she whispered through the dark.

"You don't look so hot today, Miss Pauline," said Cindy the next morning as she helped her dress. "You look like you haven't slept a wink."

"I'm perfectly fine," said Pauline, stiffening her back. She watched calmly while Cindy made the bed and dusted the bookshelf. After she'd gone Pauline faced the chest. Only two drawers remained. "I absolutely refuse to open either one," she said to the chest resolutely.

Nine o'clock passed, and she read and reread the morning paper. Ten o'clock came, and she finished her book. By eleven she surrendered. She moved to the chest and opened the next-to-the-last drawer. The slip read *a day of preparation.*

She frowned slightly, then called Cindy, who helped her wash her hair. She filed her nails while Cindy changed the bedsheets although they had only been on the bed a few days, and she directed Cindy to change the covers on the cushions of her wheelchair.

What more preparations could there be? she wondered as she lay in bed that night. She listened to the grandfather clock on the landing of the stairway. It struck ten and eleven and eleven-fifteen. At eleven-thirty she rang the bell at the side of the bed. Cindy came hurrying in.

"What's the matter?" she asked worriedly.

"I want to get dressed and into my chair," Pauline announced with such imposing finality that Cindy didn't protest. "I will wear my blue dressing gown."

Cindy helped her to dress and move into her chair. Then she stood in front of her and leaned over. "Miss Pauline, are you all right? I mean, you seem really upset, and it's weird getting up in the middle of the night like this. Are you sure everything's okay?"

"I'm fine, Cindy," said Pauline reassuringly. "You go back to sleep now."

"Okay. Well. You know, I feel funny leaving you sitting up in the dark like this. But if you say so . . ." She trailed off uncertainly, then leaned over and gave Pauline a quick kiss on the cheek. She'd never kissed her before.

Pauline touched her cheek pensively where the girl's lips had brushed it and listened to Cindy going down the hall and switching out the lights. Then she slowly edged the chair to the chest. As the clock tolled midnight she put her hand on the last drawer.

"Well," she said to the chest, "here I am."

She opened the drawer. There was more than a paper in it. The drawer held a small bundle which she lifted out. It was a miniature lady's gun wrapped in a beautifully monogrammed handkerchief. She opened the handkerchief she'd seen so long ago and studied it. How had she missed it before—the gently curved *B* entwined with the *H*? How had she not understood?

She thought briefly of writing a message of her own but rejected the idea. The mysterious chest with its cryptic fortunes in faded ink would mean nothing to anyone else. Let them wonder.

She removed the slip of paper and, holding it tightly in her hand, looked up at the chest. "I guess you have the last word," she said quietly and read the last slip.

She folded it and held it gently in her left hand while with her right hand she placed the gun beneath her breast. She pulled the trigger, and the paper fluttered to the floor.

The 365th drawer said *a taking of one's last sleep.*

MARILYN PRIBUS teaches folk guitar and works as a volunteer at a Springfield, Virginia, crisis-intervention hotline. She is married to her high-school sweetheart, and they have two teenaged sons.

A
CRIME
CHILD

H. R. F. Keating

The thieves think Friday is the perfect day for a crime, but they don't know that Brian thinks so, too.

T here are football-fact children. There are car-make children. There are train-number children. But Brian was a crime child.

He couldn't remember what had first made him interested in crimes and the detectives who solved them, but by the time he was nine—which was nearly a year ago—he had used every book token he had received for his birthday, and all the money, buying paperbacks about the way crooks operated and the way the police caught them.

He could tell you all about the great Brink's robbery, which happened in Boston, Massachusetts. And the trouble was, really, that he often did.

The football-fact fans had other football-fact fans to swap facts with. And so did the car-make nuts. And the train-number idiots. But no one that Brian knew shared his interest, and so when he started to talk about it they were usually rude.

"Well, Brian," they would say after he had produced some interesting piece of information, like how if someone comes into a store twice in an evening asking whether they've got the latest edition of the paper it means they're casing it out for a holdup. "Well, Brian, suppose they just wanted the paper."

And that made it all the more annoying once when he was in the paper shop near the school with Mike and a girl called Felicity. A funny-looking old man had come in and asked for the evening paper, and the proprietor had said, "No, I told you before, I haven't got one." So he had felt that he had to warn him that his shop was going to be robbed. But the proprietor had just laughed and said, "No, lad, that's only old Bones. A bit batty he is, and always coming in wanting a paper. So I always tell him I haven't got one. No harm in him."

"Well, Brian," Mike had said outside, "got any more sure and certain signs of a crime?"

And Felicity had giggled so much that she had spit out her bubble gum. Served her right.

So Brian never asked anybody to come with him on Friday mornings in the summer when he used to stake out the pedestrian bridge over the canal. He was afraid that nothing would happen, though he felt certain in his heart of hearts that one day it would. He had worked the whole thing out: it was bound to be the place.

Long, long ago—when he was eight—he had seen more than once on television, on "Junior Police Five," the route that a bank-robbery gang took after they had done a job.

They would come up to whichever bank it was in a car they had stolen especially. Generally that would be quite soon after the bank had opened, when it was nice and quiet. And most often it would be on a Friday, when there was a lot of money in the banks for people to draw out for the weekend. Then, once they had grabbed the loot, they would race out to the stolen car and drive away fast—till they got to someplace like the pedestrian bridge over the canal, a place where any chasing cars couldn't follow. They would leap out there, run across the bridge with the bags of cash, and jump into a different car that another member of the gang would have waiting.

And there was nowhere better for this trick than the bridge over the canal. The banks on High Street were about a quarter of a mile away. There was a good road running from there to the near side of the narrow bridge, and on the far side of the bridge lay a nice quiet side street leading nowhere, just right for a second getaway car to wait in without any trouble.

It was the ideal situation. And one Friday morning, Brian knew, some gang was going to take advantage of it. He just hoped it wouldn't be during school, because he was determined he was going to be there to see it happen if he could. And to get the car number and good descriptions of the gang members. Then when he told the police, perhaps they'd show him through the station or let him ride in a cruiser. They could pretend he'd got lost and they were taking him home. By a sort of roundabout way.

On the Friday that was different from all the others he had arrived at the special hiding place he had found on the far side of the bridge even earlier than usual. It had been raining hard all night and looked as if it were going to start again soon, so he had hurried off while he could still make his way there without getting wet. He'd once spent an hour after he'd got caught in a shower hidden in his place—it was a narrow space between two of the big iron girders that held up the bridge—

and he thought it must have been doing that which had given him such a stinking awful cold.

This Friday, almost as soon as he had settled in, a car drove up—a car with just one man in it, who didn't get out and walk away when he had parked but just sat there with the car engine running, pretending to look at a newspaper.

This is it, Brian said to himself. *I knew it would happen one day, and now it's going to.*

For just a moment he wished he'd never come. What if he got something wrong—say, he couldn't remember the car number or something? He ought to have brought a pencil to write it down with. Only he hadn't brought any paper.

But he repeated and repeated the number to himself—EJJ 238J, EJJ 238J, EJJ 238J—and hoped it would be all right whatever happened.

Then he looked at his watch. It was important to know the time of arrival of the suspicious vehicle.

It was only a quarter of nine. The banks didn't open till nine-thirty. The getaway driver was going to have a long time to wait.

It was then that he had his great idea. He'd always imagined the second car arriving only just before the men with the stolen cash came thundering across the bridge. But if this one had come so early, there would be masses of time to get to the nearest phone box and tell the police about it before the others came. Then the police could be waiting for them on the spot, and he would actually see the arrests.

He slid out of his hiding place and went quickly down the quiet side road, on the opposite side from the parked getaway car, to where on previous expeditions he had located a phone box just in case. And he knew the number of the police station and the number of the car—EJJ 238J.

He got through without any trouble. It was all going like a dream.

"I want to report some suspicious circumstances," he said.

"Yes, madam."

It took him a moment to recover from that. But he did. "I'm not a madam. I'm a boy, and I want to tell you about a getaway car that's parked on Hillingdon Road. Car number EJJ 238J."

The man at the police station listened to everything he had to say. In silence. Brian rather wished he would interrupt. Or say, "Just a moment, I'd better put out an all-stations call."

But he didn't. He just listened right to the end, and then he said, "All right, sonny. You've had your bit of fun. Now hop off the line quick, like a good lad. It might be wanted for a real emergency."

Brian thought of telling him that this was the real emergency, but he didn't think he'd be able to convince him. And then the line might be wanted for an emergency as well—a road accident, say, or some old lady losing her cat. He hung up.

Slowly and sadly he went back to the bridge, really because he couldn't think of anything else to do. He went right past the man in the car this time—he was still reading his paper—but he didn't bother to look at him. He reached his hiding place and settled down in it.

What's the good of crime? he thought. *S'pose I'll have to try and get interested in football.*

And then, round the corner at the end of Hillingdon Road, there came a police car, going rather fast, taking the corner with a squeal of tires.

It's them. It's the police. They listened. I was right.

The thoughts flashed through Brian's head. He jumped up from his squatting position and peered out along the road.

The police car drew up sharply just beside EJJ 238J. The cop who wasn't driving got out and approached the man with the newspaper.

Golly, suppose he pulls out a gun and starts firing.

But the man didn't. He just lowered his paper, switched off

the car engine, and listened to what the policeman had to say. Then he pulled out something from his pocket—it was probably his driver's license—and talked for a bit while the policeman examined it. And finally the policeman gave it back to him and returned to the cruiser. It drove away.

The man in the car sat staring in front of him. Brian could see the look of annoyance on his face even through the windshield. He dodged back into hiding.

And that was what must have given his position away. Because the next moment the man flung the car door open, bounced out, and came walking fast, straight toward him.

Oh, golly, Brian thought.

But that wasn't the worst of it. All the rain in the night had created a huge sticky patch of mud just to the side of the path going up to the bridge, and as the man came up to the place between the two tall girders his feet went right into it. His shoes sank in till the mud squelched over their tops.

So by the time he reached Brian, he was in a doubly tearing rage.

"You—you little sneak!" he shouted. "What do you mean poking your little nose in where it's not wanted, getting a good honest man quietly reading his paper in the warm because he's too early for an appointment into trouble with the police? And my license out of date, too! I've got a good mind to haul you out of there and give you what you deserve!"

Brian just shrank back farther and farther into his hiding place and wished some black doors would open behind him and let him fall into a sort of nothingness where nothing ever happened and nothing you did ever did anything to any other person ever. But at last the man ran out of nasty things to say and turned back and squished his way through the mud again to his car. When he got into it he started up the motor once more and drove away fast.

Brian sat where he was, wishing he'd never got interested in crime, that he had never learned how most bank raids happen, that it had rained all morning and stopped him coming out.

So deep was his misery that it was some time before he took it in that heavy steps, three or four sets of them, were coming thundering along the bridge above him. And that just where car EJJ 238J had been waiting another car had drawn up, plunging into its place as if it were on the point of being late.

It was it.

It was happening.

And this time it really was the right thing. Brian quickly squirmed out of his hiding place and looked up at the bridge. Yes, there were three men running along it, and each of them was lugging a pair of bulky black polyethylene sacks. The loot. The stolen cash. And the driver of the car that had just pulled up had jumped out and was flinging open its trunk ready for the others to throw in the sacks.

It was it. It really, really was.

Brian hopped up and down in sheer delight.

And that was when the driver of the getaway car saw him. "A kid!" he yelled. "There's a blooming kid there!"

Which was when Brian made his big mistake. If he had pretended just to have been playing the men might have left him to it. But he didn't pretend he didn't understand exactly what was going on. He knew he had been spotted, and he ran.

But there was only one way to go—down Hillingdon Road. He started to get over to the opposite side from the car, but it was no good. The driver was very fast on his feet, and before Brian had gone ten yards he had him firmly gripped by his T-shirt and a moment later he was pushing him painfully by the neck down onto all fours on the ground just at the edge of that sea of mud.

"Gawd," Brian heard him say, "what are we gonna do? Little bleeder's sure to have seen the car number. I told you we ought ter 'ave stolen one for this part of it, too. What are we gonna do?"

"Aw, give 'im a good kick and let 'im go," another voice said. "Little kid like that'll never be able ter describe us."

Oh, that's right, too, Brian thought, his face near the slimy mud. *I couldn't describe them. I never really looked at them. And the car number, I didn't even look at that!*

But then a sudden realization came to him.

If he hadn't been able to see the number of this car in the short time it had been there and with all the excitement of the men coming pounding over the bridge, he could see it now, despite his face being held down so close to the muddy puddle. He could see it quite clearly through his legs. JPD 269N.

Yes, but would he remember that? Would he be able to remember it with all the things that might happen to him in the next few minutes? Would he—he suddenly felt as if his stomach weren't there—would he even be around to remember it? If these men were as tough as some bank robbers, the ones who had sawn-off shotguns and used them—

But, though he felt so empty inside that he was almost not there at all, his brain still seemed to be working. Working and whirring. And coming up with an extraordinary idea. He didn't have anything to write a car number on, and held face-down the way he was, he couldn't have written anything if he had. But there was, bang in front of him, a marvelous writing surface. And he had just the thing to write on it with. His finger.

Heaving himself up a tiny bit, he got his right hand off the ground. Stretching forward just a few inches, he found a smooth area of mud that was just right. And there, digging deep into the firm sticky stuff, he traced out the number—JPD 269N.

He was lucky the driver didn't notice him because something else had been distracting his attention. "Blimey," he was saying, "that's a police siren. This side of the canal. Come on —run!"

"Yeah. Push the kid in the mud and let's go."

Brian felt himself hurtled forward into the squelching muck, hoping he had flung himself enough to the side to have missed those letters inscribed in its sticky surface, and then with mud in his mouth and in his eyes and all up his nose he didn't know what was happening for some time.

The first thing he knew was the feel of a hand on his shoulder pulling him upward. Then he realized he was hearing a voice. "It might be the kid who phoned in when we came round here earlier," it said.

Brian rolled over. Yes, it was a policeman. And the cruiser he had seen before was drawn up at the curb a few yards away.

"Listen, sonny," the policeman said. "Did you by any chance see some men get into a car here a few minutes ago?"

"JPD 269N," Brian said.

"You did? And that's the number? Hey, that's pretty good!"

"Oh, come on," said the driver of the car, who had come up, too. "The kid can't be sure of that, not after being out cold here in a puddle and all. He's making it up."

"No," said Brian. And he pointed to the sticky, firm mud at the puddle's edge, where, plain to see, the car number JPD 269N was still clearly inscribed.

"I'll get on the radio. Car computer. We could be lucky."

The driver wasn't gone very long, and when he came back his face was wreathed in smiles. "They did it," he said. "Old box o'tricks turned up trumps. Vehicle registered in the name of Arthur Blagrove."

"Awful Arthur," said his mate. "Awful Arthur Blagrove. Well, this time we've got him dead to rights." Then the two of them took down Brian's name in their notebooks, because they said he'd be a necessary witness when it came to the trial. And after that they took him home in the police car. So he did get a ride in one, and without anybody having to make excuses, either. But the nicest thing of all was what happened when they let him out.

He was walking up the garden path, a bit worried about all the mud on his clothes, when he heard just through the cruiser's open window what the driver said to his mate. "You know, that boy'll make a jack one of these days, see if he doesn't."

Brian wasn't quite sure that he remembered what a "jack" was, but he thought he had read in one of his paperbacks that it was police slang for a detective.

H. R. F. KEATING was educated at Trinity College, Dublin. His mystery novels have won awards from both the Crime Writers Association in England and the Mystery Writers of America.

DEAD-LETTER
DROP

H. R. F. Keating

David hates awful Cousin Edna, and at last he has good reason to turn her over to the police.

It's an affront to a boy of ten to learn about how spies work from a fifty-year-old spinster. But it was from his cousin Edna that David learned what a dead-letter drop is. That it is the well-chosen hiding place, like a loose brick high up in an unfrequented alleyway or a hollow place in the fourth tree from the railway bridge, that a spy uses to pass on stolen secrets to his spymaster.

It wasn't even as though David liked Cousin Edna. In fact, he hated her. Creaky and thin, with her face looking as if it were molded onto the bone beneath with candle grease, she wafted down onto him whenever she bent to kiss him, as she would insist on doing, a sickening odor of sweet face powder and strong toothpaste. Once every three months she came down from Kettering, where she presided over the typing pool at a big government research place, and stayed for two nights. David knew her "little London jaunts," as she called them, consisting as they did of a series of nagging criticisms preceded by such phrases as "I know it's not my place to say it but," were just as unpopular with his parents as they were with him.

The way he found out about dead-letter drops from such an unlikely informant was simple: one morning he followed her. She always went out for what she called "a little breath of good London air before breakfast" and, as David was practicing following people and had given himself his own breakfast a good half hour earlier, he slipped off after her and dodged along behind parked cars, keeping her in sight. So he was able to see quite clearly how she paused by the fourth tree from the railway bridge and, when she thought no one was around, reached up quickly and pushed something into a hollow place where the first branches forked.

To begin with, of course, David just wondered why Cousin Edna had done such a funny thing. And as soon as she had hurried off he went over to the tree, scrambled up its knobby trunk, and thrust a hand into the deep cleft half-filled with soft, warm, tindery wood. He found a long thin packet, a sort of envelope made of dark oily-looking paper.

He opened it, reasoning sensibly that it had been left where anyone could have found it. It was when he saw inside a narrow strip of camera film that he realized Cousin Edna must be a spy. He knew it even before he held the strip up to the light and saw that the pictures on it were of plans. Cousin Edna had referred too often to the "great big important secrets" that abounded at her place of work for him to have any doubts.

His first thought was that now he could get Cousin Edna arrested and that would be the end of her little London jaunts. But almost at the same instant it came to him that she was, after all, one of the family "in a way" and that to tell the police about her would be—he couldn't produce the word but the thought was there—a betrayal.

Then, as he pushed the film back into the long thin envelope, he thought that Cousin Edna deserved to be betrayed for being so nasty—and then that somehow because she was so nasty she deserved not to be betrayed.

And so he stood on the empty early-morning pavement with a pigeon in the leaves above him going coo-coo-coo and everything around fresh and still, and he felt hot from head to foot with torment over what he ought to do. Then, just as the pigeon flew out of the tree with a clatter of wings as loud almost as a pistol shot in the morning quiet, a policeman came into sight. He rounded a far corner and came toward David at his slow policeman's pace as if two great lead weights were swinging inside his legs.

David stayed fixed to the spot. And the knowledge blossomed inside him that when the constable reached him he would have to have chosen. He tried to find reasons for taking one course or the other, for breaching the edifice of family trust (even though Cousin Edna was not really part of it), or for gleefully handing over the hated one to retribution (when somehow the retribution, obscure and terrible, seemed too much for the offense).

Already the constable was standing on the far side of the corner twenty yards away. David felt he was being stared at with an all-seeing, penetrating vision. Would he be asked what he was doing out at this time of the morning? What could he say?

Now the constable was looking slowly to left and right. And now he was crossing. David went cold as leaden ice. And the policeman, turning his head just a little, gave him a single calm regard and walked past.

"Please," David said. "Please."

The constable stopped and turned slowly round.

"Well, sonny?"

David swallowed.

"Please," he said, "I want to report a spy."

"Do you now?" said the constable.

He didn't grin or anything, but David knew he was partly amused and partly ready to stamp on any cheekiness that went a hairsbreadth too far. Desperately he thrust the dark oily-paper envelope upward.

"This," he said. "It was in this tree. I saw her put it there."

To his relief the policeman did at least take the envelope and even examine it. And he must have caught a glimpse of the strip of film under the broken flap, because suddenly a little frown crossed his face and he turned the envelope upside down, slid out the strip, and held it up between a big red finger and thumb. Then he looked down at David with quite a different expression on his face.

"You say you saw a woman place this in the tree here?" he asked.

"Yes," said David in a croaky whisper.

"Would you be able to recognize the lady again if you saw her?"

"Oh, yes. She's my—" David stopped. "Yes," he said. "I would recognize her because I've seen her before. I think she comes here on visits."

"Well, now," said the constable, "perhaps you'd better just step along to the station with me and tell them all about it there."

At the police station David assured a coaxingly friendly policewoman that he wouldn't be missed at home, as he often went out by himself on summer mornings, and accepted a cup of very sweet tea. He was offered a pile of battered comics to read. He had gone through four of them, not skipping at all, when the policewoman came back with Mr. Lummox.

Mr. Lummox was a big shambling-looking man who wore a belted buff-colored raincoat that had seen better days. His large brick red face with two small blue eyes in it looked a little flustered. He sat down with a grunt of tiredness and at once began asking about the envelope.

Before long David had to admit to himself that an unthinkable suspicion he had begun to have almost from the very start was right: Mr. Lummox was not really at all clever. For one thing, he kept switching from asking questions in ridiculous baby talk to using words David just didn't understand. And then several times he showed quite plainly that he hadn't really been listening to the answers.

So David felt no qualms at all when he realized that he could prevent his parents ever knowing who had told the police about Cousin Edna by, instead of giving his own name and address, saying that he was Jimmy Smith and lived at No. 3 in a street four blocks away. He had come to the conclusion, after giving the matter thought, that the government could easily recognize the photographed plans as coming from the place where Cousin Edna worked and that no one else would have put them in that particular tree.

When Mr. Lummox abruptly blundered out and the policewoman came back, David accepted a ride in a police car to the corner of his own street, confident that Mr. Lummox wouldn't have passed on the false address.

His jaunty mood lasted until he set foot inside his front door. And then, suddenly, the awfulness of it all surged up and overwhelmed him. He bolted up to his room, heaved the door shut behind him, and plunged into the narrow space between the chest of drawers and the wall where he was accustomed to crouch in desperate moments and where, he believed, nobody ever thought of looking for him.

Yet, quick as his dash had been, he had been unable not to hear Cousin Edna's voice coming from the kitchen. Worse, even, when at lunchtime he had to go down and sit opposite her. He hardly ate a thing and couldn't bring himself to cast the briefest of glances at Cousin Edna, not even when she spoke to him.

"Ah," she said, "who's getting a little bit bashful with the girls? My little Davy-dee didn't used to be so shy. He used to go with his old cousin Ed—"

It was then that the front doorbell rang. David's mother went to answer it and came back looking slightly puzzled. "It's for you, Edna," she said. "A Mr. Lummox."

Cousin Edna went out, murmuring that she couldn't imagine what anybody would want with little her in great big London town.

Then after a bit she called back that she would have to go out for a wee few minutes.

David felt as if he had been sitting watching a film on television and the set had suddenly stopped working. There was a great unexpected blank. It was suddenly all over. But what he had done was still there. He had betrayed Cousin Edna. An iron collar seemed to have been fastened round his neck to weigh achingly on his shoulders.

The first chance he got he slid up to his room again, seized a favorite old comic book, and wriggled himself far to the back of his narrow hiding place.

He was still there, just beginning on the book a second time, when he heard the front door open and, a moment later, a terrible, terribly familiar voice calling out, "Yoo hoo! Anybody at home?"

He sat rigid with horror, straining to hear what explanation Cousin Edna was giving his mother down in the kitchen. But all too soon the voice ceased. And the door of his room opened.

"Out you come, Davy-dee. Old Edna knows exactly where you like to tuck yourself away."

As if he were a stringed puppet, David got to his feet and moved out into the room.

"Well, now," Cousin Edna said, "who was a clever little boy and gave a wrong name to the police? And who never guessed that he'd met a very sensible old policeman who saw he was keeping something back and told his friends in the car to keep a lookout?"

"Please—Please," David gasped.

"Yes," Cousin Edna said, "I don't expect you thought you would see me again for a very long time, did you?"

She gave a little giggle, like a rusty key squeaking in a lock.

"But what you could never have known," she went on, "was that your old cousin Edna had been asked by a very high-up gentleman in M.I.5 to pretend to give away a few little secrets to a nasty man who had asked her for them so that later she could give away some big, big secrets that were quite, quite wrong."

It was then that Cousin Edna told him what a dead-letter drop was and how she had just been with Mr. Lummox to restore the narrow envelope to its proper place. And though David squirmed inwardly at the manner of her telling, he nevertheless felt spreading up inside him a quiet and singing joy. The iron collar that he had thought he would never get rid of had suddenly disappeared into thin air.

"And you were a very brave boy, my Davy-dee," Cousin Edna concluded. "It was brave of you to tell the policeman that the cousin Edna you love so much was really a beastly spy."

She gave him a smile that curled up the corners of her candle-grease face till it looked as if she might be fixed like that forever. And then she added something else.

"We won't say a single word about it, shall we? Not one

word, either of us. My little Davy-dee's splendid act shall be our very own secret."

David did not reply. But round his shoulders he felt descending another collar of iron. And this one, he knew, nothing could ever lift off.

H. R. F. KEATING was educated at Trinity College, Dublin. His mystery novels have won awards from both the Crime Writers Association in England and the Mystery Writers of America.

THE

DEATH

TRIPLE

J. L. Pouvoir

An anachronistic journalist investigates the death of a marathon runner who knew how to prepare for the Olympic Games . . . and the Thermonuclear Games.

S trider had felt the legs coming undone on Rodeo Road, half-a-dozen miles from the Coliseum. No mystery there; every distance man ran out of glucose and met The Wall after he'd gone twenty.

Two miles later he'd sensed what Don Kardong had described at Montreal: "As if my vital organs were dropping out onto the street one by one." No novelty there, either. You ran the final four miles of an Olympic marathon on memory and instinct. Legs, lungs, and other moving parts became irrelevant.

Plodding down Exposition Boulevard, Strider felt reason leave him, too. The medals were impossible now. DeCastella was already inside the Coliseum, a minute from winning the gold for Australia. Shahanga of Tanzania was sprinting down the tunnel thirty seconds back, certain of the silver.

Salazar, the doe-eyed thoroughbred from the Boston suburbs, would take the bronze. An Englishman, a Portuguese, a Japanese were strung out behind at hundred-yard intervals. Strider, the second American, was seventh and nowhere.

The streetside faces had gone blurry on him, their voices blended to a babble. Half a mile to go now, his eyes losing focus, chest hurting terribly, pain surging everywhere, sky spinning, legs buckling, the pavement coming up to meet him.

The man from the IOC medical commission, a Belgian prince, met the world press at 9 P.M., one hour after the medals had been awarded, the flags hoisted, the Australian anthem played. A terrible thing, he said, a dreadful day for the Games.

Strider of the United States had collapsed and expired 200 yards from the Coliseum. Cause of death believed to be a myocardial infarction. In layman's terms, a heart attack. Unusual, yes, yes it was. Strider was thirty years old, thought to be in impeccable condition. But this was his third event in seven days, his second in twenty-four hours. The strain on his cardiovascular system . . . perhaps his heart was flawed. There would be an autopsy, of course. Probably not before morning. That's all the information we have at the moment.

The Europeans couldn't do much with it; the evening's last deadline had long passed in London, Paris, Frankfurt. The correspondents for the *Daily Mail,* for *L'Equipe,* for the *Zeitung* shrugged and sought the bus.

The East Coast sportswriters dashed for the rows of portable typewriters inside the press subcenter. Thirty minutes to make the city editions of the *Times,* the *Post,* the *Globe.* "Three-time Olympian T. J. Strider," they tapped, "who won two Olympic medals last week, collapsed and—"

No such urgency tugged at Sweeney. He was employed by the last afternoon daily east of Pittsburgh, a fine Baltimore relic called the *Nocturne* that had managed to survive the Six O'Clock News, crosstown traffic, and the demise of the padded armchair.

The newspaper had begun when Sweeney did, in the summer of 1922, and progressed leisurely—as he did—through the Jazz Age, the Depression, the Second War, and an assortment of regional upheavals. Breathlessness suited neither of them.

Sweeney at sixty-two was the last of the gentlemen sportswriters, gentleman and sportswriter generally being regarded as mutually exclusive. Nobody in his craft wore vested suits and watch chains any longer, but Sweeney did. Tweeds in the fall, flannels in the winter, linens in the summer, hats appropriate to the season. The functional gait, supplemented by a blackthorn stick, was somewhere between an amble and a stroll. If the afternoon newspaper did not exist, a succession of editors had grown fond of saying, it would have had to have been invented for Sweeney.

In a day when younger colleagues carried battery-powered computer keyboards with them on assignment, Sweeney still favored yellow legal pads and a fountain pen.

He wrote all dispatches longhand, in a script resembling runic, and dictated them by telephone, inserting punctuation as needed.

It was a filing procedure that demanded generous deadlines, and Sweeney was accustomed to a dozen hours. The geographical realities of Los Angeles cost him three hours; still, there were nine left to Sweeney to stroll and poke about, to make a call or two, and fiddle with the computer terminals the organizers had installed at every Olympic venue from Long Beach to Ojai.

Each of them was linked to a monster mainframe that hoarded millions of marginally applicable data shreds. Every Szechuan restaurant in Westwood. The birthdates of the entire Bolivian modern pentathlon team. The semicondensed history of the summer Games during the modern era. Memorable dates in the chronology of the city of Los Angeles and the state of California. The departure times of every Continental Airlines flight between here and Denver.

Sweeney had grave doubts about much of this business of inscribing the Library of Congress on a microchip. He viewed computers much as he viewed television—as a form of skywriting. Push a button and a vision appeared. Push another and it vanished. In the fourteenth century they burned people who did such things at the stake. *Now,* Sweeney mused, *they give them stock options.*

The technology did have its uses, though, and Sweeney had always been a man of perspective. He'd given up the Pullman car for the Whisperjet, the dial phone for the touchtone.

Now Sweeney wandered into the subcenter, where a hundred journalists from Santa Ana and Sao Paulo and St. Moritz sat pounding out their stories. He commandeered a terminal and brought it to life with an index finger. Up came the menu, the complete list of available data.

Today's schedule, today's results, total results for every sport for two weeks. Names of every athlete, alphabetically and by country. Plane, train, and bus schedules in and out of Los Angeles. Emergency numbers. Biographical sketches on each competitor.

Sweeney punched 01 and got the biographical order form. On the line reading NAME OF ATHLETE, he typed STRIDER. In half a second a screenful of green letters and numbers shimmered.

NAME: Strider, Thomas Jefferson, AGE: 30. HT.: 5-9. WT.: 150.

COUNTRY: USA. HOMETOWN: Litchfield, Conn. COLLEGE: Yale.
CLUB: Unattached.

The basics were followed by Strider's competitive history, his qualifying times, his performance in the Games.

Much of it Sweeney already knew. Strider had been at Montreal in 1976 as a Yale senior, the third American in the 10,000 meters. He'd reached the finals, pushed Finland's Lasse Viren for a while, then faded to eighth. He'd made the U.S. team again in 1980, the top man in three events, but Jimmy Carter had kept Strider and everyone else home from Moscow. A national security issue, Carter said.

Los Angeles was to be his farewell performance. Strider had run well in the U.S. marathon trials at Buffalo, hanging in with Pete Pfitzinger and Salazar once the pack broke apart, and had made the three-man team. Then he'd turned in personal bests in the track-and-field trials at the Coliseum a month later and qualified in both the 5,000 and 10,000.

The death triple, they called it, the toughest parlay in the sport. Run the 10,000 on Monday. Come back Saturday for the 5,000. Then again Sunday for the marathon, twenty-six miles through Santa Monica and Venice and Marina del Rey, then across the boulevards—La Cienega, La Brea, Crenshaw—to the Coliseum.

You could kill yourself trying the death triple, literally bust a gut, but it could be, had been, done. Zatopek had done it in 1952, winning all three. Viren had done it at Montreal and gone 1–1–5. No American had ever done it.

The computer told Strider's story. Silver in the 10,000 behind Cova of Italy. Bronze in the 5,000. DNF in the marathon. Did Not Finish. "Understatement," Sweeney murmured.

He walked to the cluster of long-distance phones in the corner and pushed 1-203-555-1212. "New Haven," he said. "Yale University. Sterling Library." Sweeney scribbled 436-8335, then pushed them. "Reference, please. . . . Yes. Could you put your hand on the yearbook for the undergraduate class of 1976?"

Five minutes passed. "Yes. Could you look up Thomas Strider and read me what it has under his name? Thank you."

Sweeney jotted notes on the back of a press release from a German shoe company listing its gold medalists for the past fortnight. At the Olympic Games, champions did not belong to countries. They belonged to Adidas, to Nike, to Tiger.

Born June 4, 1954 in New York City . . . Prepared at the Taft School . . . Lived in Davenport College . . . Major: Slavic Languages . . . Activities: Varsity Cross-Country, Varsity Track, Skull and Bones, Yale Russian Chorus . . . Future plans: Design School . . . "Cahn't thank you enough."

Now to the athletes' village, less than a mile away by black-thorn. The Americans were staying in a dormitory at USC. Odds were they'd be stuffing gear into zippered nylon bags by now, preparing for the morning flights out of LAX for a dozen points east.

With luck, Shackleford would be among them. He'd been an intermediate hurdler at Princeton when Strider was at Yale, had competed with and against him for ten years. Sweeney knew Shackleford from several forgotten Yale–Princeton–Harvard meets. The Big Three, they were called, but that was ancient history. Older than Sweeney.

Sweeney found Shackleford in the game room at the village, vaporizing a galactic cruiser. "*Mis*-tah Sweeney," he said, without glancing up.

"Old buddy, how ahh you?"

"More depressed than I was an hour ago."

"Strider." Sweeney winced. "I knew his father. I have a question for you about all that. This Russian business. Strider spoke it. Sang it. Went there."

Shackleford nodded. "And knew them. A lot of them."

"How?"

Shackleford, momentarily between cruisers, sighed. "Strider ran in Europe every summer for ten years," he said. "Oslo, Milan, Stockholm, Helsinki, Stuttgart—the whole circuit. He competed in every USA–USSR dual, went over for the Spartakiade in Moscow that year when they invited foreigners. You'd always see him hanging around with their distance types. Moseyev, Fyedotkin, Antipov, those guys. Some people said he was working for the CIA. Informal stuff, nothing serious.

"The CIA has a thousand guys like that they can call upon. Professors from Caltech, immunologists, violinists, javelin throwers. Anyone who goes to Eastern Europe in an official capacity and who might come across something interesting. When they get back, they check in with someone at Langley. Not a formal debriefing. More like lunch."

"Seems logical," Sweeney conceded. "But why Strider?"

"He studied urban planning at Harvard Design School after Yale. Knew something about the infrastructure of major cities. He could tell you how the Moscow metro system functioned. How buildings were reinforced in Leningrad. Things of that nature."

Sweeney cocked an eyebrow. "Everything you might want to know if you were preparing for the Thermonuclear Games."

"Something like that. There was talk that Strider might go with them full time after the Games. Langley's always had a soft spot for old boys who were Skull and Bones. They like the secret-society concept. Fee-fi-fo-fum and all that."

Sweeney put the notebook away. "Shack, old buddy, *always* good to see you. Sorry about the 400."

"What can I say?" Shackleford shrugged, blotting an entire imperial convoy from his video screen. "Edwin Moses is immortal."

Now, Sweeney guessed, *to call a certain lab assistant up at UCLA. How does an Olympic medalist in perfect condition die in a footrace? Only his analytical chemist knows for sure.*

From a pay phone downstairs, Sweeney rang 825-2635.

"Clinical pharmacology," a voice answered.

"Steadman, if you please," Sweeney said.

"She's fiddling with the gas chromatograph upstairs. I'll see if we can fetch her."

Steadman was a UCLA graduate student, twenty-two and brunette, and she'd been fiddling with the gas chromatograph twelve hours at a time for fourteen days, running through urine samples from a random succession of Italian fencers, German oarsmen, American weight lifters, and other sporting fauna.

The gas chromatograph, one of Silicon Valley's more complex toys, broke down the sample into molecules and spat forth a zigzag graph. If any of the molecules contained a banned drug, the chemists informed the International Olympic Committee, master of these quadrennial revels, and the committee went about the business of stripping medals, erasing records, suspending athletes, and other social pleasantries. Total time from delivery to detection: less than twenty-four hours.

Sweeney had met the gas chromatograph—and Steadman— a year earlier when he'd gone through on the lab tour they'd rigged up for the sporting press. He thought her brilliant and delightful. She thought him anachronistic and charming.

"Steadman here."

"And Sweeney here, old girl. How's the gas-passing game been going for you?"

"Pretty slowly since the weight lifting's been done with. We found enough anabolics there to choke a herd of Guernseys. Not much this week, as you've probably heard. One Venezuelan boxer swallowed some cough syrup. A little nose spray here and there. And Strider."

"Strider? I thought he'd always been clean."

"He was on Monday, after the 10,000. Last night, though, we found strychnine. You didn't hear it here, but they were going to announce it in the morning. His 5,000 is wiped from the books and the bronze goes to the Kenyan."

"Insane," Sweeney muttered. "Nobody's used strychnine since the twenties."

"Somebody did yesterday," Steadman replied. "Your boy Strider. The gas chromatograph knows all. Dump a teaspoon of sugar in an Olympic-sized swimming pool and the GC will find it."

"In your debt," Sweeney said, ringing off. "As always."

What was this, Sweeney asked himself, 1896? Do-it-yourself doping out of your medicine cabinet? Why not just drink a bottle of Sloan's Liniment? Who was that American who'd staggered in to win the 1904 marathon at St. Louis? Hicks. He'd mixed strychnine and cognac and damn near killed himself.

Nobody did crude stimulants anymore. There were more sophisticated methods available, like blood doping. A dose of strychnine might not hurt you in a 5,000-meter race, but it could kill you in a marathon, particularly if you ran both events a day apart. Why would Strider want to kill himself doing a death triple?

Precisely, Sweeney realized. Strider wouldn't, but somebody else might.

A competitor? It didn't figure. Strider had never broken 2:11.40 in any marathon; he didn't shape up as a medalist here.

Who, then? The KGB, worried about the Langley connection? But how could they get to Strider? An Olympic village was only slightly less secure than a SAC base.

The Los Angeles organizers had signed on nearly two security people for every athlete. They had state-of-the-art communications and sensing equipment. A coded photo-ID system. Fences everywhere. And a former FBI agent running the show.

Plus, Strider had never been one to go off on his own at the Games. Sweeney remembered that from Montreal. The village had whatever he needed—movies, banking facilities, twenty-four-hour cafeteria, duty-free shops, and the French women's 4×100 relay team, which Strider had taken on as a project in serial seduction. Monique, Francoise, Jeanne, and Sylvie in that order, leadoff to anchor. Qualifying time: 43.60 seconds.

Strider left the village only to go to one of the practice tracks or to the Coliseum, boarding a guarded bus each way. If the KGB wanted him dead, they had to come to Strider, and that meant getting inside the gates. And the only people with that privilege were the "Olympic family"—officials, coaches, athletes, trainers, logistical staff, the press.

Back upstairs, Sweeney sought the man from Princeton. He found him engrossed in the Robby Roto machines, surrounded by an admiring throng of Austrians. "Talk to you, old buddy? Away from these mittel-Europeans?"

Shackleford grinned. "I guess Robby Roto can chew his way through this mineshaft on his own."

"You didn't see Strider yesterday morning, did you? Before the 5,000?"

"Sure did. We had breakfast together in the cafeteria. Or at least we were there at the same time. I had the 4×400 relay final to deal with, so we were both on the same schedule. Got up about eight, ate around ten. Whole-grain toast. Fruit. Juice. An egg or two. Loosen up for an hour or so, nap for a while, bus to the Coliseum. The usual race-day ritual."

"See him with anybody?"

"A couple of West German milers. And that Russian field-events judge—you know, the one who's been at every Games since Helsinki. Florid face, square jaw, pomade hair. Smokes those cigarettes with cardboard filters. Your basic Cyrillic stereotype. Strider's known him for years."

"What's his name?"

"Vladimir. Vladislav. Valeri. Vanya. I don't know. Every Russian first name since Chekhov begins with a *V.*"

"Obligated," Sweeney concluded. "As always."

I suppose all I need to know now, Sweeney thought, *the computer can tell me.* He walked through Exposition Park just a trifle more briskly than before, displayed his photo-ID for the guard at the Coliseum gate, and made for the subcenter and a terminal.

He called up the menu, punched 17, and got the list of judges and referees, broken down by sport.

He pushed 01 and track-and-field appeared. Two-thirds of the way down, Sweeney noticed PETROV, VASILY I. (URS), and it came together for him. Petrov had judged the shot put the day before. There were no other Russians on the screen. *Has to be,* Sweeney thought.

Back to the menu. Punch 12 for the transportation schedules, 03 for the airlines. Sweeney scrolled the listings until he came to Los Angeles–Tokyo.

One flight tonight, JAL. Several more tomorrow. The menu again. Punch 16 for frequently used numbers, then 02 for airlines.

"If you please, I'm supposed to be traveling to Tokyo tonight with a Mr. Petrov, first initial *V,*" Sweeney said, "but I'm not sure of the carrier and flight. Could you assist me? . . . Flight 62, that's fine. Awfully good of you."

Once more to the menu, Sweeney told himself, *and be done with it.* Punch 13 for emergency numbers. The FBI was 272-6161.

"This is Sweeney with the *Baltimore Nocturne.* You may want to stop and search a Vasily Petrov on JAL 62. Leaves at eleven tonight. I believe he may have something to do with the death of that American marathoner, Strider. If you need me further, I'm at the Biltmore downtown. As always."

Sweeney yawned and glanced around the subcenter. Half-past ten and nobody here but the man from the *San Diego Union.* You could come in at any given hour and see the man from the *San Diego Union* at his place, transcribing tapes, the rewind button worn to a nub. Sweeney consulted his pocket watch. Barely seven hours until deadline. He drew up a chair, fished in a vest pocket for the fountain pen, and began composing the definitive account. *William Bolitho Ryall*, Sweeney thought, *we're arm in arm, you and I.*

The *Times* and the phone call from Special Agent Egan arrived simultaneously in the morning. The *Times* had Petrov nicely manacled on page 1, the bushy eyebrows arched in surprise, a federal employee at each elbow. They'd found a dossier on Strider in his shoulderbag, an empty drug vial in his room back at the village, and start lists for each event in the death triple.

"Nice piece of work, Mister Sweeney," Egan began.

"No bother," Sweeney demurred. "Late deadline, you know. Wasn't pressed for time."

"How did you figure Petrov, though?"

"All the usual elements. Motive. Opportunity. Method. Somebody wanted Strider dead and wanted to make it look as though he'd done it himself. But Strider seemed like an intelligent sort, what with the New Haven background. Yale men don't usually run around doing themselves in. It's unseemly. Not to mention unproductive."

"Why here?"

"Last good chance," Sweeney said. "Strider was going to quit running after the Games, and they couldn't be sure what Langley would do with him. The CIA can make you reasonably inaccessible if they care to. Besides, the Soviets' boycott stood to work to their own advantage."

"How so?"

"Once the Eastern bloc pulled out, most people assumed there'd be no problems with security. Oh, there were as many uniformed types walking around with holstered weapons, but the tension level was scaled back considerably. It was easy to forget that there were Russians here, but there were. They still sent their judges and officials, because the Soviets wanted to hold their ground politically in the sporting federations. And of course they had access to most areas that are restricted to the public."

"So how do you narrow it to Petrov? And Strider?"

"Strider knew more than they thought healthy about their urban infrastructure. And Petrov knew Strider. Knew his breakfast ritual and knew that Strider would have his guard down around him. Somewhere along the line, I gather, Petrov dosed him. Not all the Soviet judges are judges. A healthy number double for the KGB. They keep an eye on their own athletes, in case they have any defection fantasies. And they're available for a bit of counterespionage, too."

"But why JAL? The Russians have all their people housed aboard their luxury liner in the harbor off Long Beach. Petrov could have left with them on their Aeroflot charter today."

"Too much could have happened overnight. They would have found the strychnine during the autopsy. And somebody could have made the same deduction I did."

Egan smiled. "As I said, a nice piece of work."

"Composition without reportage falls short of journalism," Sweeney said. "Mencken told me."

J. L. POUVOIR is the pseudonym of a young Pulitzer Prize–winning journalist. "The Death Triple" is the first of a series of stories about sportswriter Sweeney of the Baltimore Nocturne. *This story was originally published in* Ellery Queen's Mystery Magazine *weeks before the 1984 summer Olympics in Los Angeles, so the winners of the marathon and the 400 hurdles were projected by the author. He was wrong about the marathon, right about the 400.*

DON'T
BE
FRIGHTENED

Celia Fremlin

Sixteen-year-old Lorna feels contempt for her mother—until she's visited by a spirit whose contempt surpasses even Lorna's own.

N ow that she had it to herself, Lorna Webster felt she could almost enjoy hating her home so much. She flung her beret onto the sofa, dumped her schoolbag down in the middle of the floor, and watched with satisfaction as the books and papers spilled out over her mother's spotless, well-vacuumed carpet. It was nice to be able to mess it up like that, without risk of reprimand.

She gazed round the neat, firelit room with contempt. Hideous ornaments—houseplants, bric-a-brac of all kinds; and on either side of the fireplace those two neat, well-upholstered armchairs were drawn up, for all the world as if a happily married couple habitually sat in them; a contented couple, smiling at each other across the hearth; not a couple like Lorna's parents, always wrangling, bickering, squabbling, the long evenings filled with temper or with tears.

With slatternly, spread-eagled violence Lorna flung herself into the nearer of the two chairs, sending it skidding and scratching under her weight across the polished wooden floor around the carpet.

That was better! Lorna spread out the length of her legs untidily in the luxurious abandonment of solitude—real, reliable, long-term solitude, a whole glorious evening of it, and a whole night to follow!

Such a fuss there had been about this simple business of leaving her alone in the house for one night! Just as if she had been a baby, instead of a young woman of nearly sixteen!

"Be sure you bolt all the doors," her mother had said, not once but ten times. "Be sure you put the guard in front of the fire before you go to bed. Be sure you turn off the oven. Be sure you don't answer the door to anyone you don't know. And remember you can always go over to the Holdens if you feel the least bit nervous."

Go over to the Holdens, indeed! Lorna would have died— yes, she would willingly have lain right here on the carpet with her throat cut—before she would run for help to that dreary Holden woman, who was both boring and sly, with her perpetual chatter-chatter over the wall to Mummy about the problems of teenage daughters. Ugh!

Ah, but this was the life! Lorna slid yet deeper and more luxuriously into the cushioned depths of the chair. Tea when she liked; supper when she liked; homework when she liked; music when she liked. Lorna's eyes turned with lazy anticipation toward the pile of pop records stacked under the record player. Ah, the fuss there usually was over those records, with Mummy twittering in and out, trying to stop Daddy being annoyed by them. "Can't you turn it down a little lower, dear? Can't you play them in the afternoons when Daddy's not here? You know how it annoys him."

What Mummy didn't realize was that actually it was quite fun annoying Daddy—a real roaring, bellowing row instead of all these anxious twitterings! And afterward Daddy would go on yelling at Mummy for hours, long after the records were finished and done with. And then next day Mummy would scuttle about with red eyes, polishing things, as if a tidy polished house were some sort of protection against quarreling!

Honestly, adults! That's why I hate the smell of polish, thought Lorna, deliberately jolting the chair on its rusty casters back and forth across the polished floor, making deep dents and scratches in the wood. *It's misery-polish that Mummy puts on everything; it's dishonesty-polish, trying to make this look like a happy home when it isn't!*

And it's all because Mummy's too cowardly, too much of a doormat, to stand up to Daddy's tempers—so she tidies the house instead. I bet she's tidied the kitchen even better than usual today, just because she's nervous about leaving me alone! She thinks tidiness is a substitute for everything!

Stirred by a flicker of resentful curiosity and also by a mounting interest in the thought of tea, Lorna dragged herself from her luxurious position and went to the kitchen to investigate.

Yes, it was immaculate. Every surface scrubbed and shining; a delicious little dish of cooked chicken salad all ready for Lorna's supper; and for her tea—just look!—a big, expensive, once-in-a-lifetime meringue, bursting with cream! A treat! Another of Mummy's pathetic attempts to provide Lorna with at least the shell of a happy home!

Irritation fought in Lorna with eager appetite. *Does she think I'm a baby or something, who needs to be consoled for its mummy being away? I love Mummy being away! I love it, I love it!*—and with each "love" her teeth sank deeper into the rare, luscious thing; the cream spurted with bounteous prodigality across her cheeks, and she didn't even have to wipe them, because she was alone. Alone, alone, alone—the nearest thing to Paradise!

Outside, the spring evening was fading. The sob and thrum of Lorna's favorite records mingled first with a pink sunset light in the pale room, then with a pearly silvery grayness against which the firelight glowed ever more orange and alive; and at last, curtains drawn, lamps switched on, coals piled recklessly into a roaring blaze, it was night; and still the records played on, over and over again. It was too lovely a time, this time of firelight and perfect solitude, to waste on anything less beautiful than the music which her parents hated so.

It was nearly nine o'clock when the telephone began to ring. It began just as Lorna had settled herself cozily by the fire with her tray of chicken salad, rolls, and a huge mug of boiling hot, sweet black coffee, whose deliciousness was enhanced by the fact that Mummy would have said, "Don't have it black, dear, not at this time of night; it'll keep you awake."

Damn! she thought, setting down the mug in the middle of the first glorious sip. *Damn! And then, Why don't I ignore it? I bet it'll just be Mummy, fussing about something. Yes, driving along those monotonous miles of highway, she'll have been thinking up some new things to worry about. Have I latched the kitchen window? Will I be sure and shut the spare-room window if it rains? Fuss, fuss, fuss, an expensive long-distance fuss from a roadside phone booth.*

I won't answer, why should I? I'll just let it ring; serve her right, teach her a lesson, show her I'm not a baby. Defiantly Lorna raised the mug to her lips once more, and calmly, leisurely, resumed her sipping.

But how the telephone kept on! It was irritating, it was spoiling this solitary, delightful meal which she had planned to savor to the full. She put down her knife and fork restlessly. Weren't they ever going to stop ringing? How long do people go on ringing before they finally give up? And just then, at last, with a despairing little hiccup, the telephone became quiet.

Silence swung back into the room, flooding Lorna with relief. She picked up her knife and fork once more and prepared to recapture her interrupted bliss. Having a meal alone by the fire like this! Alone! The joy of it! No table manners. No conversation. Just peace, delicious peace.

But somehow it had all been spoiled. The slow, savory mouthfuls tasted of almost nothing now; the new favorite magazine propped against the coffee pot could not hold her attention; and she was conscious of an odd tenseness, a waiting, listening unease in every nerve.

She finished the meal without enjoyment, and as she carried the tray out to the kitchen the telephone began again.

The shock was somehow extraordinary. Almost dropping the tray onto the kitchen table, Lorna turned and ran headlong back into the sitting room, slamming the door behind her as if that would somehow protect her from the imperious, nagging summons. All her sense of guilt and unease at not having answered before seemed to make it doubly impossible to answer now; and the longer she let it ring, the more impossible it became.

Why should anybody ring so long and so persistently? If it was Mummy, then surely she would have assumed by now that Lorna had gone over to the Holdens? Who else could it be who would ring and ring and ring like this? Surely no one goes on ringing a number *forever? Oh, please, God, make it stop!*

And at last, of course, it did stop; and again the silence filled her ears in a great flood, but this time there was no relief in it. She felt herself so tense, so tightly listening, that it was almost as if she knew, deep in her knotted stomach, just what was going to happen next.

It was a light, a very light footstep on the path out front that next caught her hearing; lightly up the steps, and then a fumbling at the front door. Not a knock, not a ring—just a fumbling, as if someone were trying to unlock the door, someone too weak, or too blind, to turn the key.

"Be sure you bolt all the doors." In her head Lorna seemed to hear those boring, familiar instructions not for the fifteenth time, but for the first. "Be sure you latch the kitchen window. Don't answer the door to anyone you don't know."

Lorna tiptoed out into the hall, and for a few moments she fancied that she must have imagined the sounds, for all was quiet. No shadowy silhouette could be seen looming against the frosted panels of the door, palely glittering in the light of the street lamp. But even as she stood there, the flap of the letter box began to stir, slowly. Lorna was looking into an eye.

A single eye, of course, as it would be if anyone were peering through a letter box; and yet, irrationally, it was this singleness that shocked Lorna most, carrying her back in an instant, beyond the civilized centuries, right back to the cyclops, to the mad, mythical beginnings of mankind. Lorna began to scream.

"Don't be frightened," came a voice from outside—a *young* voice, Lorna registered with gasping thankfulness and surprise. Why, it was a *girl's* voice! A girl no older than herself by the sound of it! "Don't be frightened, Lorna, but do please let me in."

Reassured completely by hearing her own name, Lorna flung the door open.

"Oh, you *did* give me a fright—" she was beginning, but then stopped, puzzled. For though the girl standing there looked vaguely familiar and was roughly her own age, Lorna did not know her. She had taken for granted, when she heard herself addressed by name, that she would be bound to recognize the speaker.

"Hello! I—that is, I'm awfully sorry, I'm sure I ought to know you—?" Lorna began uncertainly.

"It's all right; I didn't think you would recognize me at once," answered the girl, stepping confidently into the hall and looking around her. "I hope you don't mind my coming out of the blue like this, but I used to live here, you see."

She was a forceful-looking girl, Lorna could see now, standing there under the hall light, with strong black hair springing from a high, very white forehead; her eyes were dark and snapping-bright as if, thought Lorna, she had a quick temper and a quick wit, and very much a will of her own.

"Oh, I see," Lorna tried to collect her wits. This must be the daughter of the family that had lived here before Lorna's family had moved in, seven or eight years ago. "Oh, I see. Fancy you remembering my name! Do come in. I expect you'd like to look at everything, see how it's changed since you were here."

Already she felt that she was going to like this girl, who was looking round with such bright interest and seemed so friendly. "I'll show you my room first, shall I? I wonder if it was the same one you had? It's the little back one that looks out on the garden."

By the time they had explored the house, Lorna felt as if she and this other girl had known each other for years. They seemed to have so much the same tastes, the same loves and hates; and as they sat in front of the fire afterward, with a newly made pot of coffee between them, Lorna found herself confiding all her troubles to her new friend: Daddy's tempers, Mummy's submission and anxious, fussy housekeeping.

"I wouldn't mind," she explained, "if Mummy was *really* a house-proud sort of person—if she really got any pleasure out of making the house look nice. But she doesn't. She does it in a desperate sort of way. She clutters everything up with flowers and hideous ornaments—"

"—as if it was a substitute for making you and your father happy, you mean?" put in the other girl quickly. "You mean, since she can't give you a happy home, she's determined to give you a neat clean one, full of *things.*"

"That's it, that's it exactly!" cried Lorna. "How well you understand! But why such *ugly* things?" Her eyes swept the mantelpiece and the crowded corner cupboard. "It's as if she collected ugly things on purpose."

"I don't think so," said the other girl, glancing rapidly round the room. "They're not actually ugly, you know—not each of them taken singly. It's just that nobody loves them—your mother and father never chose any of them together, in some little curio shop, on some holiday when they were enjoying themselves. I expect your mother bought them pretending it was like that when it wasn't."

"Why, yes, I expect she did. That would be exactly like her!" cried Lorna, enchanted. Never had she found anyone before who could understand her as this girl did. "That's why I hate them so!"

"So let's smash them," said the other girl, in the same quiet, thoughtful tones. "Let's bash them to pieces on the marble fireplace there. Think how they'd crash and shatter!" There was a strange gleam in her dark eyes, and Lorna stared at her, for the first time uneasy. But she was joking—of course she was, she must be.

"Wouldn't I just love to!" Lorna gave a little laugh appropriate to such nonsense. "Have some more coffee?"

"No, I mean it. Let's! You hate them—you are right to hate them. Hateful things should be s-s-s-*smashed!*" And snatching a china shepherdess from the mantelpiece, the girl flung it with all her strength into the grate.

The splintering, shocking, unimaginable crash shocked

Lorna speechless. "Stop!" she tried to cry out as a teapot and two vases burst like spray across the hearthrug; and then, even as she finally gasped out her protests, something extraordinary began to seep into her soul. Shock, yes; but what was this joy, this exultation, this release of long pent-up anger, as crash followed crash and splinters of china bounded across the room like hail?

"Smash them, smash them!" the girl was shouting, her dark face alight with a strange joy. "Rip up the cushions! Pull down the curtains—they were sewn in misery, not in love, every stitch was stitched in misery!" With a great rending sigh the curtains came down and huddled on the floor; and by now both girls were upon them, ripping, tearing. A madness not her own was in Lorna now, and she, too, was tearing, smashing, hurling, in an ecstasy of shared destruction such as she had never dreamed possible.

Dreamed? *Was* she dreaming? Was that the telephone waking her, ringing, ringing, ringing across the devastated room? This time Lorna ran instantly to answer and snatched it from its hook.

Yes, yes, this was the home of Mrs. Mary Webster. "Yes, I'm her daughter. No, I'm afraid my father is not in. You rang several times before? Oh. Yes. What is it? What is it?"

An accident. "My dear, I'm very, very sorry to have to tell you . . . an accident . . . your mother. Yes, your mother. A truck out of a side road . . . it must have been instantaneous. . . ." And a lot more—kindly, helpful, sympathetic. Kind people on their way to Lorna right now. Lorna couldn't really take it in.

She was not surprised, when she went slowly back to the sitting room, to find that her new friend was gone. She had known that she would be gone, for she knew now who it must have been. For who else could have hated the room as Lorna hated it? Who else would have come back, at the last, to destroy it?

And, after all, the destruction was not so very great; for a ghost, even using all its strength, is not as strong as a living person. A few things were broken, the curtains crumpled and awry; and as Lorna sank down among the mussed cushions she was crying; crying with happiness because she and her mother —her real mother, the one hidden beneath the doormat exterior all these years—had understood each other at last.

CELIA FREMLIN graduated from Oxford University, England, in 1936. She won an Edgar Allan Poe Award from the Mystery Writers of America in 1959 for her novel The Hours Before Dawn.

HOW
I BECAME
A JEWELER

Louis Weinstein

Lou just wasn't meant to be a detective, despite the clever piece of work he does here.

I became a jeweler by a fluke. My father got a call one night from Harry Lubin of Lubin and Fein, manufacturing jewelers. Lubin wanted my father to investigate some thievery at the factory. But, bad as he always needed work, my father talked himself out of the job. A mature man pretending to be a skilled jeweler would be pegged as a plant right off, an Alphonse Gumshoe better with his eyes than with his fingers. The situation called for someone young enough to pass for a genuine apprentice.

Lubin got the point right away but bounced back with another idea. Maybe your boy, Lou, he suggested, would like to give it a try. He's a pretty sharp kid and probably has picked up some savvy just from being around the business. A ton of mistakes wouldn't give away a green hand.

Lou knows his way around, my father agreed. Why don't you talk to the boy yourself? If he's interested in your proposition, make your own arrangements.

That same night I found myself at the big Lubin house in the old neighborhood in Queens. Lubin knew me. His son Marvin, a year or two older than me, had been my friend before we'd moved. I'd been in the Lubin house a few times.

"Look, kid," Lubin, as gruff-voiced as I remembered, began, "Max Rubel, the furrier, recommended your father, Phil, for my problem. Okay, for Rubel your father did a great job. But for me he'd be as useful as a snowball on a pool table. But you, you'd be perfect, Lou."

"Perfect for what?" I asked. "Would you mind telling me what's the problem?"

"Gold is our problem. We make gold rings, mostly, and gold is disappearing. Not tons. Not pounds. But ounces, enough ounces to give us the hurts."

"Where do I fit in?"

"To sit at the work bench and keep your eyes open," Lubin said. "But first let me explain. My partner and I, we both work at the bench. We have four more jewelers. Three I've known since Roosevelt was president. The other is my nephew. I'd stake my life on them. They're all like family."

"Every family has a black sheep."

"True. But we don't just count on their honesty. They have to account for every ounce, every gram of gold that's handled. I check, my partner checks. The boys get so much weight for every ring, every brooch. The finished piece has to match up close. A little gets lost here and there, but most of it we pick up in the sweeps. We don't handle gold like it was Swiss cheese."

"So you think it's your partner," I said, wondering when was the last time he bought a pound of imported Swiss.

"Exactly. The question is how, not who. That's where you come in. We need a jeweler, and I handle the hiring. Hymie Farber, rest his soul in peace, died a week ago. You think you could handle a burner and file, go through the motions long enough to catch him in the act?"

"You've got a deal." I didn't hesitate. The month was June. I was fresh out of high school, and my father's income being what it was, I needed a job. Any job. There was something else, too. I'd given my father a hand with suggestions from time to time, helped him crack a few cases. I wanted to get my feet wet. My father and I were both interested in seeing how I'd do on my own. "If my father can be a milkman, a furrier, a dog trainer, why can't I be a jeweler?"

"Okay, while you're here, we'll go down to the basement and I'll give you some jiffy lessons. You have a social security number, don't you?"

"Sure," I said. "But make my name Lou Mandelbaum instead of Lou Mandel."

"Why?"

"I'm leery about using my right name."

"You want to be Mandelbaum, be Mandelbaum."

We worked pretty late in the shop I never knew was in the basement. He explained how a ring is made—the casting, soldering, shaping, finishing, polishing. He showed me how to handle the tools and seemed satisfied about how I caught on. He briefed me on some other things, too.

Next morning I got started. First I met Irwin Fein. A small, thin guy, sharp-featured, around sixty. Sallow skin. Baggy, nervous eyes. He looked harmless, almost insignificant.

Then the other guys. Benny Muster was big, paunchy, gray-haired, moon-faced. A relaxed type, delighted to have a new

pair of ears to talk at. They put me in a middle slot at one of
the two four-hole workbenches in the small loft. The loft, in
a corner of the building, had windows along two sides. Muster
was at my left, Lubin at my right, and next to him Herb
Birnbaum, his nephew.

Muster kept up a steady stream of chatter, glancing at me
to see if I was picking up on his points. He had a cure, subject
to instant change if you disagreed with his opinion, for everything wrong in the world—inflation, pollution, energy, corrup-
tion in government, pot, the youth of America. I liked him.
Once in a while he interrupted his chatter to pass along a few
tips, motioning for me to watch him while he said, "See how
I do it, like this. That's how you handle the tweezers. When
you've been at this racket as long as me, you pick up a few
tricks. Old Benny'll teach you right."

I'd try it his way and he'd nod approval. I've got to admit
I wasn't bad. I have good hands.

Pinchus Millstein, a small dry man of sixty plus, wore a
skullcap while he worked. He had skin like crumpled paper,
soft brown eyes, a wispy gray beard. With his name he should
have been a fiddler. Instead, he was an opera freak, maybe a
disappointed cantor. Pinchus ate lunch at the bench out of a
brown bag, the same menu every day—tuna and onion on a
seeded roll, a banana, and cold tea from a glass fruit jar, which
he carted back home. All day long he hummed operatic arias
in a shaky tenor. Puccini, Rossini, a lot of Verdi. Outside of
the bel canto, he was pretty quiet—a steady worker who
couldn't be rushed.

Herb Birnbaum I took to be in his early thirties. Well built.
Dark wavy hair. Good-looking, on the style of John Garfield.
A Yankee fan, the betting kind. A good dresser, changing into
work clothes instead of using an apron like the others. Herb was
unmarried, liked the night life. From his talk, a lady's man. My
impression was, it was mostly talk.

Fat Al Jacobson completed the roster. Two hundred fifty-sixty pounds piled on a five-nine frame. Moody. One day talkative and jovial, next day like a clam. The good days he bragged about his summa cum laude daughter, a schoolteacher and his only child. From her picture, a real looker, a tall shapely blond. At twenty-eight she didn't seem to show much interest in getting married. She shared an apartment with an old highschool girlfriend, also a teacher. Maybe what bothered Fat Al most about her and made him so moody was he was afraid she was living in the wrong kind of love nest. And she had expensive tastes, too—Lincoln Continental, designer clothes, cruises —and he could refuse her nothing.

Fat Al earned his poundage honestly. Most days he ate at the bench. Three cream-cheese sandwiches on rolls, followed by a big chunk of pie, all washed down by a sixteen-ounce cola. Bottle, wrappings, and bag all went into the trash can afterward. Sometimes he went out for lunch with Herb, Benny, and me, usually to the delicatessen around the corner.

I clocked Fein's routine. It was pretty regular. At about nine-thirty he went to the john. At ten-thirty, without washing first, he went to his flat-topped desk in the office for five minutes' worth of Danish pastry and coffee. Mornings, till about a quarter to twelve, he worked at the casting table along the far wall. Till lunch he got himself organized at his bench, next to Millstein. Lunch, which he ate in the office, came out of an old-fashioned black metal lunchbox. A sandwich, always nongreasy, cheese or lean meat, wrapped old-style in wax paper, plus the thermos and a piece of fruit, usually an apple.

He was very orderly, placing everything just so. On the desk top alongside the food he set down a medium-sized smoky brown medicine bottle, kept handy in case his digestive miseries—ulcer and gall bladder—flared up suddenly. He put the paper, the *Morning Press*—a pass-along from Herb—down flat on the desk and read while he ate. Like clockwork, just before one his wife called. At the first ring he got up to close the door. After lunch he worked at the bench. Around three-thirty he ducked into the office for coffee. Four o'clock was trip-to-the-john time. At six he and Lubin checked the stock and left together.

Every night Lubin phoned me. Gold was still disappearing. I was still watching Fein and the others but hadn't picked up anything definite. That was the gist of our nightly conversation.

If Fein was on my mind, I was on his, too. I would catch him pausing in his work to study me. About a week into the job I dawdled past his desk at lunchtime. The *Morning Press*, the open thermos, the open medicine bottle, the apple spread out as usual, his sandwich raised to his mouth.

I caught him staring at me. I noticed how dirty his arms seemed to be. Evidently he didn't bother to wash up before lunch. He dropped his eyes a little, then lowered the sandwich, looked my way, and smiled faintly, saying, "There's something I've been meaning to talk to you about."

"What?"

"How did Harry happen to find out about you?"

I was ready for this.

"His son, Marvin, and I are friends. Marvin told him I was looking for a job."

"What's Marvin doing now?"

"Going to medical school. For the summer, counselor at a camp in the mountains."

"Is he still playing handball? I understand he's a champ."

"Not his sport." I shook my head at the trick question. If there was anything Marvin wasn't, it was a handball champ. "He plays a little golf."

"What line's your father in?"

"A salesman. Shoe ornaments," I answered. "He's on the road a lot."

It wasn't much of a lie. My father had taken a shot at that line and missed, like always.

"So you're a friend of Marvin." He nodded. "That's all. I was just curious."

I'll bet he was curious.

That night I told Lubin.

"Nothing to worry about," he said. "I know Irwin Fein like a pinochle deck. I knew he'd get around to giving you the third degree. First day you came to work he asked me what your pedigree was. He's our man all right."

Still, I watched them all. No one made any suspicious moves. Pinchus kept crooning Puccini arias. Fat Al looked grimmer by the day. He let it drop his daughter was shopping for a mink coat. Benny solved his quota of world problems and kept telling me how well I was doing. I must say I was giving it the old college try. Even Lubin remarked I had a knack for the work. That made me feel pretty good, until I remembered the case was getting nowhere.

One morning the burner almost slipped through my fingers. I made a couple of wild swipes trying to get a handle on it. Fat Al, at his grumpiest, gave me a nasty look and snapped, "That's a burner, not a meat ax. Finesse. Use a little finesse. The way you handle it, Moishe Pipick off the street could do better."

"Leave him alone," Fein cut in. "No one was klutzier than you when you first started."

"A slip." Benny also came to my defense. "We all goof sometimes."

"Asbestos gloves," Fat Al said. "Let's take up a collection and buy him asbestos gloves."

"Size seven," I smiled at him.

"Ah," he went, and I stopped sweating.

Next day he was in a good mood.

"Forget what I said yesterday, boychik," he told me. "I've got a lot on my mind."

"Sure," I said. "No hard feelings."

But it all left me wondering.

After about three weeks Lubin started to get impatient.

"Well, Lou," he put it to me, "when do we get some action?"

"Don't quit on me yet, Harry," I told him. "Give me a little more time. I think I'm getting onto something."

"Enough time and I'll be filing bankruptcy, and that goniff Fein will be running off to Miami, laughing all the way."

I wasn't as sure as Lubin about Fein. Why should he steal from his own business, maybe put it under, kill the golden goose? In my book Fat Al was still in the running. How much of a financial bind did his daughter's extravagance put him in?

Then Fat Al faded out. His daughter was changing her mind. The mink coat was out. All of a sudden she was getting a serious rush from Mr. Right, a young professor.

That left just Fein. I tailed him home a couple of nights. I watched his apartment building to see if he went anywhere. He didn't. All I got for my trouble were bags under my eyes.

"I could have told you," Lubin remarked about this. "He doesn't budge. Not out to dinner, the movies, a walk with his wife. Weekends he sits home. His wife goes out, plays poker. A four-alarm fire in the building might get him off his backside, nothing else."

"Why is he so nervous about someone hearing his phone conversations?" I asked.

"He likes privacy, no one to know his business. He wouldn't want you to know what color Kleenex his wife uses."

"Those calls bother me," I said. "Maybe they're not all from his wife. Could you run a check with the phone company, incoming and outgoing?"

"Sure. But what would it prove?"

"Do it anyhow. If he's stealing, there's got to be a reason. Maybe the phone calls could give us a lead."

By this time a couple of things had caught my attention. I narrowed my concentrated Fein-watching to the casting and lunchtime.

We met after work one night and I asked Lubin, "Harry, what's the story on Fein's medicine bottle? It looks like a hand-me-down from Noah's ark. Did you ever see him use it? I mean, take a spoonful or a sip?"

"To tell the truth"—he thought a minute—"I never noticed. Why do you ask?"

"It hits me wrong," I said. "Why has he been nursing that same bottle for so long? If he hardly ever has to use it, why doesn't he just keep it handy in the medicine cabinet? Why put it on the desk every day and drag it back and forth from home? Another thing: I understand he takes his vacations in Florida. What month?"

"End of December, early part of January. We close the place for three weeks then. He goes to Miami. Does that mean anything?"

"Could be. He spends a lot of time looking over the racing page. Did you know that?"

"Irwin Fein is an oddball. He follows sports a little, racing included. But if he's a horse player, it's the best-kept secret since who shot J. R."

"Tropical Park has a year-end meet. Could it be that's the big Florida attraction, where he gets his secret kicks?"

"It would explain a lot." Lubin looked thoughtful. "But the idea takes getting used to."

That same night I jumped up from the dinner table, leaving my folks with their mouths open, and hotfooted it to the library. What I found out started all the other chunks of information bunching together in my mind like starlings congregating for the night's roost.

Next morning before I left for work my father had some interesting news. He'd spotted a private detective nosing around the neighborhood, a guy he knew named Chuck Brannigan. My father did some sleuthing. Brannigan, undoubtedly working for Fein, was inquiring about me. It wouldn't take much savvy for Brannigan to figure out that Lou Mandelbaum and Lou Mandel wore the same socks at the same time and that Phil Mandel and Lou Mandel were father and son. Fein was closing in on me. I had to beat him to the finish line.

Now ninety percent onto his method, I hung around at lunch, giving it a final check. Fein didn't tidy himself up. Little hunks of amber-colored wax hung onto the skin and hair of his right arm, most heavily on the underside between his wrist and his elbow. The left arm was clean as a chicken bone worked over by ants. Through eating, he crossed his arms in front of him so that his left hand lay beneath the underside of his right arm, just above the wrist. He sat that way, going through the paper from back to front. I sensed he was waiting for me to leave before his next move, so I headed out into the hall. In a few seconds I returned, slipping past him nonchalantly and mumbling something about forgetting my matches.

I saw enough. He had shifted the position of his hands. His left hand was poised over the medicine bottle, and his thumb and index finger were pressed together, mashing a lump of wax. It was the easiest thing in the world to drop the wax and whatever happened to be stuck to it—little scraps of gold, for instance—into the bottle. He had it down to a science. It was all part of the same natural-seeming movement he used to reach out for the bottle with his left hand. Casual. Neat.

Later that afternoon Lubin got a phone call and left the office for about a half hour. When he returned, as he sat down he whispered in my ear, "Meet me around the corner after work."

When we met, he said, "Lou, you smelled something. I saw my man at the phone company. Every day Fein talks to a bookie on the west side, Lenny Siegel. Not one call to his wife.

She calls him maybe twice a week. The rest of the calls are from Siegel. The days she calls, when he gets done talking to her, he calls Siegel. That's why he makes sure to close the door. Another interesting thing: Siegel lives in his building."

"That's the clincher," I said. "Right in the building is where he settles with the bookie. But we don't have much time." I explained about Brannigan. "In a day or two at most Fein will know I'm Phil Mandel's son."

"So what do you suggest?"

"I know his gimmick," I said. "Tomorrow we'll let him spill his own beans."

I outlined my plan. Maybe not great, Lubin agreed, but worth a try.

Next morning Lubin called the delicatessen. At twelve sharp a delivery boy hustled around with a big bag, which Lubin took at the front door and lugged to his desk, right next to Fein's.

Benny, on his way out to lunch, asked me, "How about a corned beef down to the deli?"

"I'll take a raincheck," I said. "Harry's already got me a sandwich. We're eating in. He wants to talk to me."

"No problem?" Benny gave me a funny look. "Jeez, I hope not."

Bless his heart, he was worried about me getting canned.

"Don't know yet." I shrugged. "I'll soon find out."

Lubin sat down. I pulled up a chair next to him, close to Fein's desk. Out of the bag Lubin dragged two mountain-high hot corned beef sandwiches and all the trimmings.

Fein looked our way and asked, "What's the big occasion?"

"No big occasion," Lubin said. "I wanted to talk to Lou about his work. But let's eat first."

We all started to eat. Lubin and I ate slowly, so Fein would finish first. I could almost hear the wheels turning in Fein's head. If he judged there was no risk, he'd do his daily thing. If not, he'd skip a day. My guess was he didn't think I could see him well enough for him to change his routine.

Fein was leafing through the main news section of the paper, and I was almost finished with my sandwich when Lubin swallowed a bite of pickle, put his sandwich down, and said, "Lou, sorry to have to break it to you, but I'll give it to you straight. I've got to let you go. As a jeweler, you make a good plumber. Your eyes wander all over the place. You're slow. We can't afford a *kolyika*, a cripple. Finish up the day but don't come back tomorrow."

"What the hell is all this?" I slammed my sandwich down, managing to catch a side glimpse of Fein. "If I'm such a washout, why'd you wait so long to tell me?"

Fein's jaw fell. He looked startled, then secretly pleased. But he wiped that expression off his face and chimed in with, "Don't be so hasty, Harry. Let's talk it over. We've had worse. He needs the job."

"What are we, a charity organization?" Lubin shouted. "You stick to your end of the business. I hire, I fire. I know when a guy can't hack it."

I doubled over and grabbed at my gut, putting on an agony act. I gasped and moaned and staggered in Fein's direction.

"Let me have the medicine," I groaned, grabbing at the open bottle, only feet away. He'd already dumped the wax into it.

I raised the bottle to my lips.

"Don't!" A cry of alarm boiled out of Fein. He jumped to his feet and lunged toward me, reaching for the bottle. "Don't drink that!"

But Lubin moved faster and stepped between us.

"Why not?" He looked straight at Fein, his voice deadly calm. "Tell me why not."

"Because"—Fein looked around, the color gone from his face—"because it's my medicine. It's just for me. It wouldn't be good for him."

"Bull," Lubin said. "Tell that to Siegel, the bookie. We've got you with your pants down, Fein. It's *aqua regia* in that bottle, and that's how you've been getting the gold out of here, a little at a time, dissolved in the acid."

"The party's over," I said.

Fein just stood there, his mouth open, his head bowed.

"Say something," Lubin roared. "Say something, you crook, you conniving skunk, you goniff. You got nothing to say? Then I'll say it. Get your tail out of here, for good. And no phone calls from lawyers or accountants either. Not while I've got this"—he held aloft the bottle he'd taken from my hand.

"Careful," I warned. "Don't wave that stuff around. If that acid dissolves gold, think what it'll do to your skin. It'll burn a hole in you."

Nitric acid and hydrochloric acid, separate, my library visit told me, were nothing to fool with. Mixed together, they would dissolve metals, like gold, that nothing else could touch. All new to me, but old hat to Lubin and to Fein. They didn't have to understand the chemistry of it any better than I did to know that certain simple chemicals, like sulfur dioxide, added to the solution would precipitate the solid gold. Or, without kitchen-sink muss and fuss, any precious-metal company would be delighted to process the solution for a reputable jeweler and buy the gold.

"Take your choice," Lubin went on. "Get out or get prosecuted."

Fein shucked off his apron, grabbed his jacket, and got while the going was good.

"I was thinking of the trade." Lubin denied any humanitarian motives for going easy on Fein. "Shenanigans like these give a firm a bad name. Keep this all to yourself, kid. I'll let the word out he suddenly got so sick he had to retire. Lou, what was it tipped you off?"

"No one thing. A lot of little things added up. Gold wasn't getting out in solid form, so it had to be some other way. Fein's fascination with the racing page. His vacations during the

Tropical Park season. His phone calls, early enough to get his bets in. Then that beat-up medicine bottle. If I'd known about *aqua regia* right away, we'd have broken the case in a day or two. Then there was that one dirty arm. Fein didn't think anyone was smart enough to catch on. Well, I guess this wraps it up here. Shall I finish out the day?"

"What's the matter?" Lubin asked. "You sound unhappy. Don't you want to leave?"

"Glad you asked," I said. "I kind of like it here. Good steady work, pay not bad, good people to work with—that's a pretty hard combination to beat."

"So stay," Lubin said. "You're getting to be a pretty good mechanic. Tomorrow we'll start you on the casting."

That's how I became a jeweler.

So next time you get engaged or married, or just want something extra nice in the way of jewelry for an extra-special occasion, stop in at Harry Lubin, manufacturing jeweler. Fine quality, good price, satisfaction guaranteed.

LOUIS WEINSTEIN's first published mystery, "How I Became a Jeweler," appeared in Ellery Queen's Mystery Magazine *when he was sixty-six years old. He is a retired City of New York dockmaster, having put in twenty-seven years on the New York waterfront.*

MR. STRANG
AND THE
PURLOINED
MEMO

William Brittain

Wholeness and place are the keys to solving the disappearance of an important document.

T he end of the school day was only minutes away, and Mr. Strang had just polished off the last of a set of general-science lab notes he was correcting when he heard a tapping at the door of the faculty room. "Yes," the gnomelike science teacher called imperiously, "what is it?"

He fully expected a student aide to peer fearfully around the half-open door and blurt out some message, quickly pulling the door closed again. The Aldershot High School faculty room was the last bastion of teacher privilege in the entire building, and students were barred from it under any and all circumstances. Mr. Strang fully intended to keep it that way.

The man who entered was wearing a dark-blue overcoat, unbuttoned, and a suit with matching vest. His hair was tinged with gray, and his face had a deep tan which, during this winter season, bespoke a recent trip to a warmer climate. "They told me in the office I'd find you here," he said. "Do you remember me, Mr. Strang?"

Mr. Strang shook hands tentatively. "I don't believe I—"

"It's been twenty-five years," the man replied, "but maybe I can refresh your memory. Think of sketches of Sherlock Holmes drawn in the margins of my chemistry experiments— the quote from Agatha Christie that began my report on alkaloid poisons—the Ellery Queen paperback you found me reading behind my open textbook."

"Charlie!" cried Mr. Strang with a broad smile of recognition. "Charlie Unsinger, as I live and breathe." And then the teacher shook his head ruefully. "You know, with all the time you spent reading detective stories when you should have been studying chemistry, you almost failed the course."

"Yeah, I remember your reminding me of that about every other day," Unsinger replied. "But I also remember you were almost as interested in them as I was."

"Oh, it was just a hobby."

"How about that time I came to see you after school—when you thought I wanted extra help."

Mr. Strang chuckled. "And all you wanted to do was talk about Poe's 'The Purloined Letter.' You'd just read it in English class."

"It was my theory," said Unsinger with mock pomposity, "that such a thing could never happen in real life; that a thorough search by trained police was bound to turn up the letter."

"I, on the other hand," the teacher added, "held that the

method employed by the evil Minister D— to conceal the letter might well confound Police Prefect G— and his men, or modern-day police, for that matter. Charlie, it's been a quarter of a century, but I'm prepared to carry on our debate if you still feel—"

Unsinger shook his head ruefully. "I concede defeat, Mr. Strang," he said. "You see, I've got a real one."

"A real one? A real what, Charlie?"

"A real purloined-letter problem. And I want you to make like C. Auguste Dupin and solve it for me."

"Me? But—"

"Mr. Strang, even as a kid I was amazed at the way you could take a bunch of odd facts and make them add up to some logical conclusion. And now—well, my purloined letter isn't anywhere near as glamorous as the one in Poe's story, but all the elements are there. For reasons I'm sure you'll understand when I tell you about it, we haven't wanted to bring in the regular police."

"We? Who's we?"

"The company I work for. I'm with Daley Electronics, out at the edge of town."

"Computers?" Mr. Strang's eyebrows shot upward. "I can remember a time when you had trouble passing elementary algebra."

"Math isn't all that important in my job," said Unsinger. "I'm in charge of plant security. Mostly we're required just to keep a close watch on workers and material in sensitive areas. Nothing much in the way of mystery until this thing came up two days ago. My men and I are completely stumped, and on turning the problem over in my mind I began to see the similarities between it and Poe's story. Then I remembered our talk that time. Look, I know it's late and you want to be getting home, but my future with the company depends on getting this thing solved and—well, I thought the time had come for extraordinary measures."

"And I'm the extraordinary measures, is that it?" Mr. Strang asked. "Sit down, Charlie, and tell me all about it. I don't know how much help I can be, but I'll be glad to listen."

Unsinger sat heavily on a straight-backed chair next to the teacher. "The 'letter,' in this case, is an interoffice memo," he began. "A single piece of paper with a diagram and a few equations on it."

"What makes it so all-fired important?"

"It's part of a process we're working on—miniaturization. If it works out, we'll be able to take a computer that's now as big as a TV set and reduce it to the size of a pack of cigarettes. Every computer company in the world is working on the same thing. Any information one company comes up with is extremely valuable to all the others. It isn't necessary to have the whole process. Any part of it might save the company weeks or even months of experimentation. And getting your product out into the marketplace first can mean millions of dollars."

"I see," said the teacher. "And I have to assume that somehow this paper was stolen. And you're afraid whoever has it will sell it to one of your competitors."

Unsinger nodded. "The memo was in an 'Eyes Only' folder. Two days ago it was passed along to one of our engineers, Warren Kirby. That was okay, because Kirby has clearance to see such material. But then the fool went and got a cup of coffee, leaving the folder out in plain sight."

"And when he returned it was gone, is that it?"

"Well, the folder was there, but the memo inside had been removed."

"Charlie, excuse my ignorance, but wouldn't it be a simple matter to ascertain who was near this Kirby's desk while he was away and—"

"Hell, we *know* who took the memo; he was seen by one of my men."

Mr. Strang looked at Unsinger blankly. "I take it I haven't yet heard the whole story," he said.

Unsinger nodded. "It was a guy on the maintenance crew—Philip Holtz. According to my man, he walked by Kirby's desk, paused for about one second, and zingo—he scooped up the memo and jammed it into his pocket."

"Then why wasn't he apprehended immediately?"

Unsinger's face reddened under its tan. "I'm afraid that was my doing, Mr. Strang. The security guard kept an eye on Holtz and called me on the interoffice phone for instructions. It occurred to me that if we let Holtz think he'd gotten away with the memo, we might be able to nab the person he was going to sell it to as well. So I told the guard not to grab Holtz but to keep a close watch on him—and anything that he handled was to be carefully examined.

"Well, an hour later it was quitting time. We're sure that when Holtz left the plant he still had the memo. Beatty, the guard, is a good man; he wouldn't make a mistake about a thing like that.

"I had two men tail Holtz home. He lives only about four blocks from the plant, in a rooming house. On the way there, Holtz didn't stop for a beer, or to talk with anybody, and he didn't come close to a trash can. He didn't drop anything, either. He went straight to the house and directly up to his room. One of my men kept an eye on his closed door, and the other made arrangements with the landlady to rent a guest room across the hall she didn't usually rent out. The point is, Mr. Strang, that when Holtz went into his room he had the memo with him. And we're sure he didn't come out again. A call was put in to me, and I went over there myself to keep an eye on things.

"About ten o'clock that evening, with Holtz sticking to his room, I began to get a little nervous. So I phoned the company president for instructions. He about hit the ceiling. He told me I had no business letting that memo out of the building, regardless of the circumstances. I was to bust in on Holtz immediately, get the memo, and deliver it to the president at home personally.

"When the boss speaks, I listen, Mr. Strang. So my men and I went across the hall and knocked on Holtz's door. When he answered and I explained how things were, he started yelling about how the whole thing was a setup just to get him fired. And he insisted on a search—right then, on the spot."

"I take it the search was reasonably thorough," said Mr. Strang with a grin.

"Thorough? I'll say it was. We took Holtz to the room we'd rented and started in on him first. First his clothes. Shoe heels, jacket lining, pants cuffs—the works. Then we searched Holtz himself. Hair, mouth, in between his fingers and toes—you name it, we looked there. He didn't have the memo on him, that's for sure."

"A question, Charlie," said the teacher. "Before you knocked on Holtz's door, did he have any inkling you were in the house?"

Unsinger shook his head. "He wouldn't have had any reason to swallow the memo or flush it down the john, if that's what you're getting at."

"I see. Go on, please."

"Then we left the other man to guard Holtz, and Beatty and I started in on his room. A really crummy place, if you know what I mean—wallpaper torn, big cracks in the ceiling and walls, only two bulbs working in the ceiling light, cigarette burns on the furniture, carpet worn almost through. And Holtz's style of living was just as sloppy. Unmade bed, empty beer cans around, the newspaper spread all over."

"I'm beginning to get the picture," said Mr. Strang. "About how big would you say the room was, Charlie?"

"Maybe fifteen feet square. A little bathroom off it, and a closet. One corner had a refrigerator and a hotplate. A bed, a dresser, three tables, a straight chair, and an easy chair. That's it.

"Anyway, we started with the junk on the floor. I got a can opener and took the tops off all the beer cans to make sure he hadn't stuffed the memo inside one of them, and Beatty looked at each page of the newspaper separately. Nothing. When we were done, we carried enough stuff out to fill a garbage can.

"Then we worked on the usual places. His clothes and the inside of the closet, the drawers in the dresser, and the kitchen cabinets. The refrigerator, the medicine chest, inside the toilet tank, and the bathroom and kitchen drains. It occurred to us he might have tossed the memo out the window, but no dice. There were storm windows on, fastened on the outside.

"Anyway, it was late by then, and we were getting tired, so I sealed the room, assigned a guard at the door, and sent Holtz to a hotel with a man to look after him. Then I went home for whatever sleep I could get under the circumstances.

"The next day—yesterday—Beatty and I were back on the job. When it came to the furniture, we didn't settle for just tapping it, like Poe's policeman. We tore open cushions and the bed pillows and the mattress and looked through the stuffing. Anything made of tube steel, we reamed coathangers through. If there was a joint in the wood, we broke it open and looked inside. After we hauled all that stuff out, there wasn't much but the bare walls."

"Your methods sound rather drastic," observed the teacher. "That memo must be extremely valuable."

"It is," Unsinger assured him. "And besides, the whole of the stuff we took apart in that room couldn't have been worth fifty bucks. Replacing it will be no problem.

"Anyway, by yesterday evening we were down to taking the plates off all the electrical fixtures and looking inside. We probed around any pipes going through the floor. We even tore off all the wallpaper and examined every square foot of it. We didn't call it quits until two in the morning."

There was a wild look in Unsinger's eyes as he stared at the gnomelike teacher. "And we didn't find the memo, Mr. Strang!" he moaned. "It wasn't there. But it's *got* to be!"

For several moments Mr. Strang considered the problem. "Charlie," he said finally, "if you think I can be of any help to you, I'll be happy to try. But I must say, your search sounds as if it covered everything. Have you considered the possibility that the letter really isn't there, that Holtz either hid it somewhere else or he never stole it in the first place?"

Unsinger shook his head positively. "I trained the security men myself," he said. "They see what they say they see, and they report it properly. If one of them says Holtz took the memo, he took it. And if they say he brought it into his room, that's where it is. I'd stake my life on it. In fact," he sighed, "I guess I already have."

"What's that supposed to mean, Charlie?"

"If I don't find that letter Holtz will sue me for everything but my underwear. False arrest, illegal detention, you name it. He may even get to keep his job. And who knows what he'll steal from Daley Electronics next time?"

"A good point." Mr. Strang glanced at his watch. "But it's getting on toward dinner time, and I'm hungry. Suppose we grab a bite somewhere, and afterward we can visit this room of yours?"

"Sure thing, Mr. Strang. How does The Aldershot Inn grab you?"

"Well—expensive."

"I'm buying. They've got a dessert there that's out of this world. I keep going back for it." Unsinger paused. "The condemned man ate a hearty meal," he concluded wryly.

The food was excellent. Mr. Strang felt a bit foolish wearing the plastic bib, but he attacked the lobster, which seemed large enough to have endangered small boats, with gusto. When they'd finished their main course, Unsinger whispered in the waiter's ear.

Shortly thereafter, the waiter returned, carrying what appeared to be a melon, whole and uncut, on a silver tray. "What's that?" asked the teacher.

"The dessert," replied Unsinger with a grin. "You'll love it."

"I don't know, Charlie. Melon really doesn't—"

"Watch, Mr. Strang." Unsinger gripped the top of the melon in both hands and lifted. The top came away, leaving the scooped-out lower half, which was filled with a mixture of fruit, ices, and thick syrups in all the colors of the rainbow. "Dig in," he ordered. "It's delicious."

"Amazing, Charlie," said the teacher. "You know, when the waiter brought this thing I'd have sworn it was whole. I never suspected it was—it was—"

Unsinger looked across the table in concern. Mr. Strang was staring fixedly at the melon as if it had some hypnotic effect on him. "Hey, are you feeling all right?"

"What?" Mr. Strang shook his head, startled back to reality. "Oh. Yes, I'm fine. Just fine."

"If you're sick or something, maybe I'd better take you home."

"Let's just finish this dessert and get a move on."

"But—"

"Eat, Charlie. Eat."

Some fifteen minutes later, on the way to Holtz's rooming house, Mr. Strang asked Unsinger to stop at an all-night grocery store. Unsinger waited at the wheel while he went in and returned a few minutes later, carrying a brown bag, inside of which seemed to be something about the size of a pint carton of milk. *Maybe the old boy has an ulcer,* Unsinger thought. All the way to Holtz's rooming house, Mr. Strang kept the bag clutched to his chest.

When the landlady let them in, she asked Unsinger irritably when they'd be finished with this searching business. He muttered something noncommittal and led Mr. Strang to the second floor. Outside the first door on the right stood a uniformed guard with DALEY ELECTRONICS/SECURITY stitched across the front pocket of his shirt.

"He's okay," Unsinger told the guard. "He's with me." He reached for the doorknob.

The teacher grasped his wrist lightly. "Wait, Charlie. I'd like to go inside alone. You wait out here."

"But I don't see—"

"Indulge me, Charlie. I had a brainstorm back at the restaurant. If I'm right, you'll know very shortly. If I'm wrong, I'd like to be alone when I fall on my face."

"Okay, Mr. Strang. Let him inside, Jake."

The paper bag in his hand, Mr. Strang entered the room and shut the door softly behind him. Two minutes passed. Three.

And then the door opened and the teacher stuck his head out. "There's no furniture in here," he told Unsinger.

"I told you, we ripped it all apart and carted it away with the rubbish."

"I need a chair."

"Mr. Strang, are you just going to sit in there and—oh, all right. Jake, get him a chair."

Jake brought a straight-backed chair and handed it to Mr. Strang. The door closed again. Another minute passed. The teacher had been alone in the room for nearly five minutes when—

"What was that?" cried Unsinger. "That sound?"

"I dunno," replied Jake. "It sounded like a gun, maybe, with a silencer on it!"

"From inside the room," added Unsinger. He tried the door. The teacher had locked it.

"Mr. Strang!" cried Unsinger in alarm. "Are you all right?"

"Just fine, Charlie," came the teacher's quiet assurance. "I wonder if you'd do me a favor."

"What's that?"

"Would it be possible to get Mr. Holtz here? I'd like to talk to him, face-to-face."

"Why in blazes do you want—" And then Unsinger shrugged. "No problem. He's being very cooperative. I guess he figures it'll help his case when he hauls me into court. Jake, go to the hotel and bring Holtz back with you."

Unsinger rattled the doorknob again. "Will you let me in now, Mr. Strang?"

"Not yet, Charlie. The first person I want to see coming through the door is Mr. Holtz himself."

Philip Holtz arrived some ten minutes later, closely watched by Jake. A thin redhead with a large crop of freckles across the bridge of his nose, he greeted Unsinger with calm self-control. "Finished tearing up my room, have you?"

"Where you're going all the furniture's bolted to the floor, Holtz," Unsinger replied.

"I doubt that. When this is all over I'll be able to afford the best money can buy. All through the courtesy of Daley Electronics. You're going to pay well for what you're doing to me, Unsinger."

"Maybe, Holtz. But first there's a man who'd like to talk to you." Unsinger rapped softly on the door.

"Mr. Strang? He's here."

"Then send him in, Charlie, by all means." There was the sound of the bolt being drawn back, and the door opened.

Holtz walked into the room. Aside from the light from the hallway, it was inky black. "Come in, Mr. Holtz," Mr. Strang said from the darkness. "You, too, Charlie. And close the door behind you."

"It's dark," Holtz began. "Put on a light."

"I like the darkness, Mr. Holtz," said the teacher. "But tell me, do you still maintain that you had nothing to do with removing the memo in question from Mr. Kirby's desk at the plant?"

"You, too?" snapped Holtz. "Man, by the time this is over I'll be suing half the village of Aldershot. But for the record, no. I didn't take nothing from the plant."

"Charlie, are you there?"

"Yeah."

"Charlie, I have a theory. I believe that lies told in darkness cannot survive the light. What say you, Mr. Holtz? Could you look me straight in the eye and still maintain your innocence?"

"I don't even know where you're *standing,*" growled Holtz.

"Then by all means, let there be light." There was a soft click, and both Holtz and Unsinger squinted against the glare. Holtz looked wildly about the small room, which looked as if it had taken a bomb blast. Paper was torn from the walls, pipes hung loosely from the bathroom sink, and there wasn't a stick of furniture to be seen except the straight-backed chair on the far side of the room in which the teacher sat gazing fixedly at the maintenance man.

"Now then, Holtz," Mr. Strang snapped. "Tell me again. Tell me you had nothing to do with stealing the memo. But only if it's the truth."

Holtz continued to jerk his head about as if expecting help to arrive through the window or out of the walls themselves.

"The truth, Holtz," Mr. Strang repeated. "Maybe a court of law will take a voluntary confession into account. But you must give it now."

Holtz lowered his head and stared at the floor.

"Get on with it, Holtz," ordered Mr. Strang.

"It was me that stole the memo out of the folder on Mr. Kirby's desk."

Only then did Mr. Strang reach into a pocket of his jacket and remove a much-folded sheet of paper. "Is this what you're looking for?" he asked blithely, handing it to Unsinger.

It was.

Later that evening, after the recovered memo had been dispatched to the president of Daley Electronics, Mr. Strang and Charles Unsinger lounged in a rear booth at King George's Arms, a self-styled English pub in downtown Aldershot. "I hope none of my students see me here," said the teacher. "Even in these enlightened times, it's not considered seemly for a teacher to be in a place like this." He sipped at a glass of white wine.

Unsinger was working on his second double scotch. "Okay, Mr. Strang," he said. "You've had your fun playing the man of mystery. How come you could find that memo when we couldn't?"

"Because," Mr. Strang replied, "as in Poe's 'Purloined Letter,' your search didn't take into account the manner in which the letter was hidden."

"Now don't go telling me the place he hid it was too obvious," said Unsinger.

"No," the teacher told him. "The place where the letter was hidden was far from obvious."

"We skinned that room down to the bare walls."

Mr. Strang sucked at his unlit pipe. "To say the letter was hidden is to imply a hiding place—a receptacle of some kind —a box or a niche in a wall or almost anything used to contain the letter itself. The question, then, is: why did you overlook such a receptacle?"

"Okay, why did we?"

"I suppose it's a matter of two qualities. One I'll call 'wholeness,' for lack of a better term. And the second is 'place.' "

"Come again, Mr. Strang?"

"Take wholeness first. Charlie, there are certain things we expect to have a quality of being whole, that is to say, incapable of being penetrated. If one grants the wholeness of such an object, one would tend to ignore it in a search. Let me give you an example from Poe himself. Do you remember how Prefect G— mentioned removing the table tops?"

Unsinger nodded. "He wanted to see if the tops of the table legs had been bored out to make a place to hide the letter."

"Yes, but never once did it occur to G— that the letter might have been hidden in the table top itself."

"Huh?"

"It wouldn't be hard to get a cabinetmaker to take a table top apart and gouge out a space on one of the inner boards. Once the letter was inserted and the table reassembled and varnished, I daresay Prefect G— would never have tumbled to the hiding place. You see, Charlie, though it's usually made up of several thicknesses of wood, a table top is expected to be solid. This is the quality—and the expectation—I call 'wholeness.' "

"Okay, but we smashed all the furniture into kindling."

"The table was only an example. Here's another. Suppose you'd opened the refrigerator in Holtz's room and found an egg. Further, suppose you lifted the egg and found it of the proper weight and density. And you observed that the shell was apparently intact, with no holes, no matter how tiny, punched in it. Would it occur to you to actually break the egg in order to assure yourself it didn't contain the memo?"

"No, I guess it wouldn't. But there weren't any eggs in—"

"Just another example. But the man who developed a method of puncturing an egg and sealing it again in a way that couldn't be detected would have a perfect hiding place for a small object, at least until his secret got out."

"Mr. Strang, this is silly. You can't—"

"Not so silly, as you'll understand in a moment. But I also mentioned the matter of 'place.' By that I mean that an object be situated where it's normally found. Take the egg I just spoke of. If you found the egg in the middle of a living-room carpet, say—out of its proper setting—your suspicions might be aroused, no matter what the egg looked or felt like.

"There's a children's game, Charlie, called 'Huckle-Buckle-Beanstalk,' which is sometimes played in our elementary schools on rainy days. Very simply, an object—a thimble, perhaps—is given to one child to hide while the rest have their eyes closed. But the one doing the hiding must place the object in plain sight. At a signal, the others open their eyes and begin their search. The first to locate the object hides it for the next game.

"A novice at the game will hide the thimble in some out-of-the-way corner, perhaps at the base of a cupboard where it can only be seen from certain areas of the room. This type of positioning, however, has occurred to each of the others, and such nooks and crannies are the first to be explored.

"The really skillful players use a superior tactic. In the case of a thimble, it might be laid beside a pincushion on the teacher's desk, or maybe worn on a finger. The searchers accept the premise that a thimble belongs with needles and pins, or on a finger, and so their eyes pass right over it without really seeing it.

"Just one final illustration. Consider a log, three feet long and a foot in diameter. If the thing's found in the bathtub during an official search, it's a very suspicious object. Such a log would be examined, x-rayed, and even chopped apart to see if it might contain the article being looked for. But put the same log inside a large fireplace and the chances are quite good that nobody'd look at it twice. The log in the fireplace has the virtues of both wholeness and place."

"But what's this got to do with Holtz's room?" Unsinger asked. "It didn't have any eggs or thimbles or three-foot logs."

"Charlie, the answer came to me earlier this evening when I saw that melon. It was in its proper place—at our table in The Aldershot Inn. And it seemed to me to be perfectly solid. Without you there to show me otherwise I'd have gone to my grave swearing it was whole."

Unsinger finished his drink. "Maybe it's the booze, Mr. Strang, but I still don't get it."

"Think, man, think. You burst in on Holtz at ten o'clock in the evening. You searched his room until all hours. And the following day you were there until two in the morning. You needed something to make those searches, Charlie, something that clearly indicated there was one part of the room you hadn't considered."

"We needed—" Unsinger began eagerly. Then he slumped in his chair. "*What* did we need, Mr. Strang?"

"You needed light! And you told me only two bulbs in the ceiling fixture were operating. Clearly then, one or more were not."

"You mean the memo was inside one of those dud bulbs!"

"Exactly, Charlie. Holtz probably prepared the thing long before he actually stole the paper. He could either part a bulb with a glass cutter, or sometimes the glass comes loose from the metal screw socket all by itself. Having prepared the thing, he came home with the memo, wrapped it around the filament rod that sticks up from the bulb's base, and held it with a rubber band. Then he glued the bulb over it, probably using one of these space-age adhesives that will stick anything together. Since the bulb was frosted, you'd have no way of knowing anything was inside without actually breaking it."

"Breaking it," mused Unsinger. "That was the sound I heard when you were in—"

"Right," said Mr. Strang. "I'd brought my own replacements from the grocery store."

"So when you turned on the lights—"

The teacher nodded eagerly. "Holtz saw that all the bulbs were working. It was a pretty good indication that his hiding place had been discovered. The jig was up, and he knew it. End of story."

Unsinger shook his head. "Who'd ever think of looking inside a light bulb? Especially one that didn't work. There it was, sitting in its socket the whole time."

"The requirements of both wholeness and place were satisfied," said the teacher. "There's really very little reason why you'd even consider looking there. But, Charlie, if I'm to remain *whole* for school tomorrow, I'd better be getting back to my *place* right now."

As they left the pub, one final question occurred to Unsinger. "The chair," he asked. "Why did you insist on my getting you a chair?"

"To stand on in order to reach the bulb," was Mr. Strang's gruff reply. "We short people have our problems, too."

WILLIAM BRITTAIN teaches junior high school in Long Island, New York. He has published more than sixty-five stories in Ellery Queen's Mystery Magazine.

A NAME

FOR

HERSELF

Alice Tufel

Lindsey doesn't rely much on the outside world—until she learns how dangerous ignoring it can be.

L indsey never reads a newspaper, although she has various magazines strewn all over her small Manhattan apartment. The magazines are all similar: book reviews, news for writers, poetry quarterlies. She doesn't concern herself with the gory details of city life. She doesn't own a television set. The prime-time shows and the news don't interest her. She is too busy writing to take the time to watch television.

Lindsey has come to New York to make a name for herself, to avail herself of the city's opportunities for young, ambitious writers. Since her arrival, she hasn't made any friends to speak of. She barely supports herself with free-lance editorial work and temporary typing jobs. Evenings and weekends usually find her immersed in a book or working on a new poem, oblivious to the sirens screaming outside her window or the raging automobile horns on Second Avenue.

An empty refrigerator or the lack of clean clothes draws Lindsey outside once or twice a week. Aside from that, there is her poetry class on Monday nights, which Lindsey attends unfailingly every week, devoted as a mailman in the dead of winter. The class, her small apartment, her writing: these make up Lindsey's world. She moves through it happily and alone.

Lindsey's poetry teacher usually has an announcement at the end of class. But tonight he rises from the long table silently. The group of aspiring poets, all of them accepted into his class because of the quality of work submitted to him in advance of the course, waits expectantly. As he reaches the door, he stops briefly and says, "Cleo Miller is reading tonight at 8:30 sharp. You should all try to catch her."

"Cleo Miller!" Lindsey says to the girl on her right. "I didn't know she was scheduled for tonight. I adore her stuff!"

The other girl shrugs. "She's okay. It's too cold for me to hang around, though. I'm going home before everything freezes over."

Lindsey grabs her handbag and her books and hurries out of the classroom to the box office at the other end of the hall. A sign reads

Cleo Miller Reading Tonight
8:30 P.M.
Tickets $6.00

Lindsey opens her wallet, hoping she has enough money. She counts out a five, a single, and a dollar in change. Enough for a ticket and the bus fare home.

"Excuse me," she says, tapping on the box-office window. "What time is the Miller reading scheduled to get out?"

"Ten, ten-thirty, I'm not sure. Do you want a ticket?"

Lindsey bites her lip, hesitating. Her poetry class is at the Y on Ninety-second Street and Lexington Avenue, almost eighty blocks from her apartment and not one of the coziest neighborhoods in town after dark. Normally she takes the bus home, but normally she leaves at eight. *Oh, why not?* she thinks. *I may never get this chance to hear Cleo Miller again.* She pushes six dollars through the little window and takes her ticket.

The reading is wonderful. Cleo Miller is pretty yet stern, all done up in leather and lace. Lindsey closes her eyes, tuning out everything but the poet's voice and words. The reading is a long one, and toward the end people start to leave. By the time Cleo Miller takes her abrupt bow and walks off stage, there is only a handful of people left in the auditorium.

Lindsey feels drained but good and sinks into the warm afterglow left by the reading. She stretches happily and then, layer by layer, wraps herself up in her heavy winter garb: scarf, sweater, coat, hat, and gloves. The clock in the lobby reads 11:05.

The wind has picked up, and a frosty mist is blowing through the already-cold night air. The street is deserted. Lindsey weighs her options for getting home. She can walk south to the Eighty-sixth Street subway or east to Second Avenue and take the bus. The subway this time of night could be dangerous, but standing alone on Second Avenue might be worse. She starts toward Eighty-sixth Street and stops. Changing her mind, she heads east for the bus stop, walking quickly, hugging her books to her chest. After what seems like forever she reaches Second Avenue.

At the bus stop, she huddles alone, stamping her feet and shivering in the cold. She strains her eyes north, searching for a bus. A cab glides past her, the sound of its tires echoing off the frozen street like a vague warning. Lindsey decides to transfer her keys and her money to her coat pocket. If anyone comes along and snatches her bag, she'll at least be able to get home.

Without warning, a voice comes from behind her. "Are the buses still running?"

She whirls around. A middle-aged man is looking at her.

"I hope so," Lindsey stutters. "I mean, I think so." She points at the schedule posted on the kiosk, not knowing if she should be relieved or afraid. The man shivers and pulls his scarf closer to his face as he reads the schedule. She stands a little apart from him. He looks all right, but . . .

They both crane their necks uptown.

Finally, a bus appears out of the blackness, but it rolls past them without stopping and continues downtown, disappearing back into the night.

"Damn," Lindsey says.

The man surveys the deserted avenue. "If a cab comes along, do you want to share it with me?" he asks.

After a moment she says, "I've only got bus fare."

"I see," he answers noncommittally.

They stand silently for a few minutes more. Then, like a mirage, a taxi approaches slowly, hunting for passengers. The man steps into the street, thrusting out his arm.

"Come on," he says to Lindsey as the cab stops in front of them.

"Oh no, really, I can't."

"Come on," the man insists. "You'll freeze to death out here."

"But I told you, I've only got the cost of the bus."

"My treat," says the man. Like a father, he takes her arm and pulls her toward the cab. "I can't let you stand here by yourself all night. I'd feel guilty for the next three months."

Lindsey hesitates, searching the man's face suspiciously, but she sees nothing. Besides, she reasons, it's just as risky to remain at the bus stop. She follows him into the cab, which continues down Second Avenue.

"Where are you headed?" the man asks.

"Thirteenth and Second."

"Thirteenth Street," the man says to the young cabby.

"Please don't go out of your way," Lindsey says. "I mean, do you live below Thirteenth?"

"Yes," the man says. "Stop worrying." He laughs. "You're making me nervous."

When he turns to look at her some blocks later, Lindsey tries to pretend she doesn't notice. She can't keep it up, though, and finally she turns toward him with a little smile. "This is really very nice of you," she says, wanting to believe it.

"You shouldn't have been standing there alone this time of night," the man says. Somehow his comment breaks the tension and she laughs with relief. "It was kind of stupid."

But the man doesn't laugh. "My wife was assaulted on Riverside Drive last winter. She wanted to save money and wait for the bus. It was late at night and she was alone." He turns his head away and stares out the window in a world of his own. The cab bumps down the empty avenue.

The cabby pulls over at Thirteenth Street and turns to look at them through the Plexiglas divider.

"The young lady is getting out here," the man says. "I'll be getting out farther on."

The cabby nods and faces front again.

Lindsey opens the door, then turns and holds out her hand

to the man. "Thank you," she says. "Thank you very much. I'm sorry about your wife."

The man grips her hand briefly and smiles. "Better get going," he warns.

She nods and runs toward her building as the cab drives away.

She gropes for her keys, relieved to be safely home. But her keys aren't in her coat pocket. Confused, she checks both pockets and then searches through her purse, her head bent down in the dimly lit alcove. Could she have dropped them somewhere between the cab and here? She stands perplexed for a moment, then buzzes a neighbor on the first floor. She waits, but no voice comes through the intercom, no buzzer sounds. She reexplores her pockets. She dumps her books on the floor and fumbles through her bag again, shaking it. She hears a jingling sound and digs deeper, her fingers racing frantically over matchbooks, her wallet and address book, papers and pens. The fear has built up again as if it had never left her.

Suddenly she freezes. The jingling sound is not coming from her purse.

"I told you you shouldn't have been standing out there alone this time of night."

Lindsey's eyes widen as the man's gloved hand flashes across the right side of her face and clamps down hard on her mouth. His other arm grabs at her waist and bears down, paralyzing her. In his left hand he's gripping her set of keys, aiming them at the door. She feels him pressed up against her back, his force desperate, as the keys move closer and closer to their target.

The first key he tries in the lock clicks into place. The man's hand turns to the right. And then, as the door starts to open, a voice comes from behind them.

"Hold it right there, Mister. Police officer."

She is shoved and sent reeling. She smacks against the door with a painful thud and crumples, stunned, to the floor. She is aware of a struggle behind her and eventually, far off, the sound of a surrendering voice. Lifting her head, she pushes herself cautiously to her feet and turns toward the sound of it. She sees a taxi on the corner, and, alongside it, the cabby who had let her off minutes before is handcuffing her molester to the outside door handle of the back seat.

"Are you okay?" he asks.

Lindsey's head bobs up and down like a puppet on a string.

"I'm an undercover police officer," he says. "I saw you both at the bus stop, and we've been looking for this character. When I heard him tell you about his wife I was almost certain he was the guy—he's told that story to his other victims—and when he asked to be let off a block south of here, I doubled back." He peers at her. "Haven't you read about this guy in the papers?"

Lindsey falls back against the door. The keys are still dangling from the lock and she snatches them up with shaking fingers. "I don't pay much attention to the news," she confesses.

"It's time you did," he says. His experienced young eyes tell her he is guessing rightly at the sheltered life she leads and that it's a life she can no longer afford.

Tomorrow she will pick up a newspaper. She'll pick up at least one of the dailies every day from now on. There is a larger world outside of the one she has brought to New York with her. She will no longer count on word-of-mouth to shape her activities. She will plan her days and protect herself. She has not come to New York to make headlines. She has come to make a name for herself. There is a difference.

ALICE TUFEL lives in New York, where she was working as an editor when her first story, "A Name for Herself," was published in Ellery Queen's Mystery Magazine *in 1983.*

NEW ORLEANS

GETAWAY

Clark Howard

Can Moss convince Keene to do the wrong thing for the right reason?

M oss Lemoyne arrived in New Orleans on the five-thirty bus from St. Francisville. He had been discharged from Angola, the state penitentiary, at eleven o'clock that morning. His face reflected the nine years he had served: a slight squint and a permanent tan from the hot sun of the fields; palms that were shiny from the wooden handle of his hoe; a habit of barely moving his lips when he spoke. He was forty-four, but his life had stopped at thirty-five. He had lost nearly a decade, and inside him somewhere was a nagging urge to catch up.

Outside the bus station, a cab driver looked him up and down and said, "Taxi, bud?"

Moss shook his head. "I'll walk. Canal Street still in the same place?"

"Unless they've moved it since breakfast, it is."

Moss tucked his extra clothes and shaving gear, which were wrapped in a brown paper parcel, under one arm and walked the two blocks to Canal Street. It was bustling, just as he remembered it: people, cars, trucks, trolleys—everything and everybody moving almost in a frenzy. *Life in the fast lane,* Moss thought. It was a saying he had heard from some young kid, a new fish who had come into the walls a while back. Feeling suddenly dizzy, Moss stepped into a doorway and stood very still. He had skipped breakfast that morning: too excited about getting out; then the bus ride; now all this noise and movement on Canal Street. *Better slow down, pard,* he told himself. *Get yourself to Coley's place and get something to eat.*

Coley's Café was on a narrow, dingy little side street just a block from the river. Moss walked past it first and went down to the edge of the wharf to look at the Big Muddy—the Mississippi River. The *Beauregard,* a tourist paddle boat, was just coming in to anchor. Upriver, near the Pontchartrain Bridge, two rusty freighters were passing each other. Across the water was Gretna, the little town where Moss had grown up. He had three brothers and three sisters, and not one of them was still in Louisiana. They were spread out all over the country now, some of them he didn't even know where. Moss shook his head briefly. *Where the hell does life go?* he wondered.

He walked back to Coley's and went in. It was a seedy little joint, long and narrow like a boxcar, with all counter stools, no booths. The place smelled of grease and fried onions and cold hush puppies, but to Moss it still smelled better than prison. There were only two customers at the counter, both bums nursing coffee. Coley was on a high stool next to the cash register, reading a racing form, picking his teeth with a toothpick. He had one leg, his right, stuck out straight alongside the stool. It was a wooden leg. Coley had lost it twenty years earlier after being shot in a bank robbery. He'd hidden out on a friend's farm, refusing to have a doctor called, and gangrene had set in. Coley was the only man on record to serve a full term for bank robbery in Leavenworth with a wooden leg.

"Hey, Coley," Moss said quietly, taking a stool next to him.

"Moss! Hey, man!" Coley's face turned on like a new bulb. He folded the scratch sheet, tossed the toothpick on the floor, and stuck out his hand. "You're looking good, boy, real good. Healthy."

"Homegrown vegetables," Moss said. Angola, the largest prison compound in the country, grew everything its prisoners ate. Some said it was the best prison food anyplace.

"They cut you loose this morning?" Coley asked. Moss nodded. "Ol' Burley still in charge of the dressing-out clothes?" Moss nodded again. Old Burley was a black man who had been in Angola for fifty-two years, since he was fourteen. He no longer believed there was an outside world; he thought it was all made up. "I bet he's seen a million guys get out," Coley said.

"At least," Moss agreed.

"You hungry?"

"Starving."

"Skipped breakfast, huh? Want anything special?"

"Anything'll do, with lots of milk."

Coley limped back to the kitchen and spoke to his fry cook. When he came back, he studied Moss Lemoyne for a moment, then asked, "What else you need?"

"A room for a couple of nights," Moss told him.

"Got one right upstairs. It ain't fancy, but the rent's free."

"And I want to find Keene Summers," Moss said.

"Keene? Hell, that's easy. He's preaching now, you know."

NEW ORLEANS GETAWAY 123

"Preaching?"

"Yeah. You knew his daddy was a preacher. Well, when his daddy passed, as the blacks say, all them people in the old man's congregation got together and made Keene their preacher."

"But Keene's a burglar," Moss said, staring at Coley.

Coley shook his head. "Preacher."

A thin young girl with ruler-straight blond hair entered the café, said "Hi, Mr. Coley," and went on back to the kitchen.

"Who's that?" Moss asked.

"My night girl. Runs the place from six 'til midnight."

"Little young for that kind of responsibility, ain't she?"

Coley shrugged. "Ain't much business at night. Just stragglers mostly. Coffee-and-pie types with no place to go, killing time. She needed a job. Anyway, she says she's twenty."

Moss grunted. "She's twenty, I'm honest."

Coley stared thoughtfully at him. "You could be, you know," he said quietly.

"Could be what? Honest?"

"Sure. It ain't so bad. Look at me, I'm doing okay. I been honest, or at least pretty near honest, for six years now."

"With you it's different. You went straight because, well—"

"Because of my leg, go ahead and say it. But you're wrong. I didn't turn honest because of my leg, I turned honest because of my head." Coley tapped his temple. "I got smart, Moss, I wised up. You could, too."

"Save it," Moss said without rancor. "I thought you said it was Keene doing the preaching. How about that room now? I'll take my supper with me."

"Sure."

Moss followed the limping man back to the kitchen where the cook had just set a large platter of steak, fries, and onion rings on the service counter.

"Put a cover over that, and put it on a tray with a pitcher

of milk," Coley told him. "Jaysie," he said to the blond girl, "show my friend to that spare room upstairs."

Jaysie carried the supper tray and led Moss up a flight of inside back stairs to a windowless room with a slanted ceiling. In the room was a cot, a round wooden table with two straight chairs, a dresser with a cracked mirror, and a small fan.

"The fan's for when it gets too hot," Jaysie said.

"Glad you told me that," Moss replied dryly.

She blushed. "Bathroom's that door we passed at the top of the stairs." She put the tray on the table and started to leave.

"What kind of a name is Jaysie?" Moss asked.

"Oh, it's not a name, really," she said, pausing at the door. "What it really stands for is my initials: J. C. Janie Carol."

Moss walked over to her. "How old are you, Janie Carol?"

"I'm twenty," she replied, shifting her eyes. She again started to leave, and Moss caught hold of her wrist.

"How old?"

"I said I was twenty."

He tightened his grip. "Try again."

"All right! I'm seventeen! Let go!"

Moss turned her loose and fixed her in a flat stare. "Coley is a good friend of mine. I don't want to see him get in any dutch over some runaway kid, understand me?"

"How'd you know I was a runaway?" she asked, almost indignantly.

"Lucky guess," Moss replied in the same dry tone he had used earlier. "Do you take my meaning about trouble for Coley?"

"I hear you," she said, half angry, half pouting. "But I wouldn't do nothing to hurt Mr. Coley. He's been good to me. 'Sides, I kind of feel sorry for him—I mean, him losing his leg in the war and all."

Moss managed to keep his expression straight. "He told you about that, did he?"

"Sure. Told me all about how he won all them medals and then lost his leg in Korea. He's a real hero."

"A real hero," Moss agreed.

After the girl left, Moss sat down and tried to control his laughter enough to eat.

The sign in front read DIXIE EZEKIEL BAPTIST CHURCH—REV. KEENE SUMMERS, PASTOR. As Moss stood looking at it, a skinny black boy, ten or eleven, came up with a homemade wooden box slung over one shoulder.

"Shine, mister?"

Moss looked down at the brown prison brogans he'd been issued the previous day. Although new, they were state-made from reject-grade leather and were incapable of taking a shine. But the kid looked hungry.

"Sure," Moss said. He stepped over to a cypress tree in the grassless, worn-down church front yard and leaned against it. The black kid got the shine box under one foot and went to work.

Next door to the church was a playground as barren as the yard: torn, limp volleyball net; bent basketball hoop; faded lines that had once been a shuffleboard court. "How come nobody's in the playground?" Moss asked the kid. The boy grunted scornfully.

"That playground ain't no good, man. Ain't got no 'quip-ment, so can't play no games. Need 'quipment to play games, you know."

The boy worked on Moss's shoes for twenty minutes, and when he finished they looked exactly like they had when he started. "Fi'ty cents," the boy said, holding out his hand. Moss gave him a dollar and the kid pretended he didn't have any change. Moss, knowing he was being worked, let him keep it all.

Inside the Dixie Ezekiel Church, Moss told a heavy-set black cleaning woman that he wanted to see Pastor Summers. She led him to a small office in the rear of the building.

"Hey, Keene," Moss said to the handsome black, ten years younger than himself, who sat behind a cluttered desk.

"Moss," Keene Summers said quietly, almost matter-of-factly, as if he might have been expecting him. He got up, came around the desk, and embraced Moss. "Moss, my friend, it's good to see you, really very good. You certainly look fit."

"Homegrown vegetables," Moss said. "But then you know that yourself."

"I certainly do," Keene said, laughing at a joke he knew to be on himself.

"I saw your name outside," said Moss. "Does your congregation know it used to have a number after it?"

"Yes, of course," Keene said. He returned to his chair behind the desk. "I grew up in this district, Moss. Everybody knows I took a fall for burglary when I was twenty-one. They all know I was sent to the adult reformatory, that I was a bad dude there and after one year got thrown behind the walls at Angola. And they know I did seven years there."

Moss raised his eyebrows. "They still let you be their pastor?"

"Not 'let,' Moss—they *insisted.* You see, my granddaddy founded Dixie Ezekiel in 1899. My daddy was pastor here for over thirty years. When Daddy passed, the church board came to me and asked me to take over. I had assisted Daddy for about five years, since I got out of prison. He had ordained me when he found out he had cancer. I tried to get out of it—Lord knows I didn't feel any calling to it. But the board, the entire congregation, insisted. They wanted me and they finally got me."

Moss smiled. "Nice work for a burglar."

Summers gazed at Moss but didn't reply to the comment.

Moss let him gaze for a full minute, then rose and removed his coat. "Warm in here," he said. Sitting back down, he carefully, deliberately, rolled up his shirt sleeves. When he got the right one rolled up, it revealed on his forearm an ugly, bluish, puffy nine-inch scar that had obviously once been a terrible wound.

Keene Summers looked at the scar, smiled tolerantly, and said, "What is it you want, Moss?"

"I remember the day I got this," Moss said, running a fingertip along the scar. "We were all in the noon chow line. You had transferred in from the reformatory a week earlier. You were right ahead of me in line, but we didn't know each other. All of a sudden, I heard the guy behind me whisper, 'Shank!' real scaredlike. I looked around and here's this big dude bearing down with a shank that had to be one of the best prison-made knives I ever seen—made out of melted tooth-brush handles, molded about six inches long, both edges and the point sharpened like a razor on the cement floor. Beautiful. Anyway, I see this dude bearing down, and I've got no idea he's the brother of a cat you had a run-in with in the reformatory. All's I know is he's getting ready to shove his Pepsodent shank into the side of your neck. I don't like to see nobody get it when they're not looking, so I threw up my arm to try to knock the shank out of his hand. Instead, I took the blade myself. Ripped my whole arm open. Took four months to heal." Moss flexed his bicep. "Never did get a hundred percent use of it back. Doc says about ninety percent. And a funny thing—it aches every time the weather's damp. Like arthritis."

Keene sat forward and put his hands together on the desk. "I know you probably saved my life, Moss. I've always been grateful to you for it. But I repeat, what do you want?"

"You said you owed me that day. You said anything, any-time. Remember?"

"I do."

"Well, this is the time, and here's the thing: I need a partner. For a vault job up in Baton Rouge."

"I'm a minister now, Moss," said Keene. "You can't be serious."

"I'm dead serious, man," Moss assured him. "Look, I think it's jake that you got your daddy's church and all; I'm glad you've got a good setup. But I *ain't* got one. I'm forty-four years old, man. I've done two stretches totaling fifteen years on the inside. I got no family, no trade, no prospects, and no future."

"But you've got something a lot of men *never* get, Moss— a fresh start." Keene's voice had turned eager. "Look, you don't need a vault job. Let me help you find a *real* job, an honest job. You're not too old to make a new start."

"Right. I'm going to make a new start, my friend, but it's not gonna be at the bottom of the ladder. I figure if I get me a nice stake, I can buy into some little business somewhere. I been keeping up on things by reading business magazines. I figure something like video-tape rentals or electronic games would have a good future. But I need that stake first." He fixed Keene in a flat gaze. "And I need a good partner. Somebody I can depend on. Somebody who owes me."

Keene Summers sighed heavily and sat back in his chair. His glance fell on Moss's scarred arm again. He imagined that scar along the side of his own face, which is where it would probably be if the knife hadn't killed him. Yeah, he owed Moss, all right. But a *vault job?* Did he owe him that much?

"Moss, I don't know if I'd be any good on a job anymore," Keene said quietly. "I've been straight for so long that I—well, I'm not sure I'd hold up well."

"On this job you'd hold up," Moss assured him. "It's a hot-car operation up in Baton Rouge. Keeps big money on hand to pay for its merchandise. The job's a snap. And your end will probably be twenty-five or thirty thousand. That kind of dough," he added pointedly, "would go a long way toward fixing up that playground of yours that don't seem to be attracting too many kids."

Keene smiled an almost embarrassed smile. "We *are* a poor church, Moss," he admitted. "But if I had twenty-five or thirty thousand dollars, I wouldn't put it into the playground. There's another, much more important project that would take priority over the playground. It's a day-care center that we've been trying to get going. We're so poor around here, and wages are so low in the black community in general, that in most families the wife has to work just to make ends meet. But she needs someplace reliable to leave her children—a place that won't charge her so much that it's not worth her while to work.

"That's where our church comes in: we're trying to set up a free day-care center. But it takes money—for cribs, youth beds, food, games, a place to put it all in, salaries for people to run it." Keene sighed almost resignedly. "You're right, Moss, twenty-five or thirty thousand dollars *would* go a long way." The young black man drummed the fingertips of one hand soundlessly on the desk top. After an awkward moment, he asked, "Where, uh—where did you get the vault job?"

"Contracted it," Moss replied, "From Henry Palmetto."

Keene's eyebrows raised and an immediate look of interest spread over his face, as Moss had known it would. Henry Palmetto was a master planner of burglaries, considered to be one of the best casemen in the business. Once an intimate of Willie Sutton, he was reputed to have set up more than a hundred of the most successful burglaries in the country, and he had never been caught for any of them. He was in prison today only because of his involvement with an unfaithful woman he had been obliged to kill. From his cell where he was serving life, he continued to set up burglaries of all sizes for a percentage of the take.

"Tell me about the job," Keene said.

"Like I mentioned," said Moss, "it's a front for a hot-car ring up in Baton Rouge. From the outside it looks like an ordinary used-car lot; they even keep a few dozen legitimate-sale cars just to make it look good. And they actually sell some of them. But the big money is in stolen cars. They specialize in American-made luxury stuff—Coupe de Villes, Continentals, Rivieras, Toronados. The cars are grabbed in other states, Louisiana plates put on them, and driven back to Baton Rouge.

"The car lot has a garage and paint shop behind it. Six hours after they get a hot car, they have it completely painted a new color, different seats in it, a new serial number burned into the engine block, and a forged Louisiana title and registration fixed up for it. Then they drive them over to Texas, run them across the border into Mexico, and sell them for six or eight grand apiece. They handle a dozen cars a week and take in seventy to ninety thousand. Palmetto says they've been operating without a hitch for a long time and never been touched. They're fat, lazy, and ripe."

"What's the layout?" Keene asked.

"The car-lot office is a one-story blockwall building in the middle of the lot. Tar-and-asbestos roof. Alarm system is a light-and-buzzer deal wired to the doors and windows only; it's connected to a security firm downtown. The vault is a War-necke triple-plate, triple-tumbler model; it'll peel or burn, whatever. There's a night watchman on the premises from the time the lot closes until it gets light the next morning. Around this time of year he leaves about six A.M. Palmetto says the best time to do it is between then and nine in the morning when they open. The best day is Monday, because the weekend car-sales money will be there, too."

"What's Palmetto's end?"

"Fifteen percent of what's in the vault. We pay our own expenses."

Keene Summers rose and walked to the one window. Standing with his hands clasped behind his back, he gazed out at the rundown, deserted playground, wondering where all the kids were who should have been playing there. Beyond the playground was a shabby, abandoned house that had been deeded to Dixie Ezekiel Church, which he hoped could be refurbished into a day-care center. There was so much to be done, he mused, and so little time, so little money. This vault job almost seemed like a gift from heaven—a gift which would permit him to free himself of his obligation to Moss Lemoyne, while at the same time securing enough money to get started on the day-care center. And it wouldn't be like he was stealing from anyone that mattered. After all, what was the place but a front for a hot-car operation? Was stealing from people who steal really stealing? Couldn't one suppose that the Savior would forgive that kind of transgression?

Keene smiled at his own reflection in the window. *Come on, boy, you know better than that,* he chided himself. *Go in on the vault job if you want to, but don't try to hustle the Lord for a partner. Maybe God will understand and maybe He won't: you'll never know until Judgment Day. Meanwhile,* Keene concluded his thoughts, *we need the day-care center* now.

Keene turned to Moss again. "I'll provide the car, the tarp, and the hand tools. You get the drill and the accessories. I think a Walsh 200-series drill ought to do it. Better get a dozen bits just in case. My Sunday-night service concludes at nine; we'll leave for Baton Rouge right after." He put his hand out to Moss. "Deal?"

"Deal," said Moss, shaking hands.

That night, in his room above the café, Jaysie brought him a tray with his supper on it. "Can I ask you a question?" she said as he sat down to eat.

"I guess."

"How old are you?"

"Old enough to be your daddy and then some," he replied.

"No, I mean it. How old are you, really?"

"Forty-four going on ninety. Don't you have work to do downstairs?"

"I'm on my break," she announced loftily. " 'Sides, there hasn't been a customer in the place for two hours. It's pouring rain out—if you had a window you'd know that. Can I sit down?"

"No."

Moss was in his undershirt, and Jaysie saw his scarred arm. "Lordy, where'd you get that?" she asked in wonder. It was the worst scar she had ever seen.

"Korean War," said Moss. "I was in the same outfit Coley was in when he lost his leg. Will you beat it now and let me eat supper in peace?"

"If you'll tell me one thing first, I'll go," she said. "How'd you know so quick I was a runaway?"

Moss paused in his eating and looked steadily at her. Her pencilthin body was almost as straight as her ironed blond hair: she had practically no hips, no bust. Her collarbone stuck out above the scoop of her blouse, and her shoulder blades stuck out under it in back. Her arms looked too skinny to do anything heavy, yet Moss knew she was strong; he knew it from when he had grabbed her wrist that first day. He suspected that her legs, which were shapely and her best physical attribute, were also strong.

"Your eyes," he said in answer to her question. "There's a vacant, hollow look in them that says tomorrow's going to be exactly the same as today. All runaways have that look. And all junkies. And all convicts. All the losers."

"Well, *I'm* not a loser," she said defiantly. She met his direct eyes and immediately looked down. "At least not a permanent loser. I'll make it someday."

"Sure you will," Moss said without enthusiasm. "Someday." He resumed eating.

Jaysie stood looking at him for a long moment, watching him eat, watching him deliberately keep his eyes averted, purposely not looking at her anymore. Finally she turned and left him to the solitude of the lonely little room.

After supper, Moss went out again. He took a bus over to an area behind the St. Louis Cemetery, where a row of small garages and repair shops occupied the limited space beneath an elevated highway. The place he went in was called Claude's Welding Shop. Claude was a rotund little man with constantly drooping eyelids that made him look sleepy or on something, Moss never could figure out which. From Claude, Moss bought, on credit, the Walsh 200-series drill he needed and ten bits, which were all Claude had on hand. He also picked up two pairs of welding goggles to protect their eyes against flying slivers of metal, two pairs of moleskin gloves to absorb the sweat from their hands when they were drilling, and two pairs of engineer's coveralls to keep the steel dust off their street clothes. Claude packed everything neatly into a black canvas bag.

"You'll get your money Monday afternoon," Moss told the sleepy-eyed little welder.

"Yeah, okay, fine," said Claude, who reiterated everything he said. "Listen, I can order them two extra bits for you. I mean, if you want a dozen, I can get two more. I can order 'em for you, you know?"

"Ten will do," Moss said. "See you Monday."

"So long. Good-bye. See you," said Claude.

When Moss got back to the café, Coley was there with a tall redhead wearing spike heels and a coral pantsuit. Coley himself had on a white linen suit and open-collar navy shirt. When he saw Moss come in with the canvas bag, he moved over to intercept him at the back stairs.

"Been to see Claude, huh?" Coley said.

Moss nodded. "Who's the redhead?"

"Estelle Dumond. She dances down at the Burgundy Club; a specialty number. This is her night off. We been making it together for about a year now." He tapped his wooden leg. "She likes me 'cause I never take her dancing. She hates dancing. Like people who work in candy factories, you know. They never eat candy." Coley glanced down at the bag. "So everything's set, huh?"

"Yeah."

"Jeez, I wish I could talk you out of it, Mossy. I'd hate to see you fall and go back inside. You'd be old and gray time you got out again."

"A man's got to play it the only way he knows how, Coley. You understand that."

"I *used* to understand that," Coley said emphatically. "Not no more. Now I know a guy can break the mold if he wants to bad enough. I done it. Keene done it. You can do it, too. Listen, I'll tell you what I'll do. Take that bag back to Claude and tell him you changed your mind. Then come to work for me. I need a new fry cook, for nights, to work with Jaysie. The guy I got is going to Miami to try to get back together with his ex-wife. Work for me a while, settle down, show me your head's on right, and then we'll sit down and talk about that little business of your own that you want: video tapes or games or whatever."

Moss's eyes narrowed knowingly. "Been talking to Keene, have you?"

Coley shrugged. "What's the diff? We're all friends, ain't we? Now getting back to this little business of yours, if the idea looks good, I'll borrow the dough and stake you. What do you say?"

Moss looked down at the floor so that Coley wouldn't see how touched he was by the offer. "I appreciate what you're trying to do, Coley. Really. But I've got to go my own way."

The redhead called to Coley from the front door. "Coley, honey, we're going to be late if you don't come on."

"Right there," Coley called back. "We're taking the supper cruise on the *Beauregard,*" he explained to Moss, "just like a couple of square tourists." For a moment then, the two men stood in awkward silence, both looking down at the floor. Finally Coley grinned and slapped him on the back. "Sure, I understand. Good luck, pal."

"Thanks," Moss said.

The café was closed Sunday night when Moss got ready to go meet Keene, so when he came downstairs he was surprised to find Jaysie sitting at the counter with an open book and a cup of coffee in front of her.

"I thought this was your night off," he said, putting the canvas bag on the floor and drawing a cup of coffee for himself.

"It is. But I like to study here 'cause it's quiet. The rooming house where I live is full of jazz musicians. They're always practicing. Makes it hard to concentrate."

Moss turned the book up to see its title. *"Basic English,"* he read. "Where you studying that?"

"At Foster Continuation School. That's a school for people who never finished high school. I'm taking spelling and typing, too. I don't intend to have that vacant look, as you call it, in my eyes forever. All of *my* tomorrows are *not* going to be the same."

"Good for you," Moss said.

His voice had such a neutral tone that Jaysie was not sure whether he meant it or if he was just being sarcastic again. She glanced down at the canvas bag. "You leaving?"

"Not tonight. But I will be soon. Probably tomorrow or the next day."

"Oh." She looked away.

Moss frowned. "You sound disappointed."

She shrugged. "It's just that Mr. Coley said that he was going to try to get you to be his night fry cook for a while. I guess you turned him down."

"Yeah, I did." Moss could not understand why he suddenly felt self-conscious. "I, uh, I've got other plans."

Jaysie turned to face him directly. "I hope whatever they are," she said firmly, "that they help *you* lose the vacant look in your own eyes. Because it is there, you know. You do have it, same as me."

Moss stared down into his circle of black coffee without replying. He could not deny it; he knew she was right. For weeks, months, years in prison, he had watched the look settle in his eyes, seen it daily in his prison-issue metal mirror: a dullness, a hollowness, an absence of anything hopeful, reflecting the knowledge that Friday would be like Thursday, Thursday like Wednesday, Wednesday like Tuesday, and all the days of his life were running together like the cells on a tier: an endless line, each the same as the one after it and the one before it.

He turned to Jaysie with a slight, sad smile. "You're right, kid. I'm a loser, too."

"Then why don't you do like I'm doing?" she asked urgently. "Try to get out of your rut. Try to make things better for yourself." She put a hand on his arm. "Take the job Mr. Coley offered you. Please, Moss."

It was the first time she had called him by name. The first time he had heard any female voice speak his name in over nine years. For some reason it moved him. But not enough. He patted the hand on his arm. "I am going to try, Jaysie. But in my own way." He glanced up at a Dr Pepper clock on the wall. "I've got to go."

Jaysie suddenly leaned forward and kissed him briefly on the lips. "I sometimes study very late," she said softly.

"Sorry," Moss said, "but I'll be out all night."

At the Dixie Ezekiel Baptist Church, Moss entered by the back door and waited in Keene's office. It was warm, and the windows were open. Moss could hear Keene preaching at the Sunday-night meeting, hear his voice loud and clear as he praised Jesus and challenged Satan, shouted the goodness of eternal salvation and warned of the tortures of eternal damnation, as he called for sinners to come forward and be saved, pleaded, cajoled, teased, and prodded them into coming forward to accept Jesus Christ as their savior. Keene's voice was powerful, moving, tenacious; it loomed above the "Amens" and "Hallelujahs" and "Yes, brothers" that mingled with his fervent message.

When it was over, the organ began to play and all the voices merged as one to sing "Just a Closer Walk with Thee." It was the first song Moss had ever learned as a kid, growing up across the river in Gretna. The words came back to him now, and he closed his eyes and sang them softly to himself:

> Through this life of toil and snares,
> If I falter, Lord, who cares?
> Who for me my burden bears?
> None but Thee, dear Lord, none but Thee.

The old gospel song swept a rush of memories through Moss's head. He saw himself again as a little white boy stowing away on the ferry to cross over to New Orleans, there to wander the levees with other little boys, some white, some colored, listening to the Creole jazz bands play on street corners, begging food at the kitchen doors of the great houses on Royal Street, watching the fancy ladies from the Quarter strut along Bourbon Street with the pride of princesses.

Life had been simple then. So very simple.

Moss was so caught up in his own thoughts that he didn't

hear the music and praying end, didn't know the Sunday-night service was over until Keene came in and said, "Hey, Moss."

He opened his eyes then, the past back where it belonged. "Hey, Keene."

"Everything set?"

"Set," Moss confirmed.

Moss watched Keene empty his pockets and wallet of everything that could identify him. Like Moss, he would carry nothing in his pockets but a little money and the business card of a good lawyer. As Keene took things out of his wallet, Moss noticed a photo of a pretty young woman with an Afro and a little girl with her hair braided in corn rows.

"Who's that?" he asked.

"My wife and daughter," Keene said.

Moss stared incredulously at him. "I didn't know you had a family."

"Sure. Little girl's four."

"Why didn't you say something?"

"What for? Would it have made any difference to you? I still owe you, Moss, whether I have a family or not."

"Yeah, but—"

"But nothing, man. Come on, let's hit the road."

They took three hours to drive to Baton Rouge, taking the back roads along the river, staying off the interstate with its fast traffic and state-police cars. They drove through little river settlements like Reserve, Romeville, Dutchtown, and Sunshine; smelled the smoky, dusky outdoor fires that the bayou people built nightly, summer and winter; smelled fish frying an hour after being pulled out of the Big Muddy; smelled the willows, the riverbanks, the okra and crawfish and greens being steamed for Cajun gumbo. And everywhere along the road there was music, all lonely, all soulful: a mournful harmonic, a blue guitar, a slow, lazy Jew's harp.

"Nothing ever changes down here, does it?" Moss said, more a statement than a question.

"Not hardly," Keene replied quietly.

They drove in silence for most of the trip and got into Baton Rouge a little after midnight. Driving past the used-car lot, they saw a light inside where the night watchman was probably sitting.

"What time's daylight, you reckon?" Keene asked.

"Five forty-two," Moss said. "I called the weather bureau long distance to find out."

They found an all-night chili joint and killed two hours there, eating a late supper, reading a discarded Sunday paper. Then they pulled onto a Holiday Inn lot, parked the car in a back corner, and slumped down in the seat to doze for a couple of hours.

At five-fifteen, they were again cruising the street that the used-car lot was on. They watched daylight come slowly, dark to gray to light. The night watchman left at ten minutes to six. They waited until six to make sure he wouldn't pull the old trick of going around the block a couple of times. Then they parked behind the building, stood on top of the car, and scrambled onto the roof. Moss carried the canvas bag containing the drill, bits, and clothing; Keene handled the hand tools and the square-folded tarpaulin with its rope and hardware.

It took them sixteen minutes to punch a hole in the roof and drop down into the office. Twelve minutes to twist screwhooks into facing walls and lash up the tarp to seal off their light and noise from the front. Four minutes to lay out their drill and bits, get into their coveralls, don gloves and goggles.

Then they were ready to drill. They took turns, one drilling while one watched the street. The drilling was hard, hot work. Sweat poured down their necks, laced their forearms, spread in a circle in the small of their backs. The Warnecke vault was one tough baby: steel on top of steel on top of steel. The first drill bit broke in four minutes, less than an eighth of an inch into the outer plate. The second one broke five minutes later; the third and fourth less than ten minutes after that. By the time they were halfway through the middle plate, they had broken three more. A total of seven dead bits.

"Good thing we got a dozen," Keene said, wiping the sweat from his face. "We'll probably need every one of them."

Taking the drill for his turn, Moss said nothing to Keene about having only ten bits. During his turn on the drill, he was very careful to keep the drill nose as level-straight as possible.

Keene took the drill again when black slivers told them they had reached the bottom plate. Immediately he broke another bit biting into it.

"Take it easy, will you?" Moss said with an edge. "Slow down a little."

"I want to get out of here, my friend," Keene said. "Besides, we've got four bits left. No bottom plate made can stand up to four Walsh bits."

Halfway through the bottom plate, Keene broke their ninth bit.

"I'll take it now," Moss said. Wetting his lips, he slugged the last bit into the drill, took a deep breath, and started to drill. He had a quarter of an inch of steel to get through. If he didn't make it, the job would go down the drain. He drilled slowly, carefully, for five minutes. Sweat, both from the effort and the tension, drenched his torso.

"Take a break, man," Keene said after five minutes. "Let me spell you again."

"I'm okay," Moss said. "Watch the street."

Keene went back to the edge of the tarp and resumed his scrutiny of the street. Several minutes later, Moss came over to him, shoulders slumped, but a look of relief in his eyes.

"We're through the bottom plate. Go punch the lock."

"All *right!*" Keene said happily.

They climbed back out through the hole in the roof at twenty past eight with the canvas bag packed with sheafs of currency. The goggles, coveralls, tarp, and miscellaneous tools were left behind; only the drill, which had a traceable serial number, was brought back out. After they got in the car, they stripped off the moleskin gloves and tossed them on the ground next to the building.

"We've got forty, maybe forty-five minutes to get across the St. Gabriel bridge before the alarm's sounded and roadblocks go up," Moss said.

"You think they'll blow the whistle?" Keene asked.

"Sure they will. All they have to say is that we hit them for the week's car-sales receipts. They'll probably call in the law just to get us caught. Then take care of us themselves later."

As they headed back south by way of the same bayou roads, Moss unzipped the canvas bag, tossed the drill on the back seat, and began counting their take. When he finished, he said, "Not as much as I hoped for. Fifty-seven thousand even." He fell silent for a moment as he figured the shares. "That's a little over eighty-five hundred for Palmetto, and about twenty-four thousand apiece for you and me."

"That's my day-care center," said Keene. "I'm satisfied, man. You?"

"Yeah," said Moss. "Yeah, I'm cool." Suddenly he frowned. "What's that up ahead?"

A white man in overalls was in the middle of the narrow blacktop road, frantically flagging them down. Next to the road, an old pickup truck was overturned in a culvert.

"Go around him," Moss said.

"Maybe somebody's hurt, Moss."

"*We'll* be hurt if we don't get over the St. Gabriel bridge by nine o'clock. Go around him."

Keene Summers flicked his eyes from the frantic man to the

overturned truck. Then he saw a child lying alongside the culvert. "Somebody's hurt, Moss. It's a kid. I'm stopping."

"Are you crazy!" Moss snapped, but it was too late: Keene was already grinding the car to a halt at the edge of the culvert.

"Can y'all help me?" the man pleaded as he ran up to them. "My little girl's hurt and my little boy's stuck inside the truck!"

"What happened?" asked Keene, leaping out. Cursing under his breath, Moss jumped out with him.

"Blew a tire," said the farmer.

"See about the girl, Moss," Keene said. "I'll try to get the boy out."

"I smell gasoline," Moss warned.

"Yeah, so do I."

Keene slid into the culvert next to the overturned truck. Through the windshield he saw a young boy lying wedged up against one door. The door was locked but the window was down several inches. "Come help me!" Keene shouted to the farmer. Keene had begun to sweat with fear; the frightening odor of gasoline was almost overpowering.

The farmer slid down beside him. With four hands exerting pressure, they managed to force the window down far enough for Keene to reach in and unlock the door. They got the unconscious boy out and scrambled back up the embankment.

"How's the girl?" Keene asked.

"I think she's got a broken arm," Moss said, kneeling, helping the tearful child sit up.

Keene turned to the farmer. "Where's the nearest hospital?"

"Over by the St. Gabriel bridge."

"Which side?" Moss asked with sudden interest.

"This side," said the farmer.

"Come on, Moss," Keene said firmly. "These kids need attention."

They put the farmer and his little boy in the back seat, Moss cradled the little girl on his lap, and Keene drove. It was twenty miles to the outskirts of St. Gabriel, where the hospital was located. And the bridge. As they drove up to the hospital emergency entrance, Moss could see that there was as yet no roadblock on the bridge. "Let's make this fast," he said urgently to Keene. The black man threw him an irritated glance which he ignored.

Keene took the boy from his father and hurried into the emergency room, with Moss carrying the sobbing girl right behind him. The trembling father of the children shouted for a doctor. It took a couple of minutes for nurses and attendants to get each of the children into an examining room. Moss saw a clock as he was being shown where to take the girl. It was ten before nine. *We still got an edge,* he thought tightly.

When the two children were finally in medical hands, Moss took Keene firmly by the arm. "That's it, man. That's all we can do. Now let's split."

They hurried back to where they had left the car. But as soon as they got outside the door, they saw that they were too late. A roadblock of two radio cars had sealed off the approach to the bridge. And a tall, uniformed policeman was walking around their car, looking it over. When they got close enough to him, they saw that his badge was inscribed SHERIFF—ST. GABRIEL TOWNSHIP.

"This your car?" he asked, one hand on his pistol butt, his eyes shifting back and forth between them.

"Yessir, it is," Keene said, trying to keep the guilt out of his voice.

Moss said nothing. He felt ill: physically sick to his stomach. Dread thoughts of Angola flooded his head: the backbreaking field work, the lumpy mattresses, the smells and noise of hundreds of men, the long nights. He suddenly knew that he would rather die than go back to prison.

"What's that there drill on the back seat for?" the sheriff asked.

"We're steel workers," Keene replied. "Going down to New Orleans looking for work."

The sheriff's expression was inscrutable. "What's in the canvas bag on the front floorboard?" he asked.

Keene shrugged. "Just clothes, sir. Personal stuff."

"Suppose you open it and show me."

Moss hung his head and his shoulders slumped. Coley's words screamed inside his head: *You'll be old and gray before they let you out again.* He looked over at the sheriff's hand still on the pistol butt. *If I run, he'll put one right in my back,* Moss thought.

"Open the bag," the sheriff said again. Keene sighed resignedly and reached in the car for the bag. Just then, the father of the two injured children came out.

"My kids are gonna be all right," he said happily to Keene and Moss. Then he saw the sheriff. "Hey, Jesse," he greeted him.

"What are you doing here, Alvin?" the sheriff asked.

Alvin told him: about the blowout, the rescue of the boy, driving both children to the hospital, carrying them inside. "Weren't for these two fellers, we might have lost Joey. He's got a punctured lung and a concussion. Doc says he could've died of shock we didn't get him here quick as we did." He turned to Keene and Moss. "Fellers, this here's my brother Jesse. He's the sheriff hereabouts. I swear I don't know how in the world to thank you boys for what you done."

"That's okay," Moss said, suddenly feeling all right again. "Your brother the sheriff knows how. Don't you, Sheriff?"

The sheriff nodded knowingly at Moss. "I reckon I do, all right."

"We was just telling him how we're in a hurry to be on our way to New Orleans to look for work. Weren't we, Sheriff?"

"That's a fact," the sheriff said. He moved his hand away from his gun. "Get in your car, boys. I'll ride with you and see you past the roadblock. Alvin, I'll be back directly to see the kids."

Half an hour later, Keene and Moss were well on their way home. Neither of them was making much conversation; it was taking them a while to get over the fright and nausea of almost being caught. But as they were driving past the New Orleans city limit, Moss felt the need to purge his conscience.

"You know that day I took the shank in my arm?" he said quietly. "I wasn't trying to keep that dude from sticking you. I thought he was coming for *me*. I had him confused with another one of those heavy dudes that I had a run-in with over some smokes that was owed me. Truth is, I hustled you into this job, Keene. You never really owed me nothing."

Keene swallowed dryly and did not say anything. He kept his anger in check, thinking, *Forgive and forget, it's all done with.* He had the money to start the day-care center now. The Lord moved in mysterious ways.

When they reached the Dixie Ezekiel Church, Moss carried the canvas bag in and opened it on Keene's desk. He counted out eighty-five hundred dollars.

"This is Palmetto's share—it goes to his lawyer. I want you to divide the rest in half. Your half you can start your day-care center with or whatever you want to do. My half I want you to use to fix up that playground out there. I want it to look brand-new again. And I want all new equipment bought—you can't play games without equipment, you know." Moss went to the door to leave. "If you want me for anything, I'll be working over at Coley's. As a fry cook."

Keene Summers was staring at his friend in disbelief. Moss paused at the door and bobbed his chin at the bag of money.

"This makes us even. It squares me for hustling you into the job, right?"

Keene smiled. "Right."

Moss winked and left the church. Outside, he ran into the little black boy with the shoeshine box.

"Hey, kid, good news," Moss told him. "The preacher is gonna fix up the playground. He's ordering all new equipment, too."

The boy eyed Moss suspiciously. "You jiving me?"

"Hey, would I lie? Honest man like me?" Moss rubbed the boy's head and hurried off down the street.

On his way to the café, he began whistling "Just a Closer Walk with Thee," all the while wondering how long it would be until Jaysie turned eighteen.

CLARK HOWARD won an Edgar Allan Poe Award from the Mystery Writers of America for "Horn Man" in 1980. "New Orleans Getaway" was nominated for an Edgar in 1983. His short story "Animals" won the first Ellery Queen's Mystery Magazine *Readers Award in 1985.*

NIGHT

RUN

Shannon OCork

Who would ever think that athlete's foot could be fatal?

He heard the footfalls at the eighth mile, where the course turned north around the west wall of the campus. *Thuk-thuk-thuk-suh, thuk-thuk-thuk-suh.* Someone was closing in in the dark, and tonight, Brad did not expect that. The only one able to challenge him after six miles was Patterson, and Patterson should be long dead by now, stiffening already. Brad was forty minutes into the race; his distance told him that. His body told him that.

Whoever it was, he was coming up fast, threatening as

Patterson usually did, just here, where the dirt path was blackest, where it swung right and ran along the stone wall for a mile and a half. The runner was back still, sixteen–seventeen paces off Brad's lead. It was too dark to identify the runner with a backward glance—the white number on his chest would not shine here under the ceiling of willow branches—so Brad didn't waste his energy in head movements. He was attuned to competition and did not panic at a challenge, especially one too early, two-thirds into a twelve-mile race that had Billygoat Hill two miles ahead. (But Patterson always threatened too early, threatened and passed and won.) So, no, Brad was not panicking, but he was surprised to hear behind him, *so close*, thudding, quickening footfalls.

Brad listened to the cadence of the running. Its rhythm was familiar and he knew it well. For three years he had run with the staccato sounds of Patterson's rabbity, toe-first strides in his ears, Patterson's jerky pounding behind, abreast, and ahead, Patterson's unorthodox loping, off-beat to Brad's own flowing heel-first roll through the foot, Brad's own textbook-beautiful *slup-sloop, slup-sloop, slup-sloop, soooo.*

The sounds behind, slight as they yet were in the night air, on the night ground, focused Brad's free-floating attention. He could tell, without consciously calculating, the approximate speed of the strides by their sounds and intervals of silence. And the runner behind was gaining.

Brad passed into slivered-moon brightness. He knew the route intimately. At this pace, he had thirty-six steps of wall bare of trees before the way was draped again by the lacey overhang of giant willows. Brad pressed a button on his Casio digital. On his wrist, black numbers glowed against white background: 41:20.9, 41:21.0 . . . He was more than forty minutes into the race.

Whoever was dumb enough to come at him here, it wasn't Patterson this time. Couldn't be. Patterson should be, by now, literally stopped in his tracks. Brad sprinted the clearing in thirty-one steps to discourage the fool who thought he could match number one. (Number one, that is, now that Patterson was removed—rubbed out with a bit of nicotine-contaminated athlete's-foot salve. Self-applied, *rub-a-dub-gone,* just like that.) Ten minutes, the medical encyclopedia had said, for pure nicotine to kill; twenty minutes tops.

Brad listened. His increased speed had not daunted the runner behind. The thunking footfalls were closer than ever now, maybe twelve paces off Brad's right shoulder, *hurrying,* in Patterson's peculiar, eccentric rhythm. *Thuk-thuk-thuk—*

Brad deepened his breathing, settled lower in his stride, and increased his time to five-minute miles. Nobody at the university could put two five-minute miles back-to-back in a long run except himself and Patterson. They could do even better when they had to. And against each other, they usually had.

Brad ran under a canopy of trees into cool night shadow. *Slap-sloop, slap-sloop, slap-sloop-soooo.*

Patterson deserved to die, there was no getting around that. Patterson (on purpose—Brad knew it was on purpose) had infected Brad with the foot fungus; he had strutted barefoot around the locker room, shower-wet, spreading his disease. Patterson had wiped his hairy, infected toes with Brad's towel. Remembering it now in the dark of the run, Brad got angry all over again. Patterson was *(had been, had been)* an inconsiderate, superstitious, narcissistic bastard. He'd even made a pass at Jeannie.

"Your friend with the kangaroo-bounce asked to run with me tomorrow. Said he'd give me some pointers. Do you mind?"

"No. Patterson's crazy, Jeannie, he's eccentric and superstitious, but he's good. I like to run with him. I push him, he pushes me, and I haven't beaten him yet at distance. I don't mind his funny ways."

And he hadn't minded, until Patterson used Brad's towel and passed along his athlete's foot. (On purpose; had to be on purpose.) Everybody knew athlete's foot was almost as contagious as TB, and just about as debilitating to a distance runner.

It happened, too, just as Brad was peaking into prime-performance condition and Patterson, overtrained, was tiring. The last time out together, a fourteen-mile run and no one else in contention, Brad had been within arm's reach when Patterson broke the tape. Two strides more and Brad would have had him. *Two strides!* Brad had collapsed at the end of that try, his toes burning up as though he'd run through fire.

The over-the-counter ointment Patterson suggested hadn't worked. That was when Brad decided to see Dr. Entwhistle.

Even if it was Patterson behind him (which it couldn't be, could it?), Brad thought he could take his rival now. He could beat Patterson on the final flat, the glass-slippery hundred-yard stretch of lawn that led to the campus gate and the white tape fluttering between the fieldstone posts.

Six–seven strides off his left shoulder now, the footfalls ran behind, gaining inches with each step. Brad was beyond the willows, at the beginning of the mile-long incline that was Billygoat Hill, a gradual, ever-rising climb. At its apex, the hill turned abruptly down into a steep half-mile descent, and then there was the tarred path that switched and swung past the university hospital and around the swamp of the parking lot and then became the relative straight of the quad yard and the final grassy sprint.

Brad risked a turn of his head. And looked dead into the white-rimmed irises of Patterson, ghostly aglow in the moonlight.

Frowning and serious, Patterson ran at Brad, four strides behind and gaining. It was summer and night, but Brad could see the gray evanescence of the expelled *swoosh* of Patterson's breath and hear the lung pull as air swished in. Patterson was clutching something round and white in his hand. When Brad turned to look, Patterson held the object high in the air and shook it, menacingly, like a stone.

Brad turned his head away. Leaned into Billygoat Hill. So Patterson hadn't used the salve after all. Damn Patterson. Damn Patterson. *Slup-slup-slup-soooo.*

And behind, coming, *thukthukthukthuk . . .*

Dr. Entwhistle was famous in the state as the leading practitioner of sports medicine. Entwhistle taught at the university, lectured throughout the United States, and had his own radio show on Sunday mornings nine to twelve. Brad didn't know anybody who didn't lie in bed Sunday mornings, no matter how long Saturday night lasted, and listen to Dr. Entwhistle. It was good, of course, to have a girl beside you then, and it was best when your girl was a runner, too, like Jeannie, who also listened, who wouldn't miss Dr. Entwhistle for anything.

The doctor wasn't as fanatical as many people seriously into health and fitness are, but Doc Entwhistle was hot on the evils of smoking. In his examining room he had a display. Under an airtight, clear plastic dome was a small saucer of colorless liquid. Above the saucer was a cardboard sign: *Nicotine $C_{10}H_{14}$ N_2. An alkaloid. In this saucer is the extract of tobacco leaves. One drop is enough to kill YOU.* To the left of the saucer was a small cardboard tombstone and, beneath that, a cigarette. The cigarette lay upon a white index-card grave, and the card read: *Cigarettes are made of tobacco leaves and contain nicotine.* A piece of white adhesive was taped to the outside of the covering dome. Printed on the tape in black ink was the warning: DO NOT DISTURB. The display sat on the counter shelf of a white cupboard to the left of the patient's chair.

Brad hadn't come to Dr. Entwhistle planning to murder Patterson. He hadn't known about the liquid nicotine; he'd never been in Doc Entwhistle's office before. He had simply gone to Doctor Entwhistle about his athlete's foot, the fungus Patterson had given him. And opportunity had presented itself.

What Doctor Entwhistle told Brad scared him. Athlete's foot, like other dermatophyte infections, sometimes never got cured. It got controlled. Unchecked, athlete's foot (Dr. Entwhistle called it *tinea pedis*) could effectively cripple Brad as a competitive runner. So daily washing was imperative, the doctor said—many daily washings—and then a careful drying of the interdigital spaces, rubbing away the softened, scaly skin, then the salve applied without fail, with gloved fingers, and finally a thick dusting of talcum powder. Brad was to go barefoot as often as he could and wear, always with shoes, clean white socks. Sweat exacerbated the condition, Dr. Entwhistle said, and, as runners' feet sweat, it was important Brad attend rigorously to this hygiene. Perhaps, the doctor suggested, Brad could ease up for a time on his workouts and competitive runs.

The suggestion that Brad ease up—that was what did it.

Brad could see how Patterson would want to share his misery. Knowing he was going sour from overtraining, Patterson had tried to halt Brad's progress, too, to keep Brad from surpassing him. So, Brad concluded, sitting humbly in the patient's chair, his eyes upon the saucer of deadly nicotine, Patterson had contaminated him with his wretched disease.

The terrible treachery made Brad seethe inside.

But he sat quietly and listened to the soft admonitions of Dr. Entwhistle. He received all with a subservient nod. He took the wide-mouthed, milk white jar of salve with its red-and-white plaid top in a grateful palm. He slumped in his chair, brooding but obedient, when Dr. Entwhistle was called into another room to attend, without delay, a university professor who'd hopped over on a break between classes to have his stomach checked—something to do with Mussels Marinara at the Faculty Club.

And just as Dr. Entwhistle went away, Brad, not thinking

it out and almost as though directed by an outer force, glanced at the closed door of the examining room to make sure he was alone. His right hand snaked out to a container of little glass tubes on the counter shelf. He extracted one of the tubelets and with his other hand, the jar of salve firmly between his thighs, he lifted away the plastic dome over the deadly liquid. An odor of decayed leaves suffused his nose.

Brad held his breath against the fumes. Leaning away, he dipped the slim length of hollow glass into the pool of nicotine. He took a cotton ball from a nearby box. To protect his finger from contact, he placed the ball between his fingertip and the end of the glass tube. Having created suction, he drew up a stemful of the toxic liquid. Then the dome down, back in place, and the top of the jar unscrewed, Brad's finger lifted off the pipestem, the suction broke, and the poison ran like gloss over the creamy surface of the salve. Still holding his breath, Brad stirred the poison into the top layer of the salve with the glass tubelet, then reset the red-and-white plaid top on the jar. He darted into the adjoining bathroom, where he flushed away the stem of glass and the cotton ball, rinsed out his mouth, and washed his hands with the deodorant soap that was there. When Doctor Entwhistle returned, Brad was sitting as before.

For some minutes the doctor continued Brad's education in the proper care of *tinea pedis,* and then Brad was dismissed. He left, feeling better than he had in days.

Three hours later, he was back. He told the doctor he'd left the ointment jar under his seat in his American History class and when he returned for it, it was gone. It wasn't true, of course. He had it snug in his running pack, ready to offer to Patterson tonight, before the run, promising spectacular results.

Dr. Entwhistle gave Brad another jar of salve, and Brad was glad to see the lid of this jar was brown.

———

Brad had barely bested the first third of Billygoat Hill, marked by the Dean of Men's mailbox, when Patterson galloped alongside, frowning, as Patterson did when he ran. Brad strained into the hill and concentrated on keeping his rhythm, but Patterson, alive and apparently well, paced beside.

Between controlled breaths, Patterson said to Brad: "Couldn't use this salve tonight, pal. I never take my footgear off once I've got my socks adjusted right." And not waiting for a reply, he tossed into the air between them the round white object he'd held in his hands like a stone.

Brad lost a stride in surprise and, from reflex, reached into the dark air and pulled down the spinning milk white jar with the plaid top. Patterson, yipping a laugh, broke out and away, ahead of Brad up the incline, two strides, three.

But even as Brad's heart sank with the realization that Patterson was not only alive and well but also winning again, adrenaline coursed through his veins. He felt new energy, a great new power within. Anger and disappointment? No, hate and fear. Hate and fear flashed red and vivid and over and over in his brain. *Get him, get him,* tom-tommed his pounding feet. *He's overconditioned, you're prime, you're fine,* his mind mantra'd. He ran into the hill, bent low into the hill, and thundered after Patterson, unconsciously gripping to his belly the jar of poisoned salve.

He caught up to Patterson where the grade was steepest. Without a word, he hurled the jar back into Patterson's hands and spurted ahead. He reached the crest of the hill six–seven lengths in the lead and dropped like a striking hawk down the sheer descent. He was hitting new times, faster speeds; he had never run so fast nor felt so well. He was beating Patterson, beating Patterson fair and square. With joy, he heard behind him, receding now in his downward plunge, the *thuk-thuk-thuk-suh, thuk-thuk-thuk-suh* of Patterson's unorthodox footfalls.

Brad was running flat-out now, saving nothing. But the power was there. The oxygen flowed from his lungs to his veins, there was no strain in his legs, no effort in his breathing. He had achieved, somehow, in his fear and hate, a new oxygen balance, a personal best.

And now he was on the flat, the tarred path under his feet. His toes burned as they slapped and gripped the warm, spongy black. He dug in, lifted off, flew on, unmindful. He was beating Patterson and that was all he cared about. He longed to hear behind him the vainly challenging *thuks,* but Patterson was too far behind, in the black of the drop down Billygoat Hill.

Brad was on a runner's high, gleeful as he flowed past the university hospital, past the dark windows of Dr. Entwhistle's office. The quarter moon jigged above him, free of cloud.

The crowd of students extended all the way to the outer fringes of the parking lot, swelled in the quad yard, flanked three deep on either side of the lane across the lawn, and then spilled haphazardly beyond the posts and the wisplike tape. Brad saw the last lap spread before him, under the moon, as in a picture postcard. Dormitory lights illuminated it all. It was a beautiful coming home.

He heard the cheering as he flashed into view. A light mitting at first, then a steady, enthusiastic clap, and then the full collegiate *yaaayyyy!* as the bystanders realized the first runner was not Patterson, who always won, but Brad, who was usually second. The spectators loved an upset, they applauded the underdog. Brad ran into the applause dazzled with happiness.

And the power was still there. He knew he could surge across the lawn, kick at the end with style, although unchallenged, alone, way ahead of the pack. The lights swam in his eyes. His own rhythms were drowned in the chanting hurrahs. He ran, ecstatic, into the tape and felt it break like a hymen against his chest. And then he slowed and wobbled and fell toward Jeannie—who was there, waiting. Just as he lost consciousness, he heard, like a faraway echo, the *thuk-thuk-thuk-suh* of Patterson, finishing second.

He came back to awareness with a blissful weariness in his muscles and the knowledge of what he had accomplished. He was lying on cool, damp grass. Jeannie was on her knees at his feet. She had unlaced his running shoes and pulled off his sweaty socks. His naked, flaming feet were cradled in a towel on her lap. And Jeannie, his own dear Jeannie, her hands protected from the fungus by rubber gloves as he'd taught her, was massaging his toes, massaging, with love in her face, the salve into the cracks and scales of his burning, fissured feet. Looming behind her, one hand holding the wide-mouthed jar, Patterson, frowning and serious, leaned into the light.

"Hell of a run," said Patterson.

"You're going to be all right now," said Jeannie.

Above Brad, and around, the students were singing "For He's a Jolly Good Fellow." And in the long grass, beside Jeannie's knees, lay the cheerful red-and-white plaid top.

SHANNON OCORK *is the author of several popular mystery novels and a number of short stories. She is currently Secretary of the Mystery Writers of America.*

THE PROBLEM
OF THE
FATAL
FIREWORKS

Edward D. Hoch

Is it a defective firecracker that kills one of the Oswald brothers, or is it murder—and if it is murder, who is the killer?

"Come in!" Dr. Sam Hawthorne urged, waving toward the vacant chair that was always at his side. "I was just pouring myself a small libation, and I don't like to drink alone. Which reminds me, I was going to tell you about the warehouse full of bootlegged Scotch we discovered back in the summer of '32 just before the Fourth of July weekend. You'll remember it was our centennial summer in Northmont and there was lots of celebrating. . . ."

The Fourth came on a Monday that year (Dr. Sam continued), and I guess Sheriff Lens had been looking forward to a peaceful holiday after all the excitement of the previous week. But early on Monday morning two well-dressed men drove into town and showed the sheriff their badges. They were Charles Simmons and James Ready from the Prohibition Bureau's enforcement division, and they'd driven in from the Boston office to take possession of the warehouse full of Scotch whiskey we'd uncovered in Shinn Corners. Though it was a different county, Sheriff Lens had found it with me, and he'd assumed temporary responsibility for it.

It happened that my nurse, April, was on vacation that week. She'd taken a cottage at Chester Lake and invited the sheriff and his wife, Vera, along with me, to spend the holiday with her. Vera, in fact, had driven up with April early in the morning, and we were supposed to join them around noon. I was in my new office in a wing of Pilgrim Memorial Hospital, having checked on a couple of patients, when Sheriff Lens phoned with the bad news.

"Doc, I don't think I'm goin' to make it to April's cottage by noon. A couple of Prohibition agents just arrived. I gotta ride over to Shinn Corners with them."

"I could meet you there and we could go on to the lake. It's on the way."

"Can't, Doc. I promised the Oswald brothers I'd stop by the garage this morning. I'll have to do that after I finish up in Shinn Corners."

I didn't want to disappoint April and Vera, so I tried to figure a way we could get everything done. "What's the problem with the Oswalds? Anything I can handle?"

"Well, maybe so. You know Max Webber has been tryin' to buy their garage. They say he's vandalizing the property to force them to sell. Somebody broke a window last night."

"I guess a broken window isn't serious enough to disrupt

your holiday. I'll swing by after I leave here and tell them you'll be over in the morning."

"I'd appreciate it, Doc."

"Then I'll drive over to Shinn Corners and meet you at that warehouse."

"Fine. I expect they just want me to show them the place and then they'll take over. None too soon for me. I've had to have deputies guardin' it all weekend."

I locked the office and drove into town, heading for Oswalds' Garage. A decade earlier there wouldn't have been a need for an auto-repair place in Northmont, but now probably half the people in town owned cars, and only the Depression was keeping the rest from buying them. The Oswald brothers, Teddy and Billy, were both in their late twenties, and they'd been tinkering with Model T Fords for as long as I'd lived in town. Their garage, opened a year earlier, had quickly become a hangout for teenage boys who shared their interest in cars. Some folks complained about the noise in the early evening, but it was never excessive.

The firecrackers going off in the town square were making a lot more noise just then. There'd be a band concert later in the day, as there always was on the Fourth, but right now the square was given over to fireworks and cherry bombs and cap guns. The sound brought back unpleasant memories of a tragic murder only a few days earlier—one that had led to the discovery of the bootleg Scotch. That was history now, and I told myself I should be happy a broken window was the worst crime Northmont had to offer on the holiday.

Billy Oswald, the younger brother, was outside the garage when I arrived. He was still a kid at heart, and I wasn't surprised to see him lighting the fuse of a firecracker as I parked the car across the street. He ran back about twenty feet and grinned as it went off with a satisfying bang. A few kids watched from a distance.

"How's the car running, Doc?" he asked when he saw me.

"Like a top, Billy. Your brother around?"

"He's inside working on a Chevy."

I followed him into the garage where Teddy Oswald was changing a tire. He was more serious than Billy but not quite as handsome. The girls chased after Billy and ignored Teddy, which seemed to be all right with both of them.

"I hear you got a broken window, Teddy," I said. "Sheriff Lens asked me to stop by and tell you he'll be over in the morning."

Teddy picked up a mallet and tried to remove a dent from the Chevy's fender. "It's Max Webber, I know it is. If I had his head here, I'd work on it with this."

Billy came around the side of the car. "It's Max, all right," he agreed.

"Why's he so anxious to get this property?" I asked. "You got an oil well under it?"

"He's got big plans for fixin' up the town. Wants to put an office building on this corner, with stores on the main floor." Billy had picked up a second mallet to help with the dent but he seemed undecided about how to proceed. Finally, Teddy sighed and took it from him, trying to show him how.

Just then, Dora Springsteen entered the garage. She was Billy's girl, a pretty blond who worked at the soda fountain in the drugstore down the street. "Where's the window they broke?" she asked of no one in particular.

"Back there," Teddy muttered. "We found that rock somebody tossed through it."

She picked up the small stone from the workbench. "This isn't much more than a pebble. You know, a big firecracker might have tossed that up in the air. Maybe it was an accident."

I had to agree with her. "There's probably nothing here for the sheriff," I said. "If you want me to, I'll talk to Max about easing off you fellas."

"Nobody talks to Max Webber," Dora said. "He comes into the soda fountain like he owns the place."

Billy Oswald opened a storage cabinet and took out two big boxes of firecrackers. "Come on, Teddy. Let's close up and go have some fun. Hell, it's the Fourth of July."

I didn't like being reminded of the fact. Back in '24, soon after I set up my medical practice in Northmont, there'd been a July Fourth killing on the park bandstand. The day had seemed jinxed to me ever since, although subsequent Independence Days had been peaceful enough. "You've got enough there to blow up the town," I commented.

Billy hefted one of the sealed packages. "These are skyrockets, for tonight. The firecrackers can go anytime—like right now!"

I followed along reluctantly as the brothers and Dora crossed the street in the direction of the park. But our trek was unexpectedly interrupted as a black sedan pulled up alongside. I recognized Sheriff Lens in the front seat with the driver.

"Doc, this here's James Ready from the Boston office. And that's Mr. Charles Simmons in back."

I smiled at both grim-faced men. Ready, in the front seat, merely grunted, and Simmons got out to stretch his legs without speaking. Maybe they didn't like working on Independence Day, either. "Glad to meet you," I told them. "I thought you'd be halfway to Shinn Corners by now, Sheriff."

"I left the keys to the warehouse at my office—had to come by and pick them up."

Charles Simmons called out to Billy Oswald as he walked by. "Wait a minute, mister. You thinking of setting off them crackers?"

"That was my idea. Who're you?"

Simmons flashed his badge. "I better look them over."

Sheriff Lens quickly interceded, sensing trouble. "We got no law against it here, Mr. Simmons. If they're careful, we let it go."

The government man grudgingly handed back the package of firecrackers. "Okay, but be careful with them." He got back into the car and closed the door.

"I'll see you in Shinn Corners," I told the sheriff as he pulled away.

"Cops," Dora Springsteen said. "All they want to do is cause trouble." She and I hung back as Billy walked across the grass of the town square. I watched him break the seal on the package and take out one of the medium-sized firecrackers. He stood it on the grass and reached into the pocket of his baggy shirt for a box of wooden matches. "Go ahead and *do* it, Billy!" his brother yelled. "Don't make such a big production out of it!"

Billy crouched down, his broad back to us, and tried to light the match. He turned in frustration, and I saw him strike it again along the side of the box. Nothing happened. Finally, on the third try, the match broke in two. Billy stood up, frustrated.

"Come on, damn it!" Teddy Oswald shouted.

Billy took out another match and again failed to light it. Finally, Teddy ran forward and grabbed the matchbox from him. He took out another match, lit it on the first try, and bent to ignite the fuse as Billy walked away, grumbling. "They're my firecrackers, Teddy. At least you could let me light them."

I saw the instant flash as the fuse ignited and I knew something was wrong. Teddy must have, too, but he had no chance to move before it was too late. There was an ear-shattering explosion and a fiery flare that seemed to engulf Teddy as it swept out to catch Billy, too.

Then people were running and screaming, and as the smoke cleared we saw them both on the ground.

Teddy Oswald was killed instantly. His brother Billy suffered burns on his back and a possible concussion. I treated him as best I could at the scene, and an ambulance rushed him to Pilgrim Memorial. Sheriff Lens and the others had heard the blast before they were out of town and hurried back to the scene. As soon as he saw what had happened, he decided to remain with me and send one of his deputies to Shinn Corners with the Prohibition agents.

"What do you think happened, Doc?" he asked as the ambulance pulled away.

"Damned if I know. A defective firecracker, I suppose. Couldn't be anything else."

The sheriff gathered up the scattered remains of the package of firecrackers. They'd been far enough from the blast so that none of them were set off, but he handled them gingerly nonetheless.

"Look at that hole!" he said as we gaped at the spot where the explosion had occurred. He examined one of the firecrackers in his hand and shook his head. "You know something, Doc? I think what went off was half a stick of dynamite. It would be just about the right size."

"How could that be? I watched Billy unwrap the package myself. It was sealed at the factory."

"What about the fuse?"

I nodded, remembering. "It flared instantly, like those long ones they use for setting off charges at mines and construction sites. Only it wasn't longer than a couple of inches, like these others."

"Doc, I could believe one mistake at the factory, but here we got two. The wrong explosive *and* the wrong fuse. What does that sound like to you?"

"Murder," I admitted. "But how?"

"You're the expert on these things."

"There's something else," I decided. "If it was murder, were both brothers the intended victims, or just Billy?"

"Billy?"

"He opened the package and tried to light that fuse, but he was having problems so Teddy took it away from him and lit it himself."

Sheriff Lens nodded. "I guess we better go talk to Billy at the hospital."

The staff doctors had done a good job of treating the burns on Billy's back, but he was still in some pain. He lay on his stomach, his head turned toward us. He was obviously in grief. "I can't believe Teddy's dead. Who would do a thing like that to us?"

"How about Max Webber?" the sheriff suggested. "You accused him of throwin' that rock through the window."

"Throwing a rock and killing somebody aren't the same thing, Sheriff. I can't believe even Webber would do a thing like that."

The sheriff had brought along the paper wrapper from the fireworks package, printed in bold red letters with the words: *One dozen Big Buster Firecrackers. Handle with Care.* "Could you show me how you opened this package, Billy?"

"I just tore the seal and ripped one side of the paper so I could take one out. I never gave no thought to it. Sam was watching me, weren't you, Sam?"

"That's right," I agreed. "He didn't choose a certain firecracker, if that's what you're thinking, Sheriff. He just reached in without looking and pulled one out. Then he put down the package and the others spilled out on the grass."

Sheriff Lens nodded. "Is there anyone else who might have a grudge against you, Billy? You gotta realize that if that match had lit you'd be dead instead of your brother."

"No one could have known I'd use those firecrackers instead of Teddy," Billy insisted. "Just last night Teddy set off some skyrockets. Could it have been a mistake at the factory?"

"We think there was half a stick of dynamite in there, Billy. And the fuse was the wrong kind, too. Doc says it flared right up when Teddy lit it."

"I wish it'd been me," Billy muttered into his pillow.

We left him then, because Sheriff Lens wanted to examine

the rest of the firecrackers and I wanted to pay a call on Max Webber.

I found him at his home on Maple Street, a few blocks from the town square, sitting on the porch reading the morning newspaper. He was a large man who more often than not had the butt of a cigar in one corner of his mouth. He was a community leader, but I hated to think that the future of Northmont depended on someone like Webber.

"Hello there, Dr. Sam," he greeted me, putting down the paper. "I hear there was an accident down at the square. My wife and daughter walked down to see what happened."

"Weren't you interested enough to go, Mr. Webber?"

He took the dead cigar from his mouth and gazed at it distastefully before replying. "The legs been bothering me. I don't get around like I used to."

"Teddy Oswald was killed in an explosion," I said. "His brother Billy was injured."

"That's too bad."

"There was dynamite in a firecracker, near as we can figure."

Webber grunted. "Awful mistake to make at the factory."

"Maybe it didn't happen at the factory. The brothers seemed to think you were harassing them, trying to force them to sell the garage to you."

"That's nonsense. I made them a reasonable offer for the property and they declined to sell. The matter is closed."

"Did you throw a stone through their window last night?"

"Certainly not!"

He sounded sincere, but so did a good many liars I'd known. I saw his family strolling back from the direction of the town square and decided there was nothing more to be learned there. "The sheriff may want to talk to you," I told him in parting.

"He knows where to find me. Either here or at my office."

I went down to the jail and found Sheriff Lens at his desk.

He was no sort of scientific detective, but I had to admit he'd done a first-rate job on those firecrackers. He'd cut off all the fuses and arranged them in two rows of six each. Then he'd taken a bit of each fuse and lit it to determine how fast it would burn.

"They're all slow burning, Doc," he said. "Just like they're supposed to be. And the firecrackers are filled with the right kind of powder. There's no dynamite or anything else unusual here."

I nodded. "So it was only chance that Billy selected the one deadly firecracker. You can't make a murder case out of that, Sheriff."

"Unless it's one of your impossible crimes, done up so clever it don't even look like a crime." He swept the fuses into the desk drawer. "Well, I'd better get back over to Shinn Corners and see what them federal guys are up to. Want to ride along?"

"I think I'll take another look at the Oswald garage. Then maybe I'll join you. I still hope we can make it up to April's cottage before the day is over."

The garage was locked up when I reached it, and I was about to leave when I saw someone in the alley toward the back. It was Dora Springsteen, and she had her hand through the glass of the broken window.

"What are you up to?" I asked, coming up beside her.

She withdrew her hand, careful not to cut it on the jagged glass. "Just testing a theory of mine. Want to hear it?"

"Sure. I love theories."

"That stone through the window didn't do much damage last night. But what if the idea wasn't merely to break the glass? What if the idea was to break into the garage?"

"It would be a tight squeeze through that six-inch hole."

"But my hand can go through. And it can reach the latch on the window."

Suddenly I was interested. I tried it myself and saw that she was right. The window could have been unlatched and opened to admit an intruder, then closed again and latched afterward in the same manner. "Why would anyone want to break in?" I asked.

"Those fireworks were kept in that unlocked cabinet. Someone could have climbed through the window and substituted a tampered package. It would be easy enough to cut a seal from a second package and glue it in place on the tampered one— if the person had the time."

I shook my head—in admiration, but she misunderstood. "Well, how do *you* think it was done?"

"Maybe the way you suggest."

"By Max Webber?"

"The thought crossed my mind," I admitted. "I stopped by to see him earlier, but he denied everything."

"He wanted them out of this building."

"I know that."

"Do you think Billy is safe at the hospital?"

"I think so. Even Webber wouldn't be foolish enough to try anything else so soon. But I might suggest to Sheriff Lens that he keep a deputy there overnight."

She looked relieved. "I'd appreciate that."

I left her at the garage and drove out of town, heading for Shinn Corners. Dora might have a point about the window, but planting a dynamite bomb where anybody might use it seemed a heartless and unprofitable murder method to me. Before I was convinced, I'd need a method by which the killer knew exactly what he'd accomplish, and that seemed impossible given the events I'd witnessed with my own eyes.

When the warehouse came into view, I saw a big truck pulled up to the loading platform. The agent named Ready was in his shirtsleeves, directing a half-dozen men who were carrying out cases of the bootlegged Scotch. I parked and walked over to him. "How's it going?" I asked.

"We're coming along."

"Heavy work for a holiday."

"We work when we have to. Criminals don't take holidays and neither do we."

I went on inside, looking for Sheriff Lens. The other Prohibition agent, Simmons, was directing work at that end, and I was surprised to see that more than half the bootlegged whiskey had been removed already. "It's our third truckload," he confirmed. "We work fast."

"Where's the sheriff?"

"He was here and then he left—said something about going fishing."

I nodded. "Good day for it."

Sheriff Lens had never fished a day in his life.

I went back outside and walked around the warehouse. There was no sign of the deputy who was supposed to be on guard.

If the sheriff hadn't gone fishing, he was still around somewhere, and that meant his car was probably still around, too. I scanned the tall weeds and underbrush in the distance, searching for something I was afraid to find.

Then I saw the unmistakable sign of tire tracks. They'd left a recent trail through uncut grass, heading toward a dry streambed just this side of the underbrush. I walked another ten feet and saw the rear end of the sheriff's car sticking out from the depression in the landscape.

"Hold it right there, Dr. Hawthorne," a voice behind me said.

Before I turned, I knew there was a gun on me. It was in James Ready's hand. "Am I violating any laws?" I asked him.

"Get back to the warehouse, wise guy. If you're so anxious to find the sheriff, I'll take you to him."

I had little choice, so I raised my hands and walked ahead of him to the warehouse. Simmons was waiting for me, also with a drawn gun, and he motioned me into a small office at the front of the building.

Sheriff Lens was tied to a chair and gagged. His deputy, a man named Oscar Frawly, was on the floor, apparently unconscious. I knew what was coming next, and when I felt the sudden movement behind me I tried to roll with the blow.

The next thing I knew I was on the floor with a splitting pain in the back of my head. But I was still conscious, though I remained still while the door to the office was closed and locked from outside. Then I gradually sat up, rubbing my head.

Sheriff Lens grunted through his gag. I got it out of his mouth, and he grimaced. "These guys aren't Prohibition agents."

"I figured as much."

"They're bootleggers tryin' to get the stuff outa here before the real government agents show up tomorrow. I recognized one of the truck drivers from a Wanted poster in my office, and then they jumped me. They hit Oscar pretty hard."

I bent to examine the fallen deputy. "He'll be all right. He's coming around now."

"Once they leave, we'll have to get to a telephone and call the state police."

"We might not be alive to do that," I warned him.

"Yeah."

I untied the sheriff, and we worked over Frawly together. His color was good, and I wasn't too worried about him. "What happened?" he asked when he was fully conscious.

"One of those hoods hit you with the butt of his gun," the sheriff told him. "Doc thinks they're going to kill us."

Outside we heard the truck starting up. Almost immediately

another one pulled in. "This'll be the last load," we heard one of the men shout through the thin partition.

"Any ideas?" I asked Frawly.

"They took my gun." He felt in his pockets. "All I got's a firecracker."

"A what?" Sheriff Lens asked, unbelieving.

"I was settin' off a few of them over in the field. It's the Fourth of July, you know."

"Give me the firecracker," I said. "Quickly!"

It was smaller than those the Oswald brothers had, but I figured it would have to do. "What you goin' to try?" the sheriff asked.

"When I light this, we all hit that door together. If this goes off at the same time, they might think we've got a gun. It's our only hope."

The door shattered under our combined weight and the firecracker gave a satisfactory crack. The man nearest us dropped the case he was carrying and raised his hands. "I've got a gun, Simmons!" Sheriff Lens shouted. "Throw down your weapons."

Frawly grabbed the nearest man and wrestled him to the floor, disarming him. Others were raising their hands, and the fight seemed over before it had begun. Except that Simmons and Ready weren't there. They were outside, running for their car.

The sheriff ran out of the warehouse after them, waving one of the confiscated guns, and for an instant I was sure that foolish act would make him a dead man. The false Prohibition agents had already started their car, heading it directly at him. But he held his ground, firing at their tires, and in the last instant the car swerved, hitting the front end of the waiting truck and almost toppling over.

"And this isn't even my county," Sheriff Lens muttered as he ran up to the car with the gun ready.

Simmons and Ready crawled out, bloody and defeated, their hands in the air.

"That was good work, Sheriff," I told him. "Your county or not."

"I wasn't about to let them escape," he told me. "I think these are the guys who killed Teddy Oswald."

After the local authorities took over, we finally were able to drive over to April's cottage on Chester Lake. It was there, sitting in big wooden lawn chairs near the water's edge, that we listened to the sheriff's theory of the case. April had cold lemonade for everyone, and Vera Lens had brought some homemade cookies along. It was a relaxing time while we watched the sailboats on the lake and waited for April's dinner, which promised to be something spectacular.

"You see," Sheriff Lens was saying, "neither Teddy nor Billy was the specific intended victim. All they wanted was an explosion, with some injuries, so's I'd stay in Northmont while they went to the warehouse. They figured one guard could be dealt with easy enough if he became suspicious, as long as I was kept away. So they stopped the Oswald brothers and made a pretense of examining those fireworks. Of course, the Prohibition Bureau has nothing to do with fireworks, and they knew it. But while he was examining the package, Simmons substituted a doctored package he had with him. It was just luck that the dynamite was in the first cracker Billy tried to light, but Simmons knew they'd set off the whole batch pretty quick. First or last, the odds were someone would be killed or injured. That's all they wanted."

Vera took a long drink of lemonade and looked sorrowfully at the water.

"They had to clean out that warehouse before the real Prohibition agents arrived. And they couldn't let anything stop them."

I got up and strolled down by the water. After a few moments April came to join me. "What's the matter, Sam?"

"I don't know."

"Is it something the sheriff said?"

"I suppose it's as good a solution as any. Why should I worry about a couple of bootleggers who probably killed half a dozen other people?"

"Other people but not Teddy Oswald?"

"I told you, I don't know. It couldn't have happened the way the sheriff says, but that doesn't mean he's wrong."

"Why couldn't it have happened the way he said?"

"Because Simmons couldn't have known Billy Oswald or anyone else would be carrying a package of firecrackers down the street at that particular moment—and he certainly couldn't have known it would be a package of Big Buster firecrackers. There was no way he could have had another package ready to substitute, and no way he could have switched something that large without one of us noticing. We were watching him every second."

"But if Simmons didn't do it, who did? And how?"

I didn't answer right away. Instead I simply stood there skipping a few stones out over the placid surface of the lake. The next thing I knew, Vera was calling us to dinner.

The food was as good as promised, and April surprised us all by producing a bottle of French brandy after dinner. "This is strictly by prescription," she announced. "I hope I'm not breaking the law, Sheriff."

"I guess I can excuse you on the Fourth of July," he said, holding out his glass.

It was after ten when we left April's cottage, and I drove the sheriff and his wife home. He was feeling good about the day, anxious to get back to Shinn Corners in the morning for a session with Simmons and Ready. I didn't want to spoil it quite yet by telling him he was wrong.

After I dropped them at home, I drove out to Pilgrim Memorial Hospital to visit Billy Oswald. He was still on his stomach, dozing restlessly, and the nurse was reluctant to disturb him. "I'll take full responsibility," I assured her.

Our voices had awakened Billy and he turned his head toward me. "How are you, Doc? Am I gonna get out of here soon?"

"I think you'll be released in a couple of days. You were lucky."

"A lot luckier than Teddy."

"Yes," I said quietly. "Tell me something, Billy. Why did you kill your brother?"

"What?" He started to rise from the bed.

"Stay there, Billy."

"That's crazy what you say, Doc! You saw me open that package yourself. If anybody tampered with it, maybe Webber or somebody sneaked in the night before!"

I shook my head. "No, Billy, it was you. The fake firecracker containing the dynamite was hidden inside your shirt. When you bent down to light the fuse with your back to us, you replaced the real firecracker with the deadly one. You made two bumbling attempts to light it, knowing Teddy would take over for you as he always insisted on doing. But you didn't get quite far enough away from the blast in time and so your back was burned."

"I tried to light those matches! They wouldn't work!"

"Probably because you'd moistened the tips in advance. You made sure the rest were dry so Teddy wouldn't have any trouble lighting the fuse as you walked away."

"You say that's what happened, but there's not a speck of proof in the world!" Billy insisted.

"The proof is in the drawer of Sheriff Lens's desk. When you were injured by the explosion, you knew you couldn't let the real firecracker be found inside your shirt, so you dropped it on the ground with the others as you fell. The sheriff picked them all up to test the wicks. I saw those wicks on his desk. There were twelve of them, one for each firecracker contained in the Big Buster package. But if Sheriff Lens collected twelve fire-crackers, that meant the explosive one didn't come from the package at all; it was a substitute. And only you could have made that substitution, Billy."

He lay there a long time without speaking. Finally he said, "Teddy wanted to tie us down to that garage forever. Max Webber made us a good offer but Teddy wouldn't even discuss it. I figured with Teddy gone I could sell the garage and move away, start a new life. I wouldn't always be in Teddy's shadow."

"I'll have to call Sheriff Lens," I told him.

"And that was the end of my involvement in it," Dr. Sam Hawthorne concluded. "Billy committed suicide in jail while awaiting trial, but I was away at the time. Then something happened that fall that almost caused me to leave Northmont forever. I suppose I'll have to tell you about it the next time we meet."

EDWARD D. HOCH has written more than six hundred short stories under his own name and various pseudonyms. His series characters number more than fifteen, with Dr. Sam Hawthorne a special favorite of Ellery Queen's Mystery Magazine *readers.*

THE
PUNCHBOARDS

Henry T. Parry

What the narrator does to help him in writing a detective story connects him with a real murder that he decides to solve.

I was writing a novel that summer about how this kid who was my age, thirteen, went out West to punch cattle for his uncle. It was all about the battles he and his uncle and his uncle's cowboys fought with this band of rustlers. Finally there is a big shootout and my hero finds himself in the middle of the street facing a rustler named Bad Sam Sears who is the fastest draw in the West. Bad Sam is standing there, holding his hands just above his two big guns, and sneering at my hero who's standing there, too, all alone, with nothing to hold his hands over.

I was walking back from my paper route one morning, trying to figure out how to get him out of this, when I saw a Ford roadster go tearing up North Main with Tommy Foulkes, our chief of police, and Johnny Herring, another policeman, in it. I ran up the street after them, figuring something big must have happened to get both of them out together.

They turned off on the road that led to the ball field. When I got there I saw that the chief had left the car just behind home plate—our ball field didn't have any fences and in the spring the outfield was sometimes used to pasture cows. He was busy underneath the bleachers, which I should explain was just a fancy name for four long homemade benches set back one above the other and shaded by a strip of canvas.

The chief, Johnny Herring, and Doc Stoneman were bent over the body of a girl. Standing behind and looking even more green than usual was Two-Dip Dorsey, who ran the Kandy Kitchen in town. Two-Dip was a pretty big fellow, but now he looked scared.

"I was taking a shortcut over to North Main on my way to open the store," Two-Dip said to me, "when I seen something white laying there. When I go closer I see it's her. So I ran back home and called Doc Stoneman and Tommy Foulkes. But it ain't no use. She's dead."

"Who?"

"Helen Handey. One of that Handey tribe lives out on the Ridge Road."

There was this big family of Handeys, the kind of people where if you walked by their place on Sunday morning you'd see Mrs. Handey and the girls all dressed up and leaving to walk to church and Old Man Handey and the boys in bib overalls with their heads stuck under the hood of a car. Somehow it worked out that the girls were all good people and the boys were kind of shiftless and plain no good. So that if it had been one of the Handey boys who had been found under the bleachers with his head busted in, everybody would have said, "I told you he wasn't coming to no good end."

"It was in the cards one of them Handey kids was going to have something like this happen," I heard Doc Stoneman say. "Looks like to me the girls ain't much better than the boys."

And what he was saying was what everybody else in town was saying, or anyway thinking, after a few days—like as if when someone is murdered it's somehow their fault. I heard them saying at Charley McCall's news store—Charley's the man I delivered papers for—that Helen Handey had put up a fight, judging from the way she was all scratched and bruised and the ground was all torn up. But I never heard that anybody agrees to be murdered, so how can it be their fault?

Doc Stoneman wasn't a doctor; he was the druggist, but he hadn't filled a prescription in years, not since Miss Hattie Snyder finished pharmacy school and came to work for him. Mostly Doc—who was a big, round man, kind of reddened and fleshy—would sit on a wire ice-cream-parlor chair under the two-bladed ceiling fan with his Panama hat on, figuring out the stock market. He took the *Journal of Commerce* that he always had to come into Charley's for because that paper didn't come in until the eight o'clock trolley from Weston while my papers came in on the six o'clock.

Doc was a spiffy dresser. He was the first in our town to have shoes of two colors and the first to wear those light striped summer suits—I think they're called seersucker—when nobody else in town would wear them because they looked like you were out on the street in your pajamas. In his lapel Doc always wore a tiny pin, less than a half inch. It was the kind of pin where the front part screws onto a back part through a buttonhole. It had three funny-looking letters on it. Eddie Heener, who jerks soda at Doc's, said it was a pledge pin for some fraternity at State that Doc had been asked to join when he went there for one term about a hundred years ago. "That ain't the real pin," Eddie explained, "but Doc's awful proud of it. It's just a sign you been asked to join. Doc puts it on whatever coat he's wearing. Them letters on it is Greek, Doc told me. When I asked Doc what they meant, he got mad and told me to get back to work. Doc only gets mad at me about five or six times a day."

Doc was a big eater, too. Often when I happened to be in his pharmacy I heard him say, "Four o'clock, Eddie," and Eddie would peel a banana, split it lengthwise, and lay it on one of those long silver sundae dishes. On top of that he'd put three dips of ice cream—chocolate, vanilla, and tutti-frutti. He'd give that a few squirts of chocolate syrup, spread on some crushed pineapple, and put a layer of marshmallow over the whole pile. I like sundaes an awful lot, but I don't think I could have eaten that even if I could have afforded it. Doc didn't have any trouble though. He'd tuck a paper napkin under his chin and start dipping away real slow, like he was trying to make it last. He was careful not to get any spots on his seersucker suit.

"Ain't a nicer man in town than Doc," Charley used to say, "so long as you don't ask him to do anything for anybody." But Charley was always saying things like that.

Besides playing the market, Doc did another thing I guess you could call gambling. That was taking a chance on one of Charley McCall's punchboards.

Every Friday morning about eight-thirty Doc would come into Charley's, put a dime down on the counter, and punch out number thirteen. Never any other number. If somebody had punched out number thirteen already, Doc would just wait until the next Friday. There weren't any numbers printed over the holes. Doc just punched out the first number in the second row, which was thirteen, because there were twelve numbers in a row.

A punchboard is made of hard, pressed paper a half-inch

thick and measuring about eight by eleven inches. It has about sixteen or twenty rows of holes, the holes plugged with rolled-up slips of paper, each slip with a number on it. You take something like a pencil or a skinny knitting needle, punch out a hole—the holes are covered front and back with paper pasted over them—and pull the rolled-up slip out from the back of the board. If the number on the slip matches a number printed on the top of the board, you win a prize. Most people didn't take the prizes they won, stuff that ran mostly to celluloid-backed brushes or Statues of Liberty made of metal so soft you expected it to melt. There were some better prizes, too, but most everybody sold them back to Charley to get the money. "Legitimate sales of merchandise," Charley called it.

For Doc, punching number thirteen every Friday morning was like somebody else being careful not to step on the cracks on the sidewalk. I heard Charley telling someone about it, and he used a fancy word. "Obsessive," Charley said. I knew it must have been a word that Charley had just heard of, because he used it about six times in the next ten minutes.

Doc Stoneman may have thought it was Helen Handey's fault that she got murdered, but Tommy Foulkes didn't think so. He got the county detectives in and later the state police. But nobody ever found out anything except that Helen had left the house around seven-thirty in the evening and hadn't come back.

The Handeys said she'd been doing this about once a week since Christmas, but she'd never say where she was going or if she was meeting anyone. *Sometimes* she said she was going down the road to meet her friend Tilly Smith, but she was all dressed up so it wasn't likely she was spending much time with Tilly.

The thing that's hard to explain is how anybody in our town could be doing something for eight months without everybody knowing it. It was pretty hard to change your mind without somebody asking how come. Anyway, a couple of weeks went by and nobody found out who had murdered poor Helen Handey—and it looked like nobody ever would.

I was still fussing with my novel—couldn't figure out a way to keep Bad Sam Sears from killing the hero in the showdown —when I got the idea that maybe I should write a detective story instead. I thought I could make the story sound more real if I visited the scene of a crime. Well, the only crime we ever had in our town was the murder of Helen Handey, so I went out to the ball field and looked around under the bleachers where Two-Dip Dorsey had found the body. It made me feel scared to think about what had happened here just a few weeks ago, right where I was standing, right in the same air space I was taking up, where someone had fought hard to stay alive and had lost.

I'd heard Charley McCall say the police had gone over the ground with a rake and hadn't found anything. Now the ground was littered over with the same stuff you always see around a ball field—wrappers from candy bars, empty cigarette packs, Crackerjack boxes, bottle caps, and empty soft-drink bottles. The grass was flattened from trampling, but there was some Queen Anne's lace and some skunk cabbage standing around the foot of one of the uprights. I figured the best way to search the place was to take away everything that was there because of people eating, drinking, and smoking while watching the game. So I picked up every bit of trash I could find and made a pile of it behind the bleachers. Then I looked carefully, down on my hands and knees, at every inch of ground.

I didn't find anything except the cap of a Moxie bottle pressed down into the ground. I pried it up and flicked it onto the trash pile. Then I saw stuck to it, under it, the pin with the Greek letters I'd seen a hundred times on Doc Stoneman's lapel. I pulled it loose and held it in my hand, just staring at it, scared of it because of what it stood for. What I had started doing just to help me in writing a story had ended up connecting me with a happening out of real life—a dark, frightening, murderous happening, nothing at all like the story that I had in my head.

I suppose I should have looked for more clues, but I had to stop because a bunch of kids were coming across the outfield and would have made a lot of smart remarks about what I was doing crawling around under the bleachers. But mostly I wanted to get rid of that pin.

When I went into police headquarters, which was a fancy name for one room on the first floor rear of the town hall, I found Chief Foulkes and Johnny Herring bent over the checkerboard. At least Johnny was bent. The chief was reading the newspaper, waiting for Johnny to move. Tommy was a big, white-haired man with blue eyes that looked like he was thinking of something else while you were talking to him. There were people in town who said that Tommy talked slow and moved slow and the only thing he did fast was think. I told them how I came to be rooting around under the bleachers, and I held out my hand with the pledge pin in it.

"Hey, that's Doc Stoneman's," Johnny said. "He's been wearing that little doohickey ever since I knew him."

Tommy proceeded to ask me a lot of questions, but I couldn't tell him much more than I already had.

"Shows Tilly Smith was telling us the truth," Johnny said. "She said she hadn't seen Helen except in church since around Christmas, when Helen said she might be getting married soon and she shouldn't tell anybody. So when Helen was going out and nobody knew where she was going, she was meeting Doc out at the ball field. They get into some kind of fracas, maybe about getting married, and Doc kills her. You know how quick he flies off the handle. Stands to reason, don't it?"

"Doc could have lost that pin while he was watching a ballgame."

"Tommy, you know as well as I do that Doc ain't never been to a game since he played for the high school. He ain't been more than five blocks from his store in twenty years."

Tommy gave a deep sigh and kept quiet. He kind of squeezed his mouth with his left hand and looked at me a long time. I kept hoping Johnny Herring would keep on talking, but he didn't.

"We want that you should keep quiet about what you found," Tommy said to me after a bit. "That would help us a lot."

Folks said that when Tommy Foulkes talked to you, it didn't make any difference if you were a kid or if you were old—say, thirty—you got the feeling he expected you to agree with him, as if there had always been some understanding between him and you about how things were. Well, that's the way I felt, and for the next couple of days I went around with this secret busting inside me. I could imagine Tommy Foulkes having meetings with the county detectives and the state police, discussing what they should do with what I'd found and probably mentioning my name any number of times. And at least two guys on my street said they could hardly stand being around anybody as important as I seemed to think I was.

A couple of mornings later—a Friday—I'd come in from my paper route and was hanging around Charley's, sneaking a free read from the magazines, when Charley asked me to watch the store, which he usually did about twice a week. This time Charley said he wanted to meet the trolley and have it out with Skooks Decker, the motorman, who Charley said was helping himself to a paper out of the bundle he brought up from Weston. I guess maybe Skooks was, because folks said Skooks had a habit of reading a newspaper while he was running the trolley.

This morning Doc Stoneman came in, plunked a dime down on the counter, and pointed at the punchboard. I rang up his dime and watched him punch out the thirteenth hole. He read the slip, tossed it on the floor, and walked out the door, not saying anything. I noticed he wasn't wearing that pin in his lapel. But if Tommy Foulkes or any of the other police had talked to him about Helen Handey, it didn't seem to have bothered Doc none. To me, he seemed the same as he always had. Noticing the slip of punchboard paper he'd tossed on the floor, this great idea came to me about how I could find out if Doc really had anything to do with Helen Handey.

I hung around Charley's as much as I could so I could pick up the slips of paper people punched out of the punchboards and tossed away. Charley asked me if I was sick or something, because he never once had seen me pick up one single, solitary, earthly thing from the floor before. I spent hours practicing printing real small on the slips I picked up.

When I had it down pretty good, I wrote out three messages on three slips. Charley generally had three punchboards in stock, so one day when I was alone in the store—Charley had gone over to the town hall to argue with Lon Adams about his tax assessment—I took a pin and carefully picked holes in the back of the punchboard around the edges of the thirteenth hole, leaving a little lid held by a hinge of uncut paper. I pushed the open ends of a hairpin into the hole, squeezed the ends together, pulled out the slips of paper, and replaced them with the slips I had written on. Then I stuck the lids back down. It's funny, people would notice right away if you tampered with the front of the board, but it never occurs to anyone to turn the board over to see if the back has been messed with. And once you've punched out a hole, you naturally expect the paper covering that hole in the back of the board to be broken open. I put the boards back in the drawer in the order I wanted Charley to take them out.

The next Friday morning when Doc came in and put down his dime, I watched him pretty close. Charley handed him the first board I doctored. Doc punched out the paper, unrolled it, and read it. He jerked his head up to see if anyone was watching, but Charley was reading the cash register and Doc hardly knew I was there. He gave his glasses a poke and went to the door to read the slip in a better light, then put the slip in his pocket instead of tossing it on the floor. When Charley said, "No luck, hunh, Doc?" Doc didn't answer; he just walked out. What I'd written on the slip was *Hi, Doc. Helen.*

The second Friday was about the same, except Charley had stepped out. I handed Doc the second board, and he punched out the thirteenth hole. He unrolled the paper and smoothed it over and over as if he couldn't bring himself to read it. Finally he did, and his face went gray and broke out in sweat. He walked out of the store, his big stomach banging against the screen door because he hadn't pushed it open ahead of him. This message read *How about it, Doc? Helen.*

I saw Doc twice in the next week, meeting him as he was coming into town on North Main Street as I was headed out with my papers. I asked him what he was doing up so early, and he mumbled something about taking a walk because he couldn't sleep. He looked like he'd been sick and that seersucker suit on him looked like it should have been worn by a much larger man, even though Doc was pretty big.

On the third Friday Doc read the slip I'd planted and groped his way out of the store. "What's got into Doc?" Charley asked. "Seems like he's sleepwalking or something." What had got into Doc was the third message: *Tonight, Doc. Same place. Helen.*

That night as soon as it got dark I said something about going downtown for a soda. I went up North Main to the ball field and sat down on the top row of bleachers, right over the place where Two-Dip Dorsey had found the body of Helen Handey. It was a beautiful night, deep summer, with a full moon, an owl beginning to stir over in Harris's Woods, and the sound of water flowing over the wall of Keller's Dam.

The road off North Main Street ends right where center field begins. I saw a car without lights stop out there where people usually park when there's a game. In the moonlight I could see a man, a big man, coming slowly in from center field, across second base, and over the pitcher's mound to home plate, where he turned around and looked at the diamond as though he was seeing again the old games that had been played there back in the days when everybody was young and the town had been a friendly, easygoing place, maybe before something was done that now couldn't be undone. I don't know. Anyway, the man turned, came around the backstop, and went around and under the bleachers. A big fear wrenched at my stomach when the thought struck me that maybe he had a flashlight. I could hear him below me, not three feet away.

"Helen."

He said it as though he wanted to talk and at the same time didn't want to talk and so had settled on a whisper. I felt myself go cold and queer, because something had come into my mind from someplace deep in it that I didn't know was there, something that made me expect to hear someone answer him, someone I'd seen lying dead on the ground below where I was sitting.

"Helen! Forgive! Please! Forgive!"

I heard him make a long moaning noise as he turned away. He went back the way he came—home plate, pitcher's mound, second base, and center field. The car door slammed.

I took off straight for the town hall to tell Tommy Foulkes

what I'd seen, but police headquarters were dark and locked up. The next morning first thing I went back to headquarters and there wasn't anyone there.

I was heading to Charley's to pick up my papers when I saw Charley and about a dozen others from up the block staring into the windows of Doc's pharmacy. It was pretty early for that many people to be hanging around, so I went to see what was going on.

I looked in the window, and there was Doc seated in his wire chair under the two-bladed fan, dressed in his seersucker suit and wearing his Panama hat. Standing behind him was Doc Simmons, who was a medical doctor, and Tommy Foulkes. Miss Hattie Snyder, the pharmacist, was in there, too, dabbing at her eyes with a paper napkin.

"Seems Hattie came in early to fix a prescription for old Miss Berger out on Second Street," Charley was saying. "She found Doc sitting there at the table with a napkin under his chin. He'd put together one of those big sundaes he had every day and had polished it off. Then, from what Hattie says, he must have fixed himself something from the pharmacy. They ain't sure yet. The coroner will have to find out."

HENRY T. PARRY was born and lives in Pennsylvania. He is a graduate of New York University and has worked as a technical writer for a large corporation.

RETURN
TO THE
OK CORRAL

Clark Howard

Kit is said to be descended from Doc Holliday—and one day a man he believes is Doc reincarnate comes to Tombstone to take care of unfinished business at the OK Corral.

The half-breed boy, Kit, was the first one to see James Halloran when he arrived in Tombstone. Kit, who was twelve, was sitting with his shoeshine box in front of the Crystal Palace Saloon, trying to pick up a few quarters shining the shoes of tourists, when he saw the Bisbee bus stop in front of the Longhorn Restaurant. When the bus pulled away, Halloran was standing there in the hot Arizona sun, a slim, pale man with dark eyes and a full black mustache. He was wearing a wrinkled gray summer suit and white shirt but no tie and carrying a battered, old-fashioned Gladstone suitcase.

Kit's eyes got wide and his mouth dropped open as he stared at the man. He watched Halloran look up and down Allen Street for a bit, then cross to the opposite corner and stand staring at the Tombstone T-Shirt Store, and finally walk across 5th right past Kit and into the Crystal Palace.

Kit grabbed his shine box and dashed across Allen, barely missing being hit by a tourist car from New Jersey. He ran the long block down 5th to Toughnut Street, where 5th ended, ran down a gully and around an open stope, and hurried behind an old adobe building that had once been a firehouse but was now an art gallery. Back thirty yards behind that structure was a little two-room house, also adobe, in front of which a bearded old man sat rocking back and forth with his eyes closed, fanning himself with a straw fan that looked as old as he did. Kit ran up to the old man and dropped to his knees in front of him.

"Miner! Miner! I seen my great-granddad!"

The old man opened tired eyes. "What are you talking about, boy?"

"My great-granddad, Miner! He just got off the Bisbee bus! He's in the Crystal Palace right now!"

"Stop talking like a fool, boy," Miner said. "Your great-grandpaw died more'n ninety years ago."

"But, Miner," the boy said eagerly, "maybe he's come *back!* You and Shepherd Man said once that if a man left his spirit behind when he died, he might come back for it."

"*I* never said that," Miner protested. "That fool Shepherd Man was the one who said it. Crazy old Indian."

"But you agreed with him, Miner."

"I was drunk." He took Kit roughly by the arm. "Listen to me, boy. Dead men don't come back, understand? Dead is dead. Now go in the house and bring me my medicine."

"Yes, Miner," the boy said, hanging his head. He went into

the cool dimness of the little adobe house and got a bottle of peach brandy from a shelf. As he started back out, he paused to look at an unframed picture tacked to the wall. A picture of a pale man with dark eyes and a full black mustache.

It's him, Kit thought. *I know it's him.*

Back outside, he handed the bottle to Miner. The old man pulled its cork stopper and took a long swallow.

"Miner?" the boy said hesitantly.

"What?" the old man asked impatiently.

"When he got off the Bisbee bus, he crossed the street and stood looking at the Tombstone T-Shirt Store for the longest time."

"Maybe he likes T-shirts," Miner growled.

"Maybe. But ain't the Tombstone T-Shirt Store where the Oriental Saloon used to be? And didn't you tell me that my great-granddad used to play cards a lot in the Oriental when it was owned by Lou Rickabaugh and Wyatt Earp?"

"Sure, I told you that," Miner grudgingly admitted. "What of it?"

"Well, I just think it could be him, is all. He could be like Shepherd Man said: re-in—you know."

"Reincarnated."

"Yeah, Shepherd Man said—"

"Shepherd Man was a crazy old Apache!" Miner said testily. "Why, he was so crazy he even said once he knowed where Cochise was buried." Miner grunted derisively. "Don't *nobody* know where Cochise is buried." He shook a finger in Kit's face. "It's a good thing that old fool finally died. He filled your head with too much foolishness."

Kit looked down at the dirt porch, at the ruts in the ground made by the rockers of Miner's chair. There was another set of ruts nearby where Shepherd Man's chair had once sat. Miner and the boy had burned the chair out in the desert when they burned the old Indian's body.

"I don't think it's a good thing he died," Kit said quietly. "I miss Shepherd Man."

Old Miner stared into space for a moment, remembering his friend of fifty years. He had to blink back tears. Putting an arm around Kit's shoulders, he drew the boy close to him. "I miss him, too," he admitted. He took another swallow of peach brandy, wiped his mouth on the back of his hand, and said, "Fetch the picture."

Kit quickly brought him the picture they had tacked to the wall. Miner stared thoughtfully at it. "You say the feller that got off the Bisbee bus looks like this picture?"

"Looks *just* like it," Kit swore, nodding his head up and down for emphasis.

"All right, we'll have us a look-see," the old man said. "Get me my walking stick."

The Crystal Palace Saloon still looked much the same as it had in 1880. A fifty-foot mahogany bar ran nearly the length of the room on the left, with a brass footrail bolted in front of it. Chandeliers that had been converted to electricity hung from the high ceiling. Polished round tables for four were spaced at intervals on the gleaming wooden floor. A single billiard table stood in back, just in front of a raised, red-curtained stage where dancing girls had once kicked high. The only thing that had changed was the customers; instead of gamblers, gunmen, and gold miners, they were now tourists in doubleknit pantsuits and walking shorts, with cameras hanging around their necks.

Halloran, the man who had come in on the Bisbee bus, sat at the end of the bar nearest the billiard table, his suitcase at his feet, a shot glass in front of him. He noticed the boy and the old man with the cane when they came in, saw them nod a greeting to the bartender and sit at a table near him, but paid no further attention to them after that. He drank quietly for an hour, ignoring the tourists who wandered in, looked around, and wandered out. The only time he moved was to lift his glass to drink, or to hold it up as a signal for the bartender to refill it. During the time Miner and Kit watched him, he raised the glass five times.

"He drinks like they say your great-grandpaw drank, that's for certain," Miner whispered to the boy.

Around midafternoon, when the desert sun was its hottest and most of the tourists had continued on their way west to Tucson or east to El Paso, Halloran called the bartender over and said, "Where can I find a poker game in town?"

"Gambling's illegal in Arizona," the bartender replied.

"If I wanted to know the law I'd ask an attorney," Halloran said easily. "But when I want a card game I ask a bartender." He laid a ten-dollar bill on the bar. The bartender picked it up and put it in his shirt pocket.

"Down the street two blocks and around the corner on 3rd. Sippy's Real Estate. Fred Sippy usually has a game in there every night. I can't guarantee they'll let you play."

"I'll take my chances," Halloran said. "Where's the quietest motel in town?"

"Down the road about a quarter of a mile farther than Sippy's. It's up on a hill—called the Lookout. Right across the road from Boot Hill cemetery. You can't miss it."

The bartender poured him another drink and went back up the bar. Halloran had just downed the shot when he noticed that the kid and the old man at the nearby table were looking at him. They had been watching him off and on ever since they came in, and Halloran was a little tired of it. He turned around on his stool and faced them.

"Any particular reason you two have been staring at me?" he asked in a neutral voice.

"No offense, mister," said Miner. "The boy here thinks you

look like his great-grandpaw. We wondered if you might be a distant relative of his."

"I don't have any relatives," Halloran said, turning back to the bar. A moment later the old man and the boy got up and came over to him.

"Begging your pardon, mister," said Miner. "We don't aim to bother you none, but would you mind taking a look at this here picture?" He handed Halloran the photo he had brought along. "This gentleman was John Henry Holliday. Most people called him 'Doc' Holliday. He was pretty famous hereabouts. Him and Wyatt Earp was best friends. He was a dentist, Doc was, at one time. Are you, uh—you a professional man yourself, sir?"

"Used to be," Halloran said. "I was a veterinarian." His light blue eyes seemed to turn dull. "But that was a while back," he added.

Miner nodded. "You sound like a Southerner. Doc, he was from Georgia. Might you be from there, too?"

Halloran shook his head. "Alabama. Sorry." He handed the picture back. "Like I said, I don't have any relatives."

Halloran picked up his suitcase and left the saloon. Kit stared after him, a look of conviction on his face.

"It's him, Miner," he said in a voice firm beyond its years. "I know it's him. I can *feel* it."

Within a week, Halloran became a regular player in Fred Sippy's nightly poker game in the office of his small real estate firm. The other regulars were Lon Metzger, a pharmacist; Gordon Toole, who had a small printshop; Lyle Linden, a trailer-park owner; Sam Manley, who had a tourist gift shop; and Fred Sippy himself. When one of the regulars failed to show up, his chair was usually filled by someone else from around town who had a night out. It was a casual, friendly game, two bits to open, half to bet, dollar to raise. On an average night, forty or fifty dollars might change hands. The men usually played from eight until midnight.

Halloran had moved into Room 120 at the Lookout. It was an end room that faced across the road to Boot Hill. When he had first checked in, he had stood in front of his door for a long time, just staring over at the old graveyard, almost as if trying to remember something. A couple of days later, before he walked uptown to start his afternoon's drinking, he crossed the road and went into the cemetery to look around. He walked slowly along Row Five, looking at the headstones, reading them silently in his mind. *George Johnson—Hanged by Mistake. Wm. Grounds—1882—Died of Wounds. Seymour Dye —1882—Killed by Indians. Delia William—1881—Suicide.*

He moved into Row Four. *Miles Sweeney—Murdered— 1880. May Doody—1881—Diphtheria. Thos. Kearney—1882 —Blown up in Mine Blast. Mrs. Stump—1884—Died in Childbirth.*

As Halloran turned up Row Three, the boy, Kit, fell in beside him. His shoeshine box was slung over his shoulder. Halloran glanced at him but said nothing.

"I could tell you about some of these dead people," Kit said. "Miner told me a lot about them. His paw told him. His paw was here in the old days."

Halloran nodded but still said nothing. He stopped at a headstone marked *John Heath.*

"This here feller was took out of the county jail and lynched," Kit said. "They hung him from a telegraph pole over by the courthouse. Miner said it stretched his neck seven inches. An' them five fellers over there," he pointed to another grave, "was all hanged legal the next month. They was his holdup gang, and he was their leader."

The man and the boy walked on.

"This here grave is Freddie Fuss, who was a little kid younger'n me," Kit said. "He died from drinking poison mine water. Real dumb. J. D. McDermott there, his horse fell on him. Crushed him flat. John King, he committed suicide. Drank stick-nine or something like that. John Beather was hanged."

They went into Row Two. Kit kept talking, but now he watched Halloran's face closely.

"Dick Toby, he was shot by Sheriff Johnny Behan. Billy Clayborne there, he was shot by Buckskin Frank Leslie. Margarita, she was a dance-hall girl that got in a argument with a Mexican girl named Gold Dollar. Miner says they was fighting over a man. Gold Dollar stabbed her. Joe Wetsell over there was stoned to death by Apaches."

Now they came to a set of three graves side by side: Billy Clanton, Frank McLaury, and Tom McLaury. On each of their stones was carved *Killed, October 26, 1881.* A taller marker standing off to the side contained all their names again and under them read *Murdered on the streets of Tombstone, 1881.*

"Them's the men from the OK Corral gunfight," Kit said quietly.

Halloran stepped in front of the grave of Tom McLaury and stared intently at it.

"Billy Clanton was killed by the Earp brothers," Kit said. "Wyatt, Virgil, and Morgan all shot him, after he shot Virgil. Frank McLaury was killed by Wyatt and Morgan." He moved over next to Halloran. "Tom McLaury wounded Morgan Earp. Then he was cut down by Doc Holliday."

Halloran, still staring at the grave, nodded.

"Doc was the man in the picture we showed you," Kit said. "The one you look like."

Halloran stared at the grave for what seemed like a long time. Then he patted Kit on the head and said, "Come along, boy. I'll walk you back to town."

———

Somehow the other card players and the people around town found out that Halloran had once been a veterinarian, and they took to calling him Doc, which pleased young Kit no end. As soon as Kit found out that Halloran was not as hard and cold as he pretended to be, the boy started following him everywhere, virtually becoming his shadow.

"Don't get yourself too attached to that feller," Miner warned. "By the look of him, he's a loner clear through. One of these days he'll up and leave, then where'll you be at?"

But Kit paid the old man no heed. He was convinced in his young mind that Halloran was at the very least a distant present-day relative, and in all likelihood even more: a reincarnation of Doc Holliday.

"Where'd the boy ever get the idea that Holliday was his great-grandfather?" Halloran asked old Miner one day. Kit had gone off for a while to shine shoes, and Halloran, running into the old man on Allen Street, had invited him into Vogan's Alley Bar for a drink. "Most people I've talked to in town say Holliday never even had a wife, much less any kids."

"Folks could be right," Miner allowed. "Doc had a woman here in Tombstone name of Kate. Some say her last name was Elder, some say Fisher. Me, I don't know. But my paw, who was here when Holliday was here, told me once that there was really *two* women, both named Kate. One of them—don't know if it was Kate Elder or Kate Fisher—got shot and killed by a drunk in a saloon down in Bisbee. The other one had a baby girl and stayed around Tombstone for a spell after the Earps and Holliday moved on. She worked for Nellie Cashman in her boarding house down at 5th and Toughnut. The daughter worked there, too, when she growed up.

"I recollect, when I was a boy of ten or so, seeing the daughter, whose name was Etta Holliday, serving meals over there. I even recollect when *she* got married and had a daughter of her own. Named her Felicity Holliday Norman. Etta's husband, Cole Norman, worked in the copper pits. Felicity went off to college somewheres around 1930 or thereabouts and married some Easterner. She came back to Tombstone twice—once to bury her maw, again to bury her paw. After that, nobody ever saw or heard from her again.

"Then one day in the late fifties sometime, a gal about eighteen years old showed up here saying she was the daughter of Felicity and the granddaughter of Etta. Her name was Naomi. Said her folks had got killed in an airplane crash and she had come back to Tombstone to see if she had any relatives out here that she didn't know about. She talked to some of the older folks in town, went through a lot of records and such at the courthouse, spent a lot of time in the old library we had here then, and finally came to the conclusion that she was the great-granddaughter of John Henry Holliday. How she decided that, I don't know. Didn't nobody argue with her over it, though. If she wanted to be Doc Holliday's great-granddaughter, that was her business.

"Anyways, a while after that she took up with an Indian named Spur. Actually, he was a breed—half Chiricahua Apache, half white—had a white paw name of Safford who worked for the Army over at Fort Huachuca. Well, Naomi and Spur got hitched in some heathen Apache ceremony where they drink out of the same gourd or something and she went to live with him on the White Mountain reservation up around San Carlos. We didn't hear nothing from Naomi then 'til about seven years ago when she showed up here again with the boy. He was five at the time. His mother was sick with the consumption, and his paw, Spur, had already died of it. So Naomi took the boy to old Shepherd Man, who was Spur's great-uncle—said she didn't have nobody else to take him to. Shepherd Man agreed to look after the boy, and Naomi went and sat out in the desert and died. Later on, old Shepherd Man died and I—well, I kind of inherited the boy. He don't remember much about his maw, but he ain't never forgot that she told him she was the great-granddaughter of Doc Holliday. Course, that would make Kit the *great-*great-grandson, but he just says he's the great-grandson and lets it go at that. When a kid ain't got nobody of his own blood, one generation more or less don't make no difference to him."

Halloran nodded thoughtfully. "And now he thinks I'm Holliday reincarnated."

Old Miner shrugged. "Well, you got to admit you do look a whole lot like his picture. And you're a Southerner like he was. Got the same *initials* he had: J. H. H. And folks have taken to calling you Doc 'cause you was once a vet. You're a heavy drinker like Doc was, and you're a card player like he was. All that's a powerful lot of coincidence for a twelve-year-old boy to swallow."

"What about you?" Halloran asked. "Do you swallow it?"

"I ain't saying I do, and I ain't saying I don't," Miner hedged. "I'm just interested in what's good for the boy."

"Well, I'm afraid that's not me, my friend," Halloran said easily. "I'm in Tombstone for a reason, and I won't be staying much longer."

"Don't suppose you can tell me what that reason is?"

Halloran thought about it for a moment, then said, "Why not?" He stared at the old man. "I'm waiting to kill a man," he told him.

The three Espy brothers arrived in Tombstone a week later. Halloran saw them drive up to the Lookout and check in. He waited until they were in their rooms, then went to see them. Victor Espy, the eldest, opened the door for him.

"Hello, Victor," said Halloran.

"Hello, James. Come in."

Walt, the middle brother, and Martin, the youngest, rose to greet him and shake hands.

"We wondered if you'd be here," Walt Espy said.

"I've been here for a month," Halloran told them. "Waiting."

"Well, your waiting is over," Victor said. "Get the map out, Martin."

Martin Espy spread a map on the bed, and the four men gathered around it. Victor leaned over and pointed to a tiny spot in northern Mexico.

"That's the town of Magdalena. The heroin was moved up there yesterday from Guaymas, where it was taken off the boat. The Clayton brothers and Benny Clough are picking it up in Magdalena and driving north with it. They're using a four-wheel-drive Jeep, so they'll probably cross into the U.S. somewhere west of Agua Prieta. Then they'll get on Route 80 and head for Tombstone. They ought to get here around one o'clock."

"What about Tim McLain?" said Halloran. "He's the one I'm interested in."

"I was coming to him. Tim McLain and his brother Floyd are driving here from Tucson to make the pickup. We'll be waiting for them. When they meet the men coming up from Mexico, we'll take them all."

"I want one thing made clear," Halloran said. "Tim McLain is mine. I want him all to myself."

Walt Espy, who had always been closest of the brothers to Halloran, stepped over and put his arm around Halloran's shoulders. "We know how you feel, James. When Tim McLain held up that hospital in Phoenix to get its drug supplies, the nurse he killed was your wife. But she was also our sister. We're giving you Tim McLain because we feel it's your right to have him. But if anything goes wrong—if you find out you can't do it, or if somebody gets you first—one of us will have to step in."

"Nothing will go wrong," Halloran replied grimly. "I'll take him out, don't worry."

"Just remember," said Martin Espy. "You're to back off

after you get him. We've all got badges—you haven't. One of us will take credit for killing him. Understood?"

"Understood," Halloran agreed. "Where's the meet going to be?"

"On Fremont Street just east of 3rd. It's in back of one of those Allen Street tourist attractions."

"Which one?" Halloran asked.

"The OK Corral," said Walt Espy.

Something in Halloran's chest jerked when Espy said it. But he kept tight control of himself and merely nodded.

"Behind the OK Corral. Right."

Halloran did not play cards that night. Instead, he bought a fifth of peach brandy and walked out behind the old fire station to the little adobe house where Kit and old Miner lived. Miner was in his chair, rocking, but there was no sign of Kit.

"Where's the boy?" Halloran asked, handing the old man the bag with the bottle in it.

"Uptown, I reckon. He thinks you're playing cards, so he's probably shining shoes at the Crystal Palace or the Bird Cage or one of them places."

He opened the bottle and took a long swallow, then stared curiously at his visitor. "Want anything in particular?"

"Not really. I'll be leaving tomorrow, on the one-thirty bus."

"I figured as much," Miner said.

"Oh? How'd you figure as much?"

Miner set the bottle conveniently next to his chair. "Simple. First I heard there was three brothers in town, all lawmen. The Espy brothers. One's a federal narcotics agent, one's a Los Angeles detective, and one's a sheriff's deputy from Phoenix. Next, I remembered what you said about being here to kill a man—and you ain't done it yet. And last, I checked my calendar and saw that tomorrow was the twenty-sixth of October. That's the anniversary of the OK Corral gunfight."

Halloran sat down on the ground, leaning back against the cool adobe of the house. "This is crazy," he said quietly.

"Sure it is," Miner said. "The Earp brothers and Holliday. The Espy brothers and Halloran. Same day. Same place. It's crazy, all right. But it's *happening.*"

"Look, the Espys are friends of mine. We all served in Vietnam together. I married their only sister. The reason we're all here is—"

"Don't *matter* what the reason is," the old man interrupted. "The only thing that matters is what it looks like to Kit."

"We've got to convince him it's all coincidence," Halloran insisted.

Miner grunted loudly. "That'll be one hell of a job." He took another long swallow of brandy.

The two men sat in silence, listening to the night sounds of the desert around them. Miner passed the bottle to Halloran, who took a drink himself. The brandy was too sweet for him. He took a silver flask from his inside coat pocket and rinsed his mouth out with bourbon. "What's going to happen to the boy when you die?" he asked.

The old man shrugged. "Nothing. He can take care of hisself."

"Doesn't he have any relatives at all?"

"None nobody knows of."

Halloran sighed quietly and drank some more from his flask. "That's a tough way to grow up."

"Like I said, he can take care of hisself."

"Sure."

After a while, Halloran got up from the ground and dusted off his trousers.

"So long, old timer," he said.

"*Adios,*" said Miner. As Halloran walked off into the shadows, Miner called out, "Good luck tomorrow—Doc!"

He heard Halloran chuckle softly in the darkness.

The Espy brothers parked their car at Swift's Chevron Station, which was down Fremont Street from the rear of the OK Corral tourist attraction. Halloran, who rode up with them from the motel, had his suitcase packed and in the back seat.

"We'll leave the car unlocked so you can get your bag after it's over," Walt Espy said. "You get out of town as quickly as you can. We'll have to stick around and help the local law make out reports. You have a gun?"

Halloran pulled back one side of his coat to reveal a .45 Colt automatic stuck in his belt.

"Here," Victor Espy said, handing him a sawed-off shotgun, "you use this. We want to make sure this gets done right."

Halloran took the ugly little shotgun and slipped it under his coat.

"All right, let's go," said Victor Espy.

The four men started down Fremont Street, two abreast: Victor and Martin Espy in front, Halloran and Walt Espy just behind them. When they got to the corner of 3rd Street, they stepped behind a fence and waited, not talking, not even moving, just watching, waiting—still, silent, solemn.

The Jeep got there first, dust-covered from its overland trip across the border. There were three men in it, equally dusty. They parked just up the street on Fremont, at the rear entrance to the OK Corral.

"That's Ira Clayton driving," Victor Espy said quietly. "His brother Bobby Clayton is next to him. Benny Clough's in the back."

As he was speaking, a white Cadillac came slowly down Fremont from the opposite direction and parked across from the Jeep.

"The McLain brothers," Walt Espy said, laying a hand on Halloran's shoulder. Two men got out of the Cadillac and crossed the street.

"Which one is Tim McLain?" Halloran asked.

"The tall one in the white shirt," Walt told him.

The men in the Jeep got out to meet the McLain brothers as they crossed the street.

Behind the fence, Victor Espy turned to his younger brothers and Halloran. "With the exception of Bobby Clayton, these men all have long criminal records. If they're taken, they face long terms in prison—and they know it. Add to it that they've got maybe a hundred thousand dollars' worth of heroin in that Jeep, and I'd say we've got a fight on our hands. Don't give them an inch, understand?"

Martin and Walt Espy nodded. Halloran just stared boldly down the street at Tim McLain, as if afraid he might disappear.

"All right, let's go," Victor Espy said for the second time.

The four men stepped from behind the fence and started down Fremont, spreading out in a line, four abreast. It was only a moment before the five men standing between the Jeep and the Cadillac saw them.

"You men are under arrest!" Victor Espy shouted. "Put up your hands!"

Four of the drug smugglers drew guns. The Espy brothers drew also. Benny Clough fired three quick shots at Victor Espy, then broke and ran down Fremont. Bobby Clayton and Floyd McLain both began firing at Walt Espy. Walt calmly aimed at Floyd and put a bullet in his stomach. Tim McLain had ducked behind the jeep and was firing at Martin Espy and Halloran. Ira Clayton, who was unarmed, stood with mouth agape until he saw Floyd McLain double up and pitch to the ground, then he ran up to Walt Espy, pleading, "Don't shoot me, man! I don't have no gun!" Walt threw him roughly aside, and Ira ran down the way Benny Clough had run.

Tim McLain, meanwhile, fired and hit Martin Espy, who was spun around by the slug entering his shoulder and slammed to the ground. In the center of the street, Bobby Clayton, the youngest of the smugglers and the one Victor Espy said had the least criminal record, was still firing, although he had been shot once by Victor and once by Walt. His right arm had been shattered by Victor's bullet, and he had switched his gun to his left hand.

Floyd McLain lay writhing in the street, blood spreading over his shirt. Halloran, slipping the shotgun from under his coat, calmly stepped around him, looking for a clean shot at his brother Tim. Bobby Clayton, shooting lefthanded, blew a hole in Victor Espy's thigh, dropping him in a heap. Clayton staggered toward the fallen lawman to finish him, but Martin Espy, lying nearby, pushed himself up and shot Clayton dead-center in the chest.

Walt Espy was pursuing Tim McLain around the Jeep, trying to force him out into the open for Halloran. McLain, in an effort to get away from Walt, ran from cover and started toward the Cadillac, running right into the waiting Halloran. Halloran let him have both barrels of the sawed-off.

"All right, get going!" Walt shouted at Halloran.

Halloran tossed the shotgun on the ground and started backing away. Bobby Clayton, miraculously still alive, fired a final shot at Walt Espy. The lawman shot him one more time and he fell, still at last. As Halloran moved away from the center of the scene, Floyd McLain rolled over on the ground and aimed his gun at him.

"You—killed—my brother—"

Without even pausing, Halloran drew his own .45 and shot him in the heart. Martin Espy, lying nearby, fired at the same time, drilling McLain in the forehead. That was the last shot fired.

The street fight was over. It had lasted less than one minute.

Halloran shoved the .45 back under his belt and walked quickly away. He went directly down to the Chevron station and got his suitcase out of the car. Then he walked up to Allen Street where the afternoon bus to Lordsburg stopped.

Kit came over to the bus to tell him good-bye.

"Lots of shooting down at the OK Corral," the boy said. Halloran nodded.

"I know you're all right, though," Kit said. "I don't even have to ask. Wyatt Earp and Doc Holliday were the only two who walked away from the gunfight. 'Cept for those cowards that run, of course."

Halloran smiled. "You never give up, do you, boy?"

"Not when I know I'm right," Kit said solemnly. He put a hand on Halloran's arm. "You've just *got* to be him, mister. There's too many things that are the same."

"But there's one thing that's not the same," Halloran told him. "I've been asking around and I've found out a few things. I found out that Doc Holliday had tuberculosis. Did you know that?"

"Sure," the boy admitted. "That's what he died of."

"I found out something about Apache beliefs, too. Shepherd Man must have told you that if a man comes back to get the spirit he left behind, he'll die the same way a second time; that's the price he has to pay to come back. So I can't be Doc's reincarnation, because I'm not sick like Doc was. I don't have tuberculosis."

Kit frowned at this new bit of logic. His young face became puzzled, then disturbed. He hardly even noticed that the Lordsburg bus had pulled up and stopped in front of them.

"Sorry, boy," Halloran said, patting Kit on the shoulder. He picked up his bag and climbed aboard the bus.

As the bus pulled away, Halloran looked back at the forlorn half-breed boy and shook his head. All those damned coincidences, he thought. But that was all they were. Just coincidences.

⬦

CLARK HOWARD won an Edgar Allan Poe Award from the Mystery Writers of America for "Horn Man" in 1980. "New Orleans Getaway" was nominated for an Edgar in 1983. His short story "Animals" won the first Ellery Queen's Mystery Magazine *Readers Award in 1985.*

SPIRIT
WEATHER

Jack Tracy

*A way station in the Rockies provides
companionship of a ghostly sort.*

G hosts again, children? You're wasting your time speculat-
ing on such things. The ruined house up on Hallard
Street is no more haunted than this one is. There are no such
things as ghosts.

Well, yes, perhaps I *am* the most obstinate man in San
Francisco. I'm also the wealthiest, and if you believe there's no
link between the two then you don't know your old grandfather
as well as you think you do.

And you puff hot air when you say I hold my opinion because

I've never had a spiritualistic experience. You know I base my beliefs on my own ken and nothing else. Of *course* I've had a ghostly experience—one that would stand your hair on end and send you shrieking beneath the bedcovers.

Of course I'll tell you the story.

I was a young man at the time, not yet twenty-turned. The year was 1851—my mercy, fifty-five years ago to the month. San Francisco was just a muddy gold camp in those days; we had no fear of earthquakes then. I saw the town grow up, and last April I saw it fall down. I guess that may signal the end of me, too. When you kids are as old as I am, they'll ask you about the San Francisco earthquake same as you ask me about the Gold Rush.

All right—this is a ghost story. Let's all assume a solemn, significant air. Switch off the electricity and light a gas lamp. Listen to it hiss. Imagine the foul things whose mouth would put out a sound like that. It's much like what I did hear, in the dark, myself, fifty-five years ago.

I hadn't seen San Francisco yet. I grew up in Illinois, as you know, and for two years we watched the flood of emigrants passing through, bound for California and Oregon and places in between, and finally we could stand it no longer. In the summer of 1851, my two brothers and I joined a small wagon party bound for the Pacific Slope.

We couldn't have picked a worse time. I say we were a small party, but you wouldn't have known it from the sight of things. As far as the eye could see, east and west along the River Platte, there were wagons and people. That's no exaggeration. The isolated wagon train upon the lonely plains may be a romantic picture, but it's fantasy. We were elbow-to-rib all the way from Council Bluffs to Fort Laramie, so thick that often there was a shortage of grass for the animals.

We followed the north side of the Platte, along the so-called Mormon Trail, because most folks kept to the south bank, even the Mormons. We weren't worried about Indians—they kept away. They were afraid of the cholera, which was especially bad that year.

We were fifty-one days getting to Laramie. That was good time, considering how unprepared we were. We were unprepared for the numbers of emigrants. We were unprepared for the cholera. We were unprepared for the cold in the Rocky Mountains in the middle of summer. We were unprepared for the irrational greed of the western trails.

West of Laramie, once you cross the Continental Divide at South Pass, the trail branches into three. You could go south along the Green River to Great Salt Lake City and get a taste of civilization, which is what many did after toiling over the Divide. You could take the Oregon route up to the northwest. Or you could do as we did and follow the middle trail along the Bear River toward California.

It was no trouble keeping to the trail. Like two straggling lines of curbstone, abandoned possessions by the ton lay on either side of the track. I can't begin to describe for you the variety of goods to be found there, and after a day lost examining all the items we couldn't carry ourselves, we pretty much lost interest in it all; it just became another part of the landscape.

You'd think people would be lightening their loads going up the Divide, but it was on the down side that they began to throw out their things. They felt they were close to the gold fields now. The gold fever took them. They lightened their wagons and whipped up their horses, and more of them died in the Nevada deserts and the California Sierras than ever came to grief in the Rockies.

We were caught up in the madness, too. Among the household goods and farm implements we found whole barrels of flour and foodstuffs abandoned along the roadside. These we took up and sold farther down the trail to the same hungry travelers who'd likely thrown them away in the first place. The prices they were willing to pay were most wonderful, and, having cleared three hundred dollars, we were carried away and began to sell our own flour, too. Soon we hadn't enough for ourselves. We had to hunt game then.

We were to take turns, and I was sent out first because I was the poorest huntsman. If I failed, it would be less critical early than late when we might have no food at all to fall back on.

And I did fail. I tramped about the mountains nearly the whole day and saw not even a squirrel. I was just turning back when I was caught in a thunderstorm.

Until you've been in a Rocky Mountain storm, you can't imagine the sudden violence of the thing. It blows up out of nowhere without warning. The wind rages and the lightning crashes about your ears, you're so near the clouds. The rain is freezing cold and comes at you sidewise in measured bursts, like a switching from some cosmic schoolmaster. You find yourself clutching at your clothes for fear they'll be torn from your body. You huddle behind a rock while the wind roars and the trees pop, and when it's over you're cold, exhausted, and feeling half drowned, as if you'd just swum a river.

It was dark now, and overcast, and I couldn't find my way. Twice more during the night I was blasted by storms. I was too nerve-shattered to sleep, too afraid I'd freeze to death to stop moving. I blundered about in fits of desperate energy, getting myself thoroughly lost, and as soon as the sun was up I collapsed and slept.

By the time I awoke it was late afternoon, and the whole nightmarish experience started over. Another thunderstorm came howling through, the night closed in. I was drenched and buffeted. I was famished now, weak from hunger and terror, convinced my time had come. I like to sobbed with relief when, during a lull between storms, I saw a light and stumbled toward it.

The place turned out to be a way station cum trading post, established by an enterprising Mormon named Fritch for the convenience of those making their way north from Salt Lake back to the California Trail. It was full of a score of stranded travelers like myself, all taking refuge from the storm, which now seemed to have blown over.

It was no hotel, and there were no beds, but there was warmth and there was food. There was plenty of companionship, too, and I was grateful just to see a human face again. I ate my fill and bought a round of beer for the house, such was my relief. I still had some money left from our flour-scavenging.

There was a big Frenchman there with a black beard up to his cheekbones and pale gray eyes you could hardly turn your gaze away from, who told me he was a trapper for the American Fur Company. He took me under his wing and made room for me near the fire to dry out. He had impressed me immediately with his masterful manner and his quiet, ever-smiling arrogance. All of us sensed it. He dominated the company without once appearing to make the effort.

We sat in a semicircle about the fireplace and smoked. The conversation naturally fell to the storm and the fearful weather of the Rockies. Every man there, it seemed, had had some little adventure to relate. One man had actually been blown off his horse. A party of Dutchmen had been half a day getting six wagons across a regular river of mud. None of us, it seemed, had known what we were in for when we'd set out from Fort Laramie.

"It's a wild country, it's true, and wild weather to match," remarked Fritch.

"It's horrendous weather," someone said.

"A cursèd climate," agreed another.

"*Spookachtig weer,*" intoned one of the Dutchmen.

"Spirit weather," translated a companion.

"True enough," spoke up a young fellow sitting down on the

cusp of our semicircle. "If there are spirits in the world, they were walking abroad tonight."

"Now, there you're wrong," said my Frenchman, speaking for the first time.

We all looked to him in some surprise.

"Do not confuse the violence of nature for a manifestation of that which transcends nature," the big man continued in a calm voice. The fluency of his English was unexpected, given the thickness of his accent. "The true spirit prefers a motionless atmosphere. And he is all the more terrible for that."

We were a little taken aback at his eloquence and the conviction with which he spoke. There was an instant of silence. Then the pup on the end burst out with a peal of mocking laughter. "Well, that's good!" he cried. "Do they make their preferences known to you personally? Or do you hide in the bushes and watch them mooning about the crossroads, flicking the mud from their ghostly shrouds?"

"Young man, I would advise you not to speak mockingly of such things."

"Would you set your phantoms on me then?" the young fellow chuckled.

"You're young," the Frenchman replied. "You don't know what you're talking about."

And with the bravado of the young, the pup sprang to his feet, dramatically tossing back his chair and leveling a finger at the trapper. "If you were anything more than a crazy hermit, I'd make you pay for that remark!" he exclaimed.

"Easy, son," our host said. "He's three times your size."

"I'm no more afraid of him than his hobgoblins!"

"It is of no importance whether you fear me," the Frenchman said in his quiet way. "But this is a matter of which I have a lifetime of experience. You would do well to show no contempt for the spirits of the dead."

"All right, then!" cried the youth. "Will you set 'em on me? *Can you?*"

"I have that power."

"Bah!" The youngster wrestled a leather wallet out of his shirt, and he threw it on the floor before the trapper. "There's five dollars, all the money I've got in the world, and that gold says you're a liar and a fraud!"

The trapper didn't touch the money, but he, too, got to his feet. The young man's taunts were having their effect on him. "I have no gold," he said. "Only furs—bear and beaver—in the care of the good Fritch, under lock and key in his cupboard yonder."

Fritch nodded agreement. Three or four others acknowledged they'd seen the Frenchman bring the peltry in and store them away.

"They're worth thirty dollars at the least," the trapper said. "Can you match that?"

"Five is all I've got," the pup said angrily.

The Frenchman shrugged. "Then there is no wager." And he sat down. It was clear he was trying to bluff his way out of proving his claim to supernatural skills, and not for the first time I found myself irritated by his manner.

"Do you really think you can start a ghost?" I asked him.

"I have that power," he repeated. "The spirits of the departed seek my will. It is my curse. It is the reason I live alone in this wilderness."

I didn't believe him. "I'll take ten dollars of that bet," I said, and, taking up the poke from the floor, I counted out two five-dollar gold pieces of my own. The wallet I lay in my lap, and upon the wallet I placed the two half eagles so that all could see my wealth.

"You see that?" the Frenchman asked the young fellow. "I *will* set the spirits upon you, my doubting young chicken, if only for a lesson. Within one hour, I will bring before you the shade of one you have known. You will recognize him. He will speak to you. He will teach you respect for the dead, or you will forfeit your sanity."

"I still have only five dollars," the youngster told him.

The other pointed at me. "Fifteen."

"Here, now," someone said, reaching into his jacket, "I'll cover three."

"I'll find you three," said another. In less than a minute, ruffled by the Frenchman's conceit and curious to see what was going to happen next, we had matched the thirty dollars at which the trapper's furs were valued.

"Give the money to the boy," he ordered. "Let him hold the stakes. I want the satisfaction of receiving it from his own hand when he is afraid to face the apparition."

The young man snorted in derision.

The giant took the fifteen dollars from my lap and handed it to the pup, who added to it the rest of the gold we had collected and tucked it away in an inside pocket.

"Come along then," the trapper said. "Out back there is a smith's house. We will use that."

The blacksmith's shack was a little earthen-floored outbuilding, not much bigger than a horse's stall, where Fritch kept his portable forge, an anvil, and some spare tackle. It had a wide door in front, barred with a stout piece of timber, and a tiny window, unglazed but too small for a man to pass through, high up in the rear wall opposite. There were no openings on the sides.

At the Frenchman's insistence, we inspected the place thoroughly and found nothing out of order. The Frenchman placed a pencil and a scrap of paper atop the anvil and, herding the rest of us outside, shut the door upon the disbeliever. The last I saw of the young fellow before the door shut he was standing, hands on hips and a knowing smile on his face, on the other side of the anvil beneath the window, the moonlight streaming in and haloing him in its pale glow.

The trapper set the bar in place on the outside of the door

and stood before it, facing us, those wonderfully piercing gray eyes riveting each of us in turn. The night was silent, with not even the call of a bird to break the hush that follows upon a storm. The air was as still and cold and damp as a tomb's.

Without warning, the Frenchman's eyes rolled back in his head and he raised his hands above his head, bent at the wrists, fingers hooked like the talons of some gargoyles I've seen. He began to chant in a low melancholy voice. It was not French he spoke, nor Latin, nor did it sound like an Indian dialect. I've heard religious fanatics in my time who claimed a gift of tongues, and it wasn't their kind of babbling either. It was a real language, or it sounded like one, but to this day I couldn't name it.

After a few minutes' chanting, he spoke in English. Still in his trance, the whites only of his eyes visible, he called out, "What do you see?"

We heard the young fellow reply from inside the shed. "There's a white mist forming inside here, up by the window."

It's only the glow of the moonlight, I thought.

"Does it alarm you?" asked the Frenchman.

"No, not at all," the young man said in a perfectly composed voice.

With a start, almost involuntarily, the Frenchman began to chant again. Again he paused before speaking. "What do you see?" he demanded.

We listened anxiously for the skeptic's answer, for the slightest hint of nervousness in his voice. But there was none. His tone was calm, measured. "The vapor is moving—churning slowly—lengthening. I can't tell whether it's descending from the window or coming up out of the ground."

Yes, it's the moonlight. I smiled to myself. *The Frenchman's got the boy's imagination playing tricks on him.*

"It's condensing," the youngster reported. "It's taking on a form—the shape of a man. Why, it's Bud Wood, who died of the cholera not five weeks back. I recognize his check trousers and the Indian blanket we buried him in. It's still wrapped around him. His face is covered, but it's Bud. It's his hair. There's the fingernail missing from the hand he caught in the coffee mill when we were kids."

"Are you afraid of it?" asked the Frenchman.

"No," came the reply without hesitation. "Why should I be afraid of Bud Wood, who's been my friend all my life?" There was a brief pause. "He just stands there, with his face covered."

The trapper seemed to smile in his trance and took to chanting again, his contorted hands still held aloft, his eyeballs rolled back, his broad back to the smithy. This time the incantation was shorter, the same phrases repeated over in various sequences.

The rest of us stood transfixed. The cold mountain air tickled the back of my neck.

And as the Frenchman intoned his plainsong, we heard a rattle and a thump, as though someone were moving about the shack. "What do you see?"

This time the boy's voice came to us from just beyond the door, as if he had maneuvered to get the anvil between him and the phantom he described.

"He's moved now. He's at the anvil. He's written something on the paper. Now he—he—"

"What do you see?"

"He's flicking the mud from his shroud—from the Indian blanket, I mean!"

"Are you afraid?"

"No! It's incredible! But I'm not afraid!"

Well, I was afraid. My heart was going like a steam hammer. Every man's mouth was standing open, his eyes bugging out of his head, and I saw one of the Dutchmen make the sign of the cross.

The Frenchman cried out again, the same phrase repeated three times in a hoarse high-pitched refrain.

"What do you see?" he howled.

The young man's voice was chillingly composed by comparison. It was almost as if their respective temperaments had been transposed, one into the other. "He's coming around the anvil toward me," he said.

I could hear the thing breathing!

It was true. I could *hear* the steady hiss of its breath, in and out, in and out, in long, inhuman sighs never made by living flesh. I *heard* it approach the door.

"He stands before me," said the young man. There was a tremor in his throat now, no doubt about it, but whether of fear or exaltation I wouldn't have wished to hazard.

"He reaches to his head. Ah, he unwraps the blankets to reveal—his face—"

"Are you afraid?" shrieked the Frenchman.

The young man's simultaneous response was a corresponding scream of utter terror that stood my hair on end. There was a frantic battering on the barred door from within, and we heard the pup crying, "Don't touch me, don't touch me, don't *touch* me!" in an unbroken wail of torment—then a piteous moan, another crash, and silence.

We had stood frozen with horror, I for one only just resisting the compulsion to run for it, but now we threw ourselves upon the door in an effort to free the young man. But the trapper, still in his trance, had collapsed back against it, pinning the wooden bar in its sockets, holding the door shut. He didn't resist us, but his size hindered our exertions for several moments. At last we succeeded in flinging him bodily to one side and burst into the shack.

Inside, we found the youngster's unconscious body on the dirt floor. Some pieces of harness had been knocked down in his struggle. Upon the piece of paper on the anvil was scrawled the signature *Wm Wood* in an uncertain hand.

The pup began to revive as we carried him out into the cold air, mumbling and thrashing about in a kind of delirium. We laid him upon the ground, but someone suggested he might suffer from the exposure so we lifted him again and brought him into the keeping room of the trading post. There on the deerskin hearthrug, in fits and rants, he quickly came to himself and rose up, breathing hard, his eyes wild.

"Where is he?" were the first words he spoke. "Where's that damned Frenchman!"

We all looked about, but the trapper was nowhere to be seen. No one could recall him coming inside. Fritch and I were going to go look for him, but the boy stopped us with frantic gestures. "No, no! I don't want to see him!" he cried. "I couldn't face his blasted smirk! He's won his bet! Let it go!"

A sudden recollection flashed across his face. In a sort of paroxysm of revulsion, he hauled the money bag out of his shirt and flung it upon the table. "There!" he shrieked, like one demented. "Take it for him! Take it all! Stay away! Leave me alone!" And he burst out the front door, leaving us standing there in confusion. Within seconds, we heard the sound of horses' hooves fading away into the still night.

So, you see, there are no ghosts. Eventually, as we waited for the Frenchman to return and claim his winnings, someone opened the poke and found it filled with worthless scrap-iron plugs. The pelts in the cupboard were blankets, such as could be picked up by the ton along the trails, wrapped in a single carrion bearskin. Searching the blacksmith's shed again, we found the hand bellows with which the pup had made the sound of the phantom's breath. The remainder of the apparition we had conjured for ourselves out of our credulous imaginations and the superb performances of the two conspirators.

They had made off with twenty-five dollars—ten of them mine—for their night's work, enough to support them for a month or more while they searched out more pickings. But they left me an experience I could learn from, and cheap at the price. I never heard mention of either of them again, but here I am, the richest man in San Francisco—and I don't believe in ghosts. And I never will.

JACK TRACY received a special Edgar Allan Poe Award in 1978 for The Encyclopaedia Sherlockiana. *Mr. Tracy has written or edited ten books on Sherlock Holmes and Sir Arthur Conan Doyle. He is the founder of Gaslight Publications, of which he is currently publisher.*

THE STATE

OF

THE ART

A. Heyst

An elaborate, foolproof security system meets its match in a computer whiz and his trusty Apple.

T he voice was dark and smooth, like chocolate pudding. "Hey, baby, stayin' secure?"

I switched the phone onto the squawk box and turned on the tape recorder. This was business.

"Last time I looked."

"Look again, baby. One of your workin' fold is spreading the green around. Like he's printin' it."

I swung around to switch on my terminal. That year I was more or less working for an outfit called IMM, a big financial house that lived on top of its own skyscraper. Normally I had a pretty good view from the window behind my terminal. Now it was all snow, flung straight at the glass by a moaning wind.

"Got a name?" I said, as I keyed up the personnel database.

"Nope. But he works nights. On the computer."

"Well, that's where the money is. Description?"

The voice turned pro, just like that.

"Male, Caucasian, five-nine, hundred and fifty pounds, reddish-blond hair, blue eyes. Could be as young as forty or as old as sixty. Can't tell with you Nordic types. Dresses like a Guindon cartoon."

"Yeah, here's a match. What's the beef?"

"No beef, baby. He's starting to attract the eye of some heavy people. Gonna start acquirin' unwanted partners. It could get messy for a lot of people."

"And you're worried. A narc with a heart of gold."

"Just returning a favor. Besides, there ain't enough of them funny little folk. Gotta protect our endangered species."

With that he hung up. I released the personnel database and started a couple of audit routines running. I took tips like this seriously. There's a law of conservation of money just like there's a law of conservation of energy, and they both say about the same thing: if it's going somewhere, it's coming from somewhere.

The snow had stopped, and the wind hadn't started. The clouds hung low and distinct above the skyscrapers like a gray lid. Snow-smoothed outlines covered the litter and made it my kind of a morning. Perfect tracking weather.

I sat across the street from the IMM employee entrance and kept watch through a little hole in my iced-up car window. It was cold, but I had been cold before.

He came out twenty minutes before quitting time. Wool cap with earflaps that tied under his chin, a great big scarf, an overcoat that was a size too big, and hightop galoshes with his trousers neatly tucked inside. Just like a Guindon cartoon.

He got a snowbrush out of his car and went to work very carefully, beginning with the roof. When he had all the snow off, he scraped every square inch of glass. Then he broke the ice off the windshield wipers. He got inside and started the engine, letting it warm up the regulation three minutes. And then we were off.

He drove west a couple of blocks and stopped at an automatic teller machine. I knew the bank. Then it was south on Hennepin to a condo near Loring Park. He didn't live there, but plenty of fancy ladies did. Not too bad, as these things go. Twenty minutes early off work on account of the snow, twenty minutes late home to mama on account of the snow, time for a quickie in between. I left him to his fun and pointed myself toward a hippie restaurant where they made their own sausage, to stoke up and warm up and wait for banker's hours.

The bank where he did his business had been taken over by a California holding company, who had hired some image outfit to do something about all that midwest stodge. The image outfit had redecorated all the banks to look like Marin County fern bars. This probably looked great in home-office presentations but lost something in a Minnesota winter, when you could practically see the ferns cringe when the door opened.

The word *security* had been too inorganic for the image outfit, so my opposite number had the title of Director of Accounts Integrity. He and I had played some very secret games together back when he and I and the world had been young.

I found him in his little office, staring at a computer terminal. The bank's inspirational message of the day was displayed as a banner across the top of the screen. It didn't seem to be inspiring him much.

"I need an account history," I said, by way of hello.

"A shocking request. Violation of personal privacy and abuse of corporate power. What's the name?"

"Johnson."

"Wonderful." There were eighteen pages of Johnsons in the Minneapolis phonebook.

"Johnson, Ingemar Ingebretson," I said, following it with the social security number.

"Hot on his trail," he said, making the keyboard sing. Someday they should stop calling us flatfeet and start calling us flatfingers.

"Ing-e-mar Ing-e-bretson Yon-son," he said in a pretty good Scandinavian singsong. "You're doing all right for a square-headed Swede."

"Dane," I said as I watched the neat pattern of prosperity displayed in green columns on the screen. "His mother was a Rasmussen."

"Racist pig. Either way, his investments are turning out nicely."

Indeed they were. The account record showed automatic deposit after automatic deposit from some of IMM's most successful money-market funds. Funds that Ingemar Ingebretson Johnson was not a member of.

"All transactions properly authenticated," my buddy said, a question of accounts integrity in his eye, "or were they?"

"Of course they were."

IMM's authentication scheme was pure state of the art. Every officer with funds-transfer authority was issued a new password every day. The password was used by a cryptographic technique called Beelzebub to encode every transaction, just the way spies encode messages. If you didn't know the password, you couldn't decode the transaction, and if you couldn't decode a transaction, you couldn't forge one. I knew the scheme was close to perfect. I had installed it myself.

One way to react when you discover that somebody has punched a hole in your system is to assume that something small has happened and to go off on a search for tiny cracks. Anybody with half a crypto background knew there weren't any tiny cracks in Beelzebub. I had considerably more than half a crypto background, and I went off looking for the impossible.

The search took me up and down phone lines, through program and data files, and into a lot of binary back alleys. In the course of it I found plenty of impossible things, all lying around as sharp and clear as Johnson's tracks in the snow. They led me right up to his front door.

It opened off a tiny little porch at the end of a well-shoveled walk in the old part of town. I stood there for a moment and listened to him get it for the way he had stacked the teacups. She had to be his wife to talk to him like that. Her voice cut right through the storm windows. On the other hand, maybe it was cutting through the brick. I blotted it out with the doorbell.

He opened the door. His hair was thinning, but his eyes were bright and lively. He was wearing a patched sweater and a pair of old-fashioned carpet slippers, and he looked as if he were expecting me.

"Come in," he said. She was still going on from the kitchen about the teacups. "Marybeth," he called back, "it's somebody from the Apple Club at work. Come to see my machine. We'll be downstairs."

We went through rooms and short corridors. The place had a kind of desperate tidiness about it, with things piled neatly in unlikely places. He talked over his shoulder as we went down the basement stairs.

"I said what I did to keep from upsetting Marybeth. She upsets easily."

"I heard."

"You have to understand Marybeth. She has a college degree."

I knew he didn't, and I said nothing. In college they would have taught him to think the way they thought, in neat categories. What he had done was neat, but it didn't have anything to do with a college professor's categories.

He opened a door at the bottom of the stairs, and we stepped into a little room that had probably been the coal bunker in the old days. An Apple with a green-screen monitor and a hard disc sat on a table. Homemade bookshelves lined the walls. They held a very select library on cryptography—every issue of *Cryptologia* from the beginning, all of the papers by Diffie, Hellman, and Rivest, and some very hard-to-find things by Friedman. I was impressed.

"Nice hobby," I said, trying to get things started. I was better at a keyboard than I was at this business.

"Something to think about while the tapes spin," he said. "Being a computer operator gets duller every year. Drink?"

I tried not to sound surprised.

"Sure."

He pulled a copy of *The Codebreakers* off the shelf and fetched a pint bottle from behind it.

"Marybeth objects to drinking. Says it clouds your mind."

Not yours, brother, I thought as I let him pour me a shot of pretty decent brandy.

"Well," I said after a polite interval, "I guess you know why I'm here."

"Of course. You wanted to meet the man who broke Beelzebub."

It was his moment and I let him have it. He had earned it. I had only one question.

"On an Apple?"

"I have an M68000 board for it. Runs almost as fast as a VAX in machine language. I can break a transaction back to cleartext and extract a password in a little over twelve hours."

It took a moment and another sip of brandy to let that sink in. Beelzebub had been certified by the codebreaking agency that is so secret it doesn't have a name. Those boys had used machines a million times faster than Johnson's to try and crack Beelzebub and failed. But then a talent for codebreaking is one of those things that pops up in unlikely places. A lot of people who have it treat it as a hobby. The rest, like the boys in the no-name agency, are deadly serious.

"Well, now, we're going to have to figure out what to do about this."

"Oh, you won't do anything about it. I only take what I need to make my life bearable, which isn't much. And if you prosecute, my defense will involve explaining how I did it. You know what that means."

I knew. Since Beelzebub had been certified it had become, with a little pushing, the standard code technique for commercial systems. It protected—or used to protect—a hell of a lot of sensitive and expensive information. I drained my drink, saluted him with my glass, and got out of there.

The big boss at IMM had his desk placed in the far back corner of a ballroom-sized office, so that you got to sweat plenty on the way to the hot seat beside it. It was a trick he had learned from Mussolini.

He had learned a lot of other tricks, including hiring independents to follow along in my footsteps. No way did I want some headhunting cowboy to stumble over this situation. So I had made various appointments, paid my respects to various flunkies, straightened my tie, and ridden up to the fortieth floor. Just to test the temperature of the water.

"There's a little leak," I said when I finally got to the high-backed chair beside his desk.

"How little?" he said, peering over the glasses that gave him the look of a scholarly reptile.

"Three, five grand a month."

"Plug it."

"I don't think we want to."

He looked at me, his face as cold as the air outside. He made a science of that sort of thing. It intimidated people who, unlike me, had never been seriously intimidated in their lives.

I continued. "This fellow is onto some basic flaw in the system. If we close in on him, he may go for a big killing. In any case, it will cost a lot more than the lossage to fix the problem. Not to mention the publicity."

He dismissed my statement with a wave. It was a very expressive wave. I was just a tiresome underling, unable to break out of my parochial mindset.

"Can you track it down?"

I became alert, trying not to show it.

"Sure."

"Then find whoever is doing this and make him disappear."

"I don't understand."

"Of course you understand. I know where you've come from. I heard it, very discreetly you understand, at an affair for supporters of the current administration. And I want you to know that I approve. This country has just sat back and taken it for too long."

He paused to let that sink in. It sank in.

"And so it's very simple. You know how these things are done. A threat arises, you deal with it. So find this person. And make him disappear."

I sat for a moment, trying to think.

"There's a bonus in it for you."

I stood up.

"I'll see what I can do," I said. And then I hurried out to set a contact marker.

It looked the way safe houses always do: reasonably clean, reasonably new, and not a human touch anywhere. Harry sat on the sofa, his feet up on a coffee table, flicking his cigar ash on the floor to give the sanitization team something to do. It was an old habit of his. I knew all his old habits. He had been my case officer for a long time.

"My cover's been blown. Somebody talked out of school at a political shindig."

"Sure. Last administration it was left-wing dingbats blowing covers because intelligence work is immoral. Now it's right-wing dingbats playing James Bond at cocktail parties." He spat out a flake of tobacco. Harry wasn't exactly above politics, he was more to one side. "I was about to pull you out of that place anyway. That three-piece suit is starting to get on my nerves."

Harry shifted his cigar from one side of his mouth to the other without taking his eyes off me. It was his way of asking a question without asking it. This had been a shallow-cover mission from the start. I had been sent into IMM to install Beelzebub as part of an operation to strengthen financial institutions from attack by the next generation of terrorists. The next generation will raise their war chests using keyboards in a place like IMM, not by robbing banks. A hole in my cover wasn't enough reason to pull a Marylander like Harry up into the snow country. I answered the unasked question.

"IMM has a genius working for it."

"What kind of genius?"

"A cryptographic genius. Meek little computer operator. He broke Beelzebub. Using an M68000-equipped Apple, of all things."

This caused Harry to take the cigar out of his mouth, something that seldom happened. "Tell me more."

"Not much more to tell. He must have discovered a flaw in the basic principle, because he can break it back in twelve hours on that little machine. I didn't ask how he did it. The top-secret part of my brain is already full."

He was awed. "That was certified algorithm."

"Well, he just decertified it."

"Are you sure?"

"Absolutely. He left a trail a mile wide. He wanted to get caught so he could have somebody to show it off to."

"This is serious."

"The big boss at IMM thinks so. He's ordered me to make Johnson disappear. In the interests of financial security."

Harry clamped his cigar back in his mouth, gave me his best Churchillian glower. "Who'll miss him?"

"Nobody much."

"Then you make him disappear. In the interests of national security."

Making people disappear takes a lot of staff work. Briefings have to be given, clearances obtained, supplemental budgets approved. Then you have to wait for the right kind of weather. And your immediate reward is a brief, ugly moment of staring down into a terrified face.

"I really hate to fly," he said.

"It'll be over before you know it."

I peered out the window of the operations shack of the little country airfield we had hired and plowed for the event. The owner clearly thought we were running drugs and just as clearly didn't care. Nobody but our people was within five miles of the place.

The Learjet was painted pearl gray and seemed to simply materialize out of the snowladen clouds. It flared over the perimeter fence and touched down in a little storm of its own making. It taxied over to us and wheeled in a half circle. We heard the nearside engine spool down, and the little door in the side opened like a drawbridge.

Johnson clutched his shopping bag full of notes and working papers, now so highly classified that officially they didn't exist. I started wondering if we were going to have a hard time getting him on the airplane.

"Look," I said, "you'll love it. Six acres of supercomputers in the basement. Barbed wire and triple electric fence to keep out any distractions. People to talk to about your work. Plenty of problems to work on. A whole new life."

"I get airsick. It's terribly embarrassing."

"The steward will give you something. You can sleep all the way if you like."

Then he visibly screwed up his courage and marched out to the airplane. He turned and waved just before he stepped in. The door closed, the engine spooled up, and he was gone in a cloud of snow.

I was back at IMM the next morning, up on the fortieth floor with the big boss.

"Johnson's wife just reported him missing."

"Oh, really?"

"In a couple of days the cops'll find his car at the airport. Nobody will remember seeing him. It will be a very small mystery for a very short time."

"Very good. Very good indeed."

"State of the art," I replied.

A. HEYST is a pseudonym. The author won first prize for "The State of the Art" in the annual short story contest sponsored by the Cabrillo Suspense Writers Conference in California.

THEY NEVER EVEN SEE ME

EVEN

SEE ME

J. N. Williamson

Poor Raymond died sometime Thursday night between Johnny Carson and school . . . and no one even notices.

My name is Raymond Kelnover. I'm fifteen years old and I died last night, sometime between 1:00 A.M. (when Johnny Carson went off) and the time I saw that my three brothers had gone to school. It was extremely quiet, like always when we've all gone (including Pop) and Mom's still in bed. I can't really say any closer than that what time it was when I died.

Maybe you wonder (I guess I should have spelled it with a capital *Y*) how I know it's all quiet after we've left, if I'm gone, too. I wouldn't want you to think I'm lying. I don't even know, really, if I'm talking to myself in my mind, but I sure hope you're listening. And it seems awfully important that you get things straight. I think truth sounds more truthful when somebody has got all the details down pat.

So it's that sometimes I'm—and the other guys—sick in bed. Both Pop and Mom are very strict about waking them up. So when we're home, we wait till he takes off for work before we slip upstairs and watch cartoons on TV. (Mom whines a lot, for sympathy, when we get her up. With Pop it matters more that we're just quiet.)

Of course, if you know everything you know all this and probably what time I died also. But I'm not like old Louie who takes dumb chances with everything and I'll bet would take chances now, too. He even used to wake Pop up, Louie did, till after Pop had his gall bladder out and said that it was Louie who caused it. Every time Pop sent the hospital or doctor or something a payment, if Louie was around he'd say loudly, "There's another installment in the real-life story of a self-made jerk."

Don't think (please) that Pop is a very mean fellow who don't care about people's feelings. Well, I guess he doesn't, much. But you see, we're Mom's kids first. Pop loved her so much he didn't care about us four children with her first husband, but he cares now. Especially with one of his own, who is Joanna. She's in kindergarten now and a darling little girl.

I just tried to get up again and nothing happened again. Since you know I'm dead and all, I don't know how much I'm supposed to tell you. But there doesn't seem to be any way that I can talk out loud, or move, or nothing. Since I sleep on my back, all I can see is the ceiling unless I squinch around, inside some way, and then I can make out Louie's area.

That's what Pop, who hated the army but learned a lot from it, calls where we sleep in the basement room—our areas.

We're each responsible for our own, and since nobody at all remembers about it and Mom's too busy working her part-time job on the main floor of the house to bawl us out any—well, each area's pretty screwed up.

Pardon me. Disorderly, I mean.

Louie's the worst though, like in everything. A real mess.

I wish I could have waked up and been Louie. Instead of whatever it is I am now.

Friday Nite

I scared myself pretty bad, thinking like that about who I am. Even if I'm dead I'm still Raymond Kelnover, fifteen years old.

I started wondering when they are going to find me. After school the guys came downstairs, and after a while I saw Louie messing around in his area. He asked me if I was sick or something, and when I didn't answer him (I tried) he just ate the brown sugar he'd cobbed out of the kitchen and took off again.

The others didn't say anything to me at all. So I have been thinking about how that can be. You'd think a person would look a little bit different, being like dead. But it probably hasn't started changing me yet.

Partly I guess it's my fault anyway. Not being noticed, I mean. Start with Louie who's about two years younger than me. He is tough, really a tough kid, for thirteen. Back when we were small I had to fight him a whole lot, and I never could make him give in. I swear to God—

Pardon. But really you had to practically kill old Lou just to get him to shut up, and he never really gave in. I wanted to go ahead and kill him, if you want the truth, all of it. Sometimes I thought he wanted me to do it.

Since I got in the eighth grade and then graduated, though, it was kind of weird what happened. He just understood some way that I couldn't fight him no more. Not till he went to high school, too, at least. And then we quit talking altogether.

Then there's Carter, and I don't know how old he is. A tall skinny kid with blue eyes who goes his own way, kind of. Maybe you've noticed him? I mean, we're brothers and all, but he was always too little for horsing around with. Carter digs cemeteries and poetry.

Ted's the youngest, till Joanna came along. All Ted does is try to be like Louie, and sometimes I hit Ted just to wise him up some. But mostly Louie and me both ignore him, and he winds up playing with the baby. Joanna. She's in kindergarten and a darling little girl.

Well, now everybody is upstairs eating dinner and there's a lot of noise like always. Pop is trying to get Mom to not work so hard when Louie has her all nervous, and Pop's so worried about her health that he's started yelling at her. Mom is being quiet except she just told Carter to eat and now she's bawling out Ted for wetting his bed. "Aren't you just a little too old for that, Ted?" she asks. And Ted stays quiet as usual. This burns both Mom and Pop up, when Ted don't answer. I think Ted knows it.

Joanna says can she go out and play after supper (Mom calls it that, but Pop says "dinner," because he isn't like all the miserable conformists in the neighborhood who may make more money but don't know anything intellectual). Mom says yes, Joanna, you can go out. Pop says no, but because he can't stand either one of them being hurt he just tells her to come in when it's getting dark. We have to watch out for Joanna, all of us, cause she's different than us.

Friday Nite, Later

Is this sleeping that I do when I'm gone a while—from everything?

Pardon me, but aren't even you going to notice what's happened to me? Would you sort of look at the records and see if there's anything written down for Raymond Kelnover? That's me. I'm fifteen. I got blond hair which grows too fast to suit Pop, and my feet are very large for my age, size eleven.

They sent Ted down to bed early for getting Joanna's dress dirty, and I can hear him over in his area swearing to himself. "Damn Pop damn Pop damn Pop I hate him I hate him I hate ole damn Pop." I guess that sounds sort of terrible to you, with your line of work, but I laughed out loud.

Or thought I did. Ted looked up a second, I think, cause he stopped cursing. Then he took up again where he left off.

I've been figuring out why they didn't ask about me at supper. See, it's Pop's idea that till I'm a junior, at least, I ought to be in bed at the regular time. He used to fuss with Mom over it, but she would get very very quiet until he thought she was getting sick again. Mom doesn't act like it, yet I think she likes me some. Because she allows me to go and come when I want and says things like, "I trust you, Raymond, and I know that you wouldn't let me down."

Look. Do you keep records on everybody up there?

I was wondering. So, anyways, Pop pretended I wasn't there at all—that he didn't notice I was gone—and Mom figured I had taken off again without telling her where. They'll notice I'm gone any time now, I hope.

Saturday Morning

Isn't that what you call it, after midnight but way before dawn? I'm back now from wherever it is that I keep going to, and they still haven't missed me, so far as I know.

In case you're interested, I've tried to get up and talk again, but nothing still happens. I've studied Louie's area until it's almost memorized. Okay, now I'm not looking. There's the bed with the sheet torn off and a hole in it. A gob of his clothes are everywhere, even in my area. But now I can't throw them back. An inner tube, a broken corrugated box with old toys slopping out, two or three of my books, and he's cobbed my good ballpoint pen again, plus I can see the edge of the empty brown sugar box and some other wrappers from stuff he stole and hid under the bed.

I can't see it, but there's a real filthy book stuck under his mattress, and I keep trying to get him to throw it away before Joanna sees it. She wouldn't understand probably, but it wouldn't seem right for such a darling little girl to see such a neat book.

There's more stuff in his area, but I'm tired. Will I wake up in heaven this time?

Saturday Morning (Really, it's about 11:00)

Louie and Ted, Carter and Joanna are watching cartoons upstairs, and I remember most of the lines from the Popeye that's on now. So do they. Any time now Pop will wake up and get mad because the set's turned on too loud. Maybe then he'll think about me, since I usually hold it down.

I've just found out that I can sort of read back over what I've been saying to you, and I think maybe you felt like I was criticizing Pop or Mom. So let me level with you.

Pop is very very loyal to Mom, and he works hard. Mom works hard, too, and neither one of them drink much or use many dirty words, and I don't think they hate us at all. Well, I used to think so (with Pop). But then I got to be about as tall as he was and we'd tell jokes and kid each other and stuff. He's okay.

Mom is modern in a lot of ways, she says. She believes that a guy has to have some independence, to learn a sense of responsibility. So she hasn't kissed me since I was about seven or eight. I can come and go about like I want, or could till I died last Thursday, and I'm pretty sure that I love Mom. She has nice dark hair.

Joanna came down a minute ago and it was pretty awful. I didn't want her to find me, after all. She's just a little girl and wouldn't know what to do with a dead person. (If you want to know, I knew it was her by her footsteps. They're a-tap-and-a-trip, always about to fall, and she stopped at the foot of the stairs and just stared at me.)

Then this crazy thing happened. She climbed up and leaned over on my bed, and there were these beautiful eyes looking down at me. I tried to, you know, close my eyes so she'd think I was asleep, and for a minute there I thought I was going away again. But Joanna kind of patted my cheek and then put this thing right under my chin and went away.

For a long time now I been trying to figure out what it is, this thing under my chin. I can't feel anything, not really, and I can't move or pick it up. But now I finally got it. It's a picture she made at kindergarten, one she's been working on the whole semester. There are a lot of colors in it, great crayon work, and these letters *Jo* printed in the corner, very very big and important and proud.

She's a darling little girl.

Saturday Nite, Early

There is no use arguing about it, I'm kind of invisible. Not actually, because they can see my body and all. But it's being invisible anyway. Mom came down to go into the utility room and put some junk in the washer and didn't even see me. I almost died.

I mean, I'd have almost died if I was still alive. God, how I wanted Mom to notice—to see that I existed.

But she was busy working. She had her own thing to do. And I'm not it.

Sunday Morning

My name is Raymond Kelnover and I'm fifteen years old and I died Thursday night, between Johnny Carson and school. That's all I know. Every bit of it. Except I'm stuck—really stuck—and that's mainly why I was real scared for a while, just now.

But I just got this great idea. I feel better just thinking about it. Look. Next Wednesday is my birthday. I'll be fifteen— maybe I stretched it some, at first—and they always have this big cake and Grandma on our birthdays. They'll simply have to notice I'm gone. Besides, school ought to notice tomorrow, too. This can't go on much longer. Mr. Frazier, the gym teacher, he'll probably be the first to find out. I was supposed to help him with the frosh basketball team tomorrow.

But even if he don't realize I'm gone, Grandma will on Wednesday. Somebody has to open those presents she buys on birthdays, don't they?

Listen, have I told you why Pop doesn't know I'm dead? It's cause he doesn't come down here. He's afraid he might break his neck, the way we don't fulfill our responsibility in the area and keep things neat.

Louie went to church this morning, like he does most Sundays. This absolutely breaks Pop up. "Little Adolf goes to mass," he'll say, doing his imitation of somebody I never heard of. Kind of high and sarcastic-mean sort of. Now Pop's coming downstairs, but I don't get my hopes up any. He won't come near me, and he wouldn't be able to see me if he did.

"Raymond?"

Pop! I'm here!

"Raymond, where the hell have you gone to this time?"

Nowhere, Pop. Nowhere. I've been here all along, right here.

"Damn kid can always be underfoot when I don't need him, but he's never around when I want him for something." He's backing away from the steps. "I've tried to give him everything he wanted, just like all the rest." Pop's talking to himself and hoping Mom hears him. "But just want one miserable thing, just one. Joanna?" His voice is different now. "Joanna, honey? Are you up in your room?" She don't answer. Pop laughs. "Bet she's gone next door to Robin's. What a little darling she is."

Monday Afternoon

I've been gone a long time now, and I do not know where. I must still be lost because I am looking at the ceiling again. There are all these white squares, with Kool-Aid and cupcake and dead fly stains as far as the eye can see. It's all spread before me, a world of white squares with these little spots, like an upside-down landing field. And off to the corner of my eye Louie is sitting on the edge of his bed.

"Boy, you are something, Raymond. You know that?"

I tried to ignore him, which of course I did.

"How long you been out of school now? What a soft life. You go and come like you want and nobody asks nothin' of you."

Then suddenly he gets up and comes over to the side of my bed. He has this angel's face, big eyes and kind of just-right forehead and ears with a whole bunch of yellowish hair that falls around it. He's a nice-looking boy. "Raymond, tell me something."

I don't answer.

"Raymond, just answer me one question." Louie poses like a big deal threat, fists jammed into his sides and head cocked. "Raymond. Are you dead?"

I almost died again. I mean—well, you know what I mean.

"Look, I just want to know. I won't tell, Raymond. I promise."

I glare hard at him, or feel a hard glare at him.

"What I want to know for, is, Raymond, if you are dead then I'm the oldest. Right, Raymond? And if I am shouldn't I be the guy to get all your gifts Wednesday?" He paused. "Raymond, if you don't answer me I'll declare you dead."

I don't answer him.

"You're dead," he says.

Wednesday Morning (Getting Late)

My name is Raymond Kelnover. I'm fifteen today. Grandma came over, and they waited a real long time for me. I heard her say finally, "If that's not just like teenagers today. Well, in my day birthdays were something special. You looked forward to them."

No one answered. Then Louie said, "If he ain't here, then I should get his presents. Right? I mean, you can't take 'em all back, right? So can I open 'em now?"

"Certainly not!" Mom says.

"Louie, m'boy, you'd pick the gold right out of his teeth if he dropped dead in front of you," Pop says.

"But he is dead! He really is dead, Pop, so can I have his gifts now?"

There is a lot of silence, and I have some hope.

Grandma clears her throat. "Such an imagination. Really, he watches too much TV, that one. I almost believed him."

"Don't worry," Mom says. "We'll see to it that Raymond gets his gifts, Mother."

I hear Mom and Pop get up and start putting packages up on the shelf in the front closet. "Heaven knows when he'll be home to open them," Mom says with a sigh.

"Don't blame me. I've told you before that a boy takes advantage of you when you let him run around free that way."

She doesn't answer Pop at all—not a word.

After a while it got quiet in the house again. I think, maybe, it will stay that way now. Happy Birthday, Raymond Kelnover. Happy Birthday to me.

J. N. WILLIAMSON is a free-lance writer whose widely varied work experience has included Pinkerton detective and assistant publicity director for the Indianapolis 500.